MARIA FURLONGER

The Phoenix Twins

Risen From The Ashes

This book was professionally typeset on Reedsy. Find out more at reedsy.com

Acknowledgement

I would like to thank all of my beta readers and my friends:
Iva Dimitrova
Karen Frombach
Anna-Marie Birchley
Derek Weaving
Alan Drewett
for keeping me motivated throughout this very long project.
An extra special thank you goes to my husband, Emerson
Furlonger. He had to read through my work twice!
I am hugely grateful to you all.

Prologue

3rd August 1994. Gloucester, England

Alfie sat on the kerb. He flicked his lighter as he dragged from his cigarette, tapping the ash onto the floor. Next to him rested his best friend Bobby; they'd been friends since primary school, and they were now in their second year of secondary school. They were tight, doing practically everything together. On the other side of the small street, sitting opposite them, chewing gum with his mouth wide open, was Kevin. His surname was 'Short,' which was ironic as he was the tallest boy in school, standing a little over six feet tall. They met a couple of years ago in the first year, and an instant friendship was formed. He wasn't exceptionally bright, but he was a laugh. As they listened to rave music on their ghetto-blaster, the bass thumped, and they bobbed their heads to the beat, earning them disapproving stares from people walking by. Bystanders gave them a wide berth, likely intimidated by their raucous music. They wolf-whistled at a few girls as they walked by, which was met with cold glares. The boys found it hilarious, it was the summer holiday after all, and there was lots of skin on show.

Alfie was casually scraping his foot over the gravelly street when he saw someone turn the corner and approach them; it seemed as though the boy was listening to a Walkman and hauling a plastic carrier bag. Alfie's face flashed with recognition; he lived just over the road from him. He was an odd-looking boy; with his teeth crooked and yellowing, dimpled skin, and long skinny features, Alfie thought he ever so slightly resembled something out of a horror movie. Alfie knew the boy didn't go to a mainstream school. His parents told him he went to a special school. They often saw him around and liked to shout at him, but he didn't react, as if he couldn't hear them; either that or he ignored them. Alfie didn't appreciate being ignored. Alfie flicked Bobby's knee.

"Hey Bobby, look who it is." He pointed. Bobby stood up and moved in front of the boy, blocking his path.

"Hey, freak. What you listening to?" Bobby whipped the earphones off of the boy's head and put them up to his ear, a menacing grin spreading across his face. Indeed upset by the sudden assault, the boy stretched out his lean hands to reach for his property. In a flash, Bobby dodged him, bouncing backwards and cackling with venom.

"That's some pussy girl shit you're listening to there. Are you a pussy girl?" Bobby stepped into the boy's face with confidence. The boy tried to turn his head away, but Bobby kept repositioning himself to remain eye-to-eye.

"G-g-go away," the boy stammered. Tiring of his attempts at peace, Bobby shoved him, and he fell roughly to the asphalt. Alfie and Kevin howled with laughter. Wanting to join the fun, Alfie pushed himself up and walked over to the boy who was now on his knees and shoved his boot into the boy's stomach, causing him to double over, coughing and spluttering. Alfie smirked at the sight and circled him. Spotting a relatively large stone next to the kerb where he'd been sitting, he picked it up and launched it hard, hitting his target and striking the boy on the side of the head. As the boy covered his head with his arms, Bobby and Kevin howled with enjoyment and joined in, each picking up stones of various sizes. Distraught, the boy curled up on the floor in a foetal position as he tried to shield himself from the onslaught of flying missiles. They were disrupted from their enjoyment when they heard a girl shouting over the chaos.

"What the hell do you think you're doing? Leave him the hell alone."

Alfie recognised her. She went to his school; although she was this boy's younger sister, he thought it hilarious this girl believed she could have the ability to stop what they were doing. She was pretty odd herself; she used to be overweight and wore thick-rimmed glasses. He and his mates would often give her a hard time as well. It was a bit of a drag since she didn't bite back or cry, but he knew they got to her; he could tell by her face. Now she was older, he had to admit, she was starting to look quite hot. She'd slimmed down a bit and had some incredible boobs on her.

"Hello," said Alfie, producing a long, low whistle. "What do we have here?" He strutted toward her, studying her up and down. She was wearing a low-cut summer dress that showed off her best features. He grabbed his crotch and bit his lip. The girl stopped. Bobby stayed with the boy, but Kevin joined Alfie, and they stood before the girl.

"Stay away from me and stay away from my brother." The girl's voice trembled, but she stood her ground.

"What exactly are YOU going to do? There are three of us and only one of you," Alfie sneered at the situation. "Grab her,

Kev." Without hesitation, Kevin ran up behind the girl and grabbed her. She tried to fight him off, but he was almost twice the size of her and effortlessly pulled her arms backwards. As she yelped in pain, Kevin transferred his arms to hold her around her shoulders and chest. The girl was forced to watch as Alfie and Bobby continued to hurtle rocks at her brother, witnessing the blood trickling from his face and his cries of pain.

"Stop, you're hurting him!" the girl yelled. Kevin was laughing hard, paying no attention to her struggles. He was so much stronger than her; it was like holding a wiggling kitten. She grabbed his arms, and Kevin was vaguely aware of her nails digging in; it didn't hurt; they were short and blunt. All at once, he started to feel a warming sensation, not bothersome at first, but then it got hotter and hotter- a bit like a heating radiator- to the point where it began to feel as if his skin was burning. Becoming flustered, Kevin tried to pry her hands off of him, but she had a firm grip, intensifying his pain. He screamed in agony as he felt his skin blister and bubble under her grasp. He tried to push her away, struggling violently, and she eventually released him. Kevin looked at his forearms, and red hand marks appeared, the smooth flesh now boiling with blisters. The girl turned her back on Kevin, but not before he caught what he thought to be a fiery red glow in her eyes. His mouth fell open in shock.

"Stop. Now," The girl growled. Alfie turned, now looking into the girl's glowing red eyes; his own eyes widened with disbelief.

"She burned me, man; Look," Kevin yelled. He raised his arms for Alfie to see.

"What the fu-" began Alfie. Bobby was still throwing rocks,

oblivious to everything going on, and the girl turned her gaze to him. He didn't see her attack coming. Bobby was far too busy laughing and revelling in the morbid enjoyment of hurting her brother. Alfie watched in horror as the girl fixed her glowing eyes on Bobby, and within seconds, he became a whirling ball of fire. When the girl's brother realised rocks were no longer battering him, he slowly got up and stared at the scene materialising in front of him.

Alfie inhaled sharply. His best friend was on fire, and this girl was doing it to him. Fury burning inside of him, he sprinted to the girl and tackled her to the ground. They scrambled about, and Alfie managed to connect his fist to her cheek. Her head snapped to the side, but she turned it straight back and stared deep into his eyes. Her already crimson eyes somehow become brighter. Petrified, Alfie tried to move away, but she grabbed his ears with her hands, holding her terrifying stare. He squealed as her touch scolded his oversized ears. Alfie pulled himself loose from her grip, his melting skin clinging to her fingers and stretching like the stringy cheese of a pizza slice. He scrambled away from her, and Kevin helped him up from the ground as he cried in agony.

"Come on, mate, we gotta go, she's a freak too, and she's lost it," said Kevin, his eyes wide and frightened. Alfie looked over at the fireball that was his friend.

"But what about Bobby?" Alfie asked in horror. Bobby was his best friend; they were like brothers. Alfie ran to Bobby; he took off his light jacket, grabbed his friend, and started rolling him around on the ground with it. He looked up at the girl. She was in a trance, her eyes still glowing. Alfie saw the boy hobble over to his sister. He grabbed her by the shoulders and was shaking her, but it was like she'd gone somewhere else; she finally snapped out of it. Both the boy and girl looked at Alfie one last time and then ran away down the street. Alfie hadn't realised he was holding his breath, but he let out a massive sigh of relief. The fire was out now, but Bobby was unconscious, and the smell of burning flesh and hair assaulted his nose. Alfie ordered Kevin to find a phone and call an ambulance. The sides of Alfie's head were excruciatingly painful, and feeling helpless, he could do nothing more than look at his smouldering friend and sob.

Chapter 1

The old red Vauxhall exceeded the speed limit as it sailed around the bends of the narrow, country lanes of Herefordshire. It was early in the morning, and the sun was yet to come up. Mae tried to suppress her moans with little success, and she clung to her seat as Anthony took sharp corners way too fast. She was grateful for the speed; the pressure pushing against her cervix told her there wasn't much time.

"Will you stop that bloody racket. You're giving me a headache," Anthony growled. Mae rolled her eyes; she had a damn sight more than a headache right now, "this better not be Braxton Hicks; otherwise, this will all be a waste of my time."

"It's not Braxton Hicks. It literally feels like something is trying to come out right now, so you need to hurry." Said Mae. She was becoming breathless; there was another contraction coming.

"Who do you think you are, ordering me around?" he snapped. Mae shrank into her seat. She felt the car immediately slow down. It was now a dead straight road, and he was

7

braking for no reason. Well, for no good reason anyway, she knew why he was doing it.

"I'm sorry. I didn't mean to sound like that; it's just because I'm in pain and I'm scared. Please could we hurry?" asked Mae softly. The car started to accelerate again.

"Only because I don't want a mess in the car." He muttered. Mae sighed; she hoped she would make it.

They arrived at the hospital in a rush and headed for the main hospital reception, where a nurse greeted them. She directed them to the maternity unit, and Mae made a bee-line for the toilet. Anthony went about asking for some assistance. Mae flushed the empty toilet; it was strange how contractions made you think you needed to poo. Mae shuffled into the waiting room. She could hear Anthony was getting agitated about something.

"No! No men at all, especially not a Paki."

"Mr Newton! We will not tolerate any racism here. If you continue, we'll be asking you to leave. What you don't understand is that your wife has just gone into labour six weeks prematurely. The midwives can deliver the babies, but we have to have two doctors in the delivery room, one doctor per baby. They will be tiny and may need help with their lungs or heart. There are no female doctors on staff today, but we will make sure that your wife is protected; there will be many midwives in the room, she is at no risk."

"What's going on?" Mae was afraid to ask since she'd heard some of the conversations.

"Apparently, two doctors have to be in the delivery room. There are no female doctors, so they are going to be men. Tell them, tell them this cannot happen. You were raped; the only man you trust is me," he yelled.

It wasn't true; she'd never been raped. It was only a story they'd told the doctor when they moved back from Cornwall. She wanted to know why Mae waited so long to see a doctor about the pregnancy. The truth was, there were only male doctors at the surgery in Cornwall, and Anthony didn't want her seeing a man. He said male doctors were perverts, and unless she wanted to be molested by one someday, she shouldn't want to see a male doctor either. The same went for any male professional, dentists, police, etc. He didn't want her telling the lady doctor he was the one with the issue; it had to be about her, so he suggested Mae claim that she was raped and had a fear of men. Mae looked at the nurse desperately, not because of what Anthony just said but because she had no idea how to get out of this. Another contraction had Mae crippled in pain, and she sank onto a nearby chair. The nurse crouched down in front of her.

"We won't worry about this right now. Let's get you into a ward, and we'll take a look at you, see how far along you are, okay?" Mae nodded. Anthony didn't follow.

"I'm going for a fag." Anthony grunted. He approached Mae, and it appeared to anyone who may have been watching that he was hugging her. "If a guy gets anywhere near you, I'll have nothing to do with those babies. They'll be tainted. You'll be allowing a strange man to look at your twat, which would make you a dirty, filthy whore, and you'll be sorry for disrespecting me." He kissed her on the cheek, and Mae cringed. She was frightened, as if it wasn't already enough to be giving birth for the first time and to twins. Now she also had to worry about the people that would be around her. Anthony angrily left the corridor and headed for the stairs. Just as he left, Mae turned to the nurse.

"Please don't let those doctors near me," she said, her eyes wide and watery.

"They won't go near you, sweetie. Please try not to worry, honey. You have more pressing things to worry about at the moment. Come, I'll take you to your room, and we'll take a look at you." The nurse took Mae gently by the elbow. She was lovely, her voice was calm and sweet, and she introduced herself as Cheryl. Mae had a room to herself which she was incredibly grateful for. She was instructed to dress in a backless gown. Mae had been wearing trousers; she didn't own any dresses or skirts. She wasn't allowed to wear them, but her trousers were sodden. She sat on the bed and tried to remove her shoes and socks, but it was a struggle. Her centre of gravity was off, and as the painful contractions continued to grow in intensity, she felt as though she wanted to push. Once she changed, she lay on the hospital bed and reclined back. It was good to be able to lie down finally. Cheryl asked her to raise her knees, and she lowered her head between Mae's legs. She felt a bit self-conscious as her last shower was the other day. Anthony was stingy when it came to the use of hot water, and with the events of this morning, she wasn't feeling remarkably fresh down there.

"Well, honey, I can already see the top of the head," Cheryl said, smiling. "Baby number one is coming." Mae felt as though she was going to hyperventilate or be sick, or both.

"Oh my god, I can't do this. I'm not ready; they're too early. I haven't got things ready yet." From then, Mae could hear a disturbance outside of the room: "What's going on out there? Is it Anthony?" Cheryl excused herself whilst she checked, asking another midwife to be with Mae until she got back. She was only gone for a couple of minutes, but Mae felt an uncontrollable urge to push within that time. She saw at the corner of her eye two men in white coats enter the room. Mae scrambled for the bedsheet and urgently covered herself.

"What are they doing here? They can't be here! I need them to leave!" Cheryl was back at Mae's side.

"Relax, honey, they have to be here for the babies, those babies are early, and they're going to need their help. Don't worry. There are two midwives here and two nurses, including myself. They won't see anything, and they won't be near you. You see them over there? By the trolley," Mae could see them behind her at the end of the room; they were several metres away. Mae sobbed. It really didn't matter where they were in the room, they were still IN the room, and as far as Anthony was concerned, she'd still be a dirty whore for allowing it.

"But you don't understand," she cried. As she let out a sob of frustration, she was overcome with the urge to push again, and she let out a cry of pain. "Where's Anthony?" Cheryl looked at Mae with regretful eyes.

"I'm sorry, honey, but we had to ask security to take him outside to calm down. He was getting aggressive with one of the doctors. He'll be allowed back in when he's cooled off. Unfortunately, he won't be able to be here for the birth. But don't worry, we're here to support you." Mae sighed. She thanked God for small mercies but then cursed him too.

Mae gave birth to a beautiful boy and girl. The boy was the smallest of the two. But still, they were both ridiculously tiny. Mae wondered how such fragile beings could be alive; they looked so vulnerable. Cheryl reassured her that both of the babies were as well as could be expected, but they had to go straight to the Special Care Baby Unit.

The nurses cleaned her up a little, and Anthony finally came in and saw her. Mae held her breath, just waiting for the whore and slut insults to come spewing out of his mouth. Mae was pleasantly surprised when he walked in completely calm and even had a smile on his face. He walked up to Mae's bedside and kissed her forehead.

"Well done love, I've seen the twins; they're perfect." Mae wondered if Cheryl could see the confusion on her face, and then it dawned on her; this was just an act; he had an audience to perform to. He'd already allowed them to see his nasty side, but as far as they were concerned, his nastiness was aimed at people he barely knew. He wanted to prove he was the doting husband and the proud father.

"I've called your mum and dad. Your dad will be here soon. Your mum said she couldn't get here at the moment. She is working and doesn't finish 'till late, but she said she'll give us a ring when she can see you. You'll probably be home by then. I'd think you'd probably be out in a couple of hours."

Cheryl kept her distance to give some privacy, but when she overheard what Anthony just said, she walked over to the bed.

"Actually, honey, it's been recommended that you stay overnight, you have a high temperature, and you're very anaemic. We want to keep an eye on you. Any excessive bleeding could make your condition escalate very poorly, especially with such a low iron count; it's at quite a dangerous level. Don't worry; we'll take good care of you." Mae could see Anthony forcing a smile. He didn't like this; he didn't like it at all. She was so pleased Cheryl was there, although she did wonder why Cheryl was loitering. She wasn't doing anything in particular, she was just making herself look busy, but Mae couldn't tell exactly what she'd done. Mae wondered if Cheryl knew; Did she learn her husband was a monster just waiting for that moment alone?

Certainly frustrated by their lack of alone time, Anthony said he would go out and pick up Janet and Brendan. These were his children from a previous relationship; they lived with their mother. Janet, in particular, was very excited to come and see her new baby brother and sister. Mae knew it would be an hour and a half round trip, so she allowed herself to relax. Cheryl left the room to let her rest, and she leaned into her pillow and closed her eyes.

Mae napped for half an hour when Mae's dad arrived. He carried two colossal teddy bears and pink and blue helium balloons. Mae was overjoyed by seeing her dad. It had been a while. They went to see the babies. Her dad wheeled her to the SCBU in a wheelchair. Once they arrived, they tracked down the twins. Mae sat with her little boy and her dad with his granddaughter. They didn't say much to each other. They just stroked the babies hands through the small holes in their incubators and basked in their perfection until Mae's dad spoke up suddenly.

"Hey Mae, have you seen this?" Mae looked up. She went over to her dad. He lifted a foot that was no bigger than a fifty pence piece. There was a small red mark on the side of her heel just under the ankle of her right foot. It was most likely a birthmark, but Mae had never seen a birthmark shaped like a perfect triangle before. Mae went to the boy's incubator; she checked his right foot, there was nothing there. Mae reached for his left and turned it, and there it was. There was another birthmark, shaped like a triangle, but his one was inverted.

"Dad, look. He has one too, but on the other foot, it's slightly different in that it's upside-down." They marvelled at the sight and were utterly baffled by it. They put it down as a strange "twin" coincidence.

Mae was struggling to stay awake. The baby unit was hot and quiet. The faint hum and rhythmic sounds of life support machines were lulling her eyes shut. Mae's dad could see her drifting, and he offered to help her back to her room. When they arrived back, Anthony and the children were already there. Mae's dad took this as his cue to leave.

Cheryl walked in as her dad was collecting himself, and she confidently advised Anthony it would soon be time for Mae to be left on her own as she needed to rest. It would have been okay for him to stay with her alone but not the children; they had to comply with visiting hours, and that was over in ten minutes. Anthony told Mae he would take the children home and come back in the morning. Mae's dad left, and Cheryl followed close behind. Thank goodness the children were still there. This would mean he still needed to watch what he said. However, he would have no qualms about calling her names in front of them; he'd done it many times before. Mae waited; she knew it was coming.

"So. My whore wife." His voice was low and quiet. "You opened your legs in front of two guys; what's worse is one was a paki! You liked it did you? Being the centre of attention. I guess you're no stranger to showing any guy your twat." Mae hated herself for crying yet again; she knew he got a sick satisfaction from it.

"No men saw anything, and I had midwives and nurses around me; the doctors were behind me, they wouldn't have seen anything," Mae tried to keep her voice low too, but she couldn't keep the desperation out of it.

"Why the fuck would I believe you? You're a fucking liar." He chewed the inside of his cheek and clenched his fists. "They can't make you stay the night. Why didn't you insist on coming home? Are you going to hook up with someone? Is that your plan?" Mae guffawed, her eyes wide.

"Don't be ridiculous; I just gave birth to twins. I had to have stitches down there, so the last thing I want to be doing is THAT." Anthony didn't respond immediately; he turned to check on the children. Janet was sat nicely in a chair whilst Brendan was tucking into some drawers, making a mess.

"I'll be back in the morning, and you ARE coming back tomorrow, you understand?" Mae nodded curtly. Shortly after, Cheryl entered, telling Anthony visiting hours were now over. Cheryl's eyes were cautious as she detected the thick atmosphere in the room. Anthony left with the children graciously and without incident.

Mae was horrified by his behaviour from start to finish. After the birth of their children, most couples would be hugging, crying with joy and picking out baby names. They hadn't even come up with any names yet. At that moment, their wristbands read *Newton Twin 1* and *Newton Twin 2*. There was absolutely nothing ordinary about their relationship.

Mae wished the night would last forever. It was like a huge weight was lifted from her shoulders, and she was about to have a minimum of twelve hours away from Anthony. But much like the time she spent with her dad earlier, tomorrow would soon come. She knew the babies wouldn't be returning with them, and it would just be her and Anthony. Mae was at a loss as to what to do; she was afraid all the time, she didn't want this life anymore, and she didn't want this life for her children. It was then she made the decision. She was going to leave him. It wasn't going to be easy, but she had to, if not for her, then for them. She needed to keep them safe. She had to think of a way out, and soon.

* * *

Mae awoke early from a peaceful sleep. It was great to be able to have the chance to be herself. She felt pretty gory; even though the nurses tried to clean her up, she was consistently bleeding profusely, and she longed for the smell of soap instead of the rusty smell of dried blood and sweat, so she took a deep and relaxing hot bath.

It bothered her that the babies weren't in the room with her; she wanted to hold their hands and for them to know mummy was there. Her legs were feeling stronger, so she quickly put on her robe and slowly made her way to the SCBU. There was no limit to how long you could be in there. She sat between the two incubators, her right hand with the girl and her left with the boy. She needed to name them something; boy and girl just seemed inappropriate. After some deliberation, she called them Catherine and Toby. She spoke softly to them.

"I promise that once you come home, I'll have a plan. I won't keep you there longer than necessary. I won't let him hurt you," she whispered. "Don't worry, I'll come and see you every day; I love you so much." Tears began to fall, and they didn't stop until Cheryl told her Anthony had arrived. She wiped her face dry and took a deep breath. For the first time in a long while, she felt strong and determined.

Anthony was there waiting in her room to take her home. Unfortunately, the twins needed to stay in hospital for a while, but she knew this from the start. More tests needed to be done, and their lungs weren't yet developed enough for them to breathe properly on their own; they needed extra oxygen. The doctors wanted Mae to stay another night, her temperature was still running high, but Mae told them she felt well enough to go home, and she would regularly visit to see the babies. She felt she could get away with the previous night, but there was no way Anthony would allow another night without suffering severe repercussions. Hence, they provided her with some iron tablets, and she was told to return soon for further blood tests to ensure levels went back to normal.

Mae felt sick with anxiety; she could only imagine how awful things would be when they got home. He'd taken his kids back to their mother this morning, so without them around; he wouldn't have to hold back. Of course, he was sweet and light around the nurses, he thanked them for their work, and he even brought Mae a bunch of flowers. Mae gushed her appreciation as a wife would when a husband gets his wife flowers, but she knew this was an act, a performance, and she was his leading lady. Cheryl wasn't fooled, and she glared at him, her stony gaze unwavering. Anthony didn't see it, but Mae did. Their eyes met, and Cheryl's seemed to say, *Look after yourself.* Mae's eyes replied *I'll try.* The hospital laundered the clothing Mae arrived in since Anthony hadn't bothered bringing some fresh clothes from home for her. They weren't maternity wear, but they were very stretched, the clothes now hanging on her thin frame. She was still very sore and moved around very slowly. Anthony was hurrying her around, but as Cheryl remained in the room, he kept it civilised. Mae was thankful to her for doing that.

They left the hospital. In the car, it was quiet, and Mae chose not to speak as she didn't want to trigger a fight, but the atmosphere was palpable. When they arrived home, he parked up outside the house, came around the car's passenger side, opened the door, and helped Mae out. The performance had to continue until they got into the house. They had neighbours who knew she'd been pregnant, so she was confident there would be curtain twitchers as an audience. As they shuffled into the house, he slammed the front door behind them. The bang made Mae flinch; the tension was already unsurmountable, and this had been brewing for over twenty-four hours. Mae immediately went to the sofa in the living room; she was so tired, she just wanted to lay down.

"Where do you think you're going?" Anthony demanded. Mae assumed it was a rhetorical question on the basis it looked pretty obvious where she was headed, so she didn't say anything; she just stood and gave him a blank look. "You know I had to take the kids back early this morning, then I had to come and get you. That seemed to take forever because apparently, you're as slow as fuck, I've not had any breakfast, and it's now lunchtime. I've been running around all morning; I'm knackered. Do you really think I'm going to make my own lunch?" Again, Mae said nothing as he continued, "I want four pieces of toast and a cup of tea to go with it." With that, he barged past Mae and collapsed on the sofa, switching on the TV and making himself comfortable. Mae stared at him with her mouth open. When Anthony saw she still hadn't moved, he put down the remote and stared back.

"Got something to say?" He tilted his head and chewed the inside of his cheek. He always did this when he was being confrontational, which was regularly, so it was surprising he hadn't chewed through his face by now. Mae's shoulders sagged.

"Nope, I have nothing to say." Mae turned and dragged her feet to the kitchen. In a way, she was relieved; it could've been worse and demanding his lunch wasn't going to kill her. She'd expected a barrage of abuse, but this was what he did. He was unpredictable. This was what made him so scary to be around; he liked to keep Mae on her toes and for her to be constantly walking on eggshells. Sometimes he was friendly; he had to be; otherwise, Mae would have left a long time ago. He had to make her think there was some good in him. He would do a small deed that would make her give him the benefit of the doubt, but the nice and nasty scale was tenuous; the minutest thing could shatter a good mood. Once, they were watching "You've been framed", a programme where people do the silliest things and usually hurt themselves in the process. They'd been laughing together after watching some very clumsy cats humiliate themselves, but then a video came on the screen where a row of Scottish men lifted their kilts and mooned the cameraman. Mae was foolish enough to laugh at it, Anthony didn't, and he looked at her with those cold eyes and called her a dirty slut for watching it. Then that was it; the good mood was gone. The problem was, he was a clever guy. Every time he flew off the handle, he made Mae believe it was her fault, and she would promptly apologise for it. She didn't see his behaviour as possessive or abusive, she saw it as protective, and it wasn't till later, as he worsened, that she realised it was all a mind game.

Mae tried to leave him several times, twice in a month once, but he convinced her she had nowhere to go, she had no friends, and she hadn't seen her family in months. He told her they didn't care for her anymore and he was all she had. He'd ground her down so much that she believed it. He'd be nicer to her afterwards to enforce the idea he was the best thing for her, and it worked. Mae felt foolish for being so naïve, but no more, she could see through him now.

Mae promised the twins she'd see them every day, but unfortunately, Anthony broke that promise on her behalf. He'd said there was no way to afford to go to the hospital daily; the fuel cost would be too much. Mae was so upset that she told him she'd take the bus if she had to, and this led to a horrendous argument, which resulted in him locking all the doors in the house and hiding the key. If that wasn't enough, he then threatened to leave the children at the hospital for good and never to go back, so Mae backed down; she needed to do this on his terms. In the end, they only saw the twins a maximum of twice a week and only provided two packs of nappies once a week. This did not see them through, and the hospital regularly asked for more, but Anthony kept telling them they couldn't afford it, despite being paid child benefits for two children. That money was better spent on cigarettes and cans of lager. In his mind, the hospital wasn't likely to allow the children to lay in soiled nappies, so whilst the hospital continued to supply them, why should he buy them? This broke Mae's heart, she ached to see them every day, and she wanted to provide for them. The more weeks that went by, the more they had their eyes open, and she was devastated to know they looked upon nurses more than their mother. She cried herself to sleep most nights. She wouldn't go to bed until she was sure Anthony was asleep, and she faked sleep on the sofa so that he would leave her to it. One night, he shook her awake hard, and when she opened her eyes, he demanded she come up to bed with him. He advised her that he had needs. This was too much for her, she was still in a lot of pain, and she plainly did not want to have sex with him, ever. She refused him. As usual, he accused her of getting 'it' elsewhere. She screamed back at him.

"I don't want to have sex with you because I hate you," His eye twitched, and he chewed his cheek as Mae continued to yell, "I can't do this anymore, you've kept me from my family, you've kept me from my babies, and you treat me like shit. I'm leaving you, Anthony; I can't stay here another minute." In an instant, Anthony lurched at her and grabbed her throat. He'd never hit her, and he didn't start now, but he pushed her against the wall; she could still breathe, but it was uncomfortable.

"I don't think so," he growled. "I will *never* let you leave. If you ever walk out that door, I'll come after you. I would track you down, I would take those children and throw them in the canal whilst you watch, and I'll drag you back, and you can live the rest of your life knowing it was your fault that they died." Spittle was splashing Mae's face as he spoke. Mae's eyes stung, but she held the tears back; she wasn't going to give him the satisfaction of crying. He yanked her away from the wall and threw her onto the sofa. Mae sat herself up and defiantly stuck out her chin.

"I'll call the police. I'll get a restraining order. You can't just murder two children and get away with it," Mae cried, and Anthony grinned. "Perhaps I'll go for a murder that looks more accidental, but either way, are you willing to take that chance? If you leave, whether I get away with it or not, those twins' days will be numbered, and you'll be left to live with it." His grin turned to a sneer, and he knew she wouldn't risk it. She had an idea of what he was capable of. But this wasn't over, she would have to get creative, and she didn't have long.

After four weeks of being without the babies, they received a call to say their health checks were much improved and the twins could go home. Mae was ecstatic; she couldn't wait to bring them home so she could hold them whenever she wanted to, feed them, bathe them and love them. But she was worried; after she attempted to leave just two weeks before, Anthony had been the model husband since their altercation, and this made Mae suspicious. *Why bother? You just threatened to kill my children if I leave.* She did wonder if it was remorse. She did believe he loved her in his own twisted, psychotic way, but no amount of good behaviour was going to make her ever love him or even remotely like him ever again. The nice guy wasn't around for long, though.

The car seats were prepared, and the cots were built, and the house was ready for them at last. Anthony's doubtful comments monopolised the whole trip to the hospital as to how well Mae would look after the twins.

"Don't expect me to get up in the night; that's your responsibility. I'm assuming your milk has dried up now?" During the pregnancy, Anthony made it very clear that Mae wasn't to breastfeed under any circumstances. He claimed it was disgusting and unnatural, and any mother that did it had some sick sexual interest in their child. Mae knew very well this was ridiculous and that he was an ignorant asshole, but she knew better than to argue with him. It was hard for her after the birth; it was difficult for Mae to get comfortable. Her breasts were so engorged with milk she was constantly leaking, soaking through several breast pads over the hour. Eventually, it did stop. The moment it happened, she didn't feel like a real mother anymore. She'd squandered the liquid that was supposed to nurture her babies, and it wasn't even her decision. She saw herself as a shitty mother already bringing these children into this awful existence, and she didn't need Anthony to bring her down further.

"Yes, the milk stopped a while ago now," Mae replied. She turned her head to look out the car window; a pesky tear escaped, and she didn't want him to see it.

"Good, I don't want to find you secretly feeding them with your tits; it's fucking sick." Mae didn't say anything; she just let him carry on and tried her best to block him out. He could say whatever he wanted now; Mae didn't care. She had an exit strategy. Hopefully, within the next couple of weeks, she and the children would be away from him, and they could start a new life. Well, she didn't have the resources to have a literal new life, but she could protect the children. She hoped.

They finally arrived back at the house. Mae was looking forward to getting the twins inside; it would be the longest amount of time she would have spent with them so far, and she was keen to experience motherhood as it should be. As close as she could get to it anyway, she knew Anthony would make things more complicated than it had to be. He wasn't particularly pleased when he'd found out she named the children without consulting him. It took him long enough even to notice. He didn't mention it again on the way home. The trip was reasonably quiet.

Two weeks passed. During that time, Anthony had his good days. He played with the babies, made silly faces and blew raspberries on their tummies. Then most of the days, he was awful. He ignored the children when they cried. He shouted at Mae when they awoke at night. He kept telling her to do things that didn't sound right, like letting the children cry out. He would say, *"you'll spoil them, and you'll make a rod from your own back".* The baby book she had, stated that a newborn couldn't be spoilt. Anthony did have two children already, and despite his poor ability to be a good husband to her, they turned out alright. Janet was the sweetest little girl, so she listened to his advice.

Mae was delaying her plan to leave, but only because it was risky; the scheme's success would depend heavily on whether Anthony went on the defensive or the offensive, and there was just no way to know.

It was just after one-thirty in the afternoon, and they'd just had a Sunday lunch. Anthony was having a nap on the sofa, as was his custom after a large meal. He was usually out for a couple of hours, so she had time for what she needed to do. The twins were sleeping peacefully in their cots. Mae quickly packed their clothes. It didn't take long; they didn't have much, probably a total of fourteen vests and fourteen baby grows; technically one per child for each day of the week, but it didn't work out that way. Lots of washing needed to be done because they went through about six pieces of clothing between them daily. Anthony was so tight on what money he spent on them. He felt the more money spent on them, the less there was in his beer fund. If all went well today, that would change, and she would spend every penny on them. After packing just a few things for herself, the bags were ready. It was time for the hard part.

Mae entered the bathroom and stared at her reflection in the mirror. She looked ill, her hair was dull, her face was drawn and pale, and the dark circles around her eyes made her face look hollow like a skeleton. Her cheekbones were too sharp, her lips didn't even have colour and her reflection almost looked like a black and white photograph. Mae picked up the ornament she kept on her bathroom window sill; it was like a snow globe but not hollow; instead, it was filled with a resin, making some pretty flowers appear alive. It created a weight in her hand, but it was not too heavy. She gritted her teeth as she held the ornament at arm's length to her right side, then she swung it like she was about to throw a ball, but instead of letting go, she guided it toward her face, striking herself in the eye socket. She was careful not to make a sound, but she couldn't help but let out a little squeal. Her skin already turned red. She watched herself in the mirror, but she wasn't convinced it had done enough damage. Now that she knew how much it hurt, she was reluctant to do it again, but she knew she had to. She repeated the action. This time she missed her target, and it stuck more towards her brow; the blow made her feel dizzy. She then saw a slight seepage of blood coming from a small split where she'd last hit. Perfect. This would cause a nasty bruise in time, but she needed something more evident for now. She grabbed a clean scouring pad that she would typically use to scrub the bath. On the same side of the cut, she started to rub the abrasive side against her cheek and chin; it was burning, and she decided to scrape her nose as well. Once she was finished, it definitely looked as though she'd been beaten up; her face was a mess. The scourer made her look as though she'd been dragged on her face.

Hurriedly, she grabbed the old laptop they bought second hand. They had a dongle to get mobile internet, but it wasn't capable of much. It did, however, have a built-in webcam. Anthony didn't know she knew, but she'd found the dating sites he'd been browsing, and she was confident he'd met people too. She didn't care. When he left the house for a couple of hours in the evening, she was pleased to see the back of him. She would get Cat and Toby out of their cots to have proper cuddles, whether they were crying or not, and she felt like an actual mother when he wasn't around. Mae shut the twins' room door and positioned herself on the floor with the cots in the background. The laptop was set directly in front of her. Mae pressed record on the webcam.

When she was finished, she put the children in their car seats already in the bedroom. She grabbed all of their bags. She needed to call her dad, but she didn't have her own phone, she needed Anthony's, and she also needed the key. He was still locking the doors, and he always kept both the key and phone on him; she needed to wake him up.

Mae placed the bags and the twins by the door; they were still sleeping peacefully. The living room door was the first door on the left, it had glass panes, and she could see Anthony, who was still snoring loudly with his mouth wide open. She silently opened the door, and she tiptoed over to the sofa, then knelt beside him nearest to his head. She reached out and shook his shoulder, and his eyes flung open, making Mae jump. He sat bolt upright the moment he saw her face.

"What the fuck is going on? Did someone break in and attack you? Where are they?" He was looking around, very panicked. Mae shushed him and touched his arm; he gazed at her quizzically.

"No one broke in, and I wasn't attacked, although it looks like I could've been attacked, doesn't it?' Mae circled her face with her finger and smiled. Anthony was naturally paranoid, so he was immediately suspicious about what Mae was up to.

"What the fuck are you playing at?" he growled as Mae stood up.

"I'm leaving you, and I'm already packed. I have everything ready to go, that includes the twins. All I need to do now is have the key and to call my dad, so I need your phone." Anthony stood and smirked.

"Oh yes, of course, you do. Well, let's just say I'm not going to let you go, and I don't give you the phone or the key. I think you better go back upstairs and unpack those bags before I do something that you'll regret," said Anthony. He chewed his inside cheek, just daring her to defy him. Mae smirked back at him.

"Well, this is where my beat-up face comes into it. You see, I already guessed you wouldn't cooperate, so I made a video. I emailed it to my old friend Annie. I asked her to email the video to the police if I don't call her, letting her know I'm okay. The police don't take too kindly to woman beaters and child abusers." Anthony's face suddenly became serious and dark; he scowled. Mae was backing him into a corner, and he wasn't used to it, especially not from her.

"Is that right? I always knew you were an untrustworthy whore. You met someone, didn't you?" Anthony challenged; this angered Mae. The guy was obsessed, like that would be the ONLY reason she could possibly want to leave him.

"For Christ sake, NO. You suffocate me. You call me a whore, a twat, and you call our children bastards, and you threaten to smother them. You are the worst husband any woman could have. Don't you think that's reason enough for me to want to leave you?" Anthony surprised Mae by suddenly bursting into tears. She didn't expect that. He dropped back down onto the sofa and put his head in his hands. Mae wondered if she should be feeling sympathy for him, but she felt nothing. Everything he'd done to her just made her feel cold, in some ways heartless. There was no way he could feel the hurt that she'd felt since they'd been together.

"If I promise to trust you more and to be better towards you, will you stay?" He sounded pitiful.

"No, Anthony. Too little too late, I'm afraid." Mae's voice was flat, and he began to sob.

"Can I at least see the children? I am their father." Mae was dreading this part; she predicted he would bring up access rights.

"The thing is, Anthony, I can't trust you with them. I'm afraid you'll hurt them to hurt me, which was why I made the video. I can't have you in their lives; it'll be no different to staying with you. I'll be scared all the time. I'm sorry, but I have to ask you to let us go. For good. If you come near us, I will use the video to press charges against you." She knew she needed to be careful, she cornered the animal, and he didn't like it. "Please don't make this any harder. Could I have the phone so I can call my dad to pick us up? As soon as the twins and I are safe, I will call Annie to let her know I'm okay and you can continue your life as normal. Please, let me have the phone?"

Anthony took his phone out of his jeans pocket, reluctantly holding it out to Mae. She went to take it, but he wouldn't let go. Mae tugged at the phone again, but Anthony grabbed Mae's hand with his free hand, squeezed it hard, making Mae scream in pain, and she let go of the phone. Anthony twisted her arm as he swiftly stood up, and pushed her face-first into the sofa and then let go of her. She quickly flipped over onto her back and saw a fist surge towards her face, and everything went black.

When Mae came to, she didn't know how long she'd been

unconscious for; it could have been seconds, or it could have been hours. She was still on the sofa in the living room, but she was alone. She could hear one of the twins crying, and the sound was coming from upstairs. Mae leapt up from the sofa and sprinted up towards the bedroom. She entered the room. The curtains were drawn, so it was dark. She saw Toby was still in his car seat, sleeping in the far corner of the room. The other car seat was next to him, but it was empty. On the bed, Mae could see a shadow. The whites of Anthony's eyes glowed in the dim light. Anthony was sitting against the headboard with Catherine right next to him. The computer was in his lap; he opened the lid, which lit up his face creating deep shadows where his eyes were. There was something demonic in the scene unfolding in front of her. Mae's hairs grew stiff on her arms.

"Anthony, give Catherine to me." Her voice remained level and calm. Anthony leaned forward and grinned wickedly. His left hand was concealed behind his pillow; when his hand finally emerged, it revealed he was holding a large kitchen knife; the blade glinted as the light caught on the shiny metal. Mae immediately lunged towards Catherine.

"Hold on." Anthony quickly placed the knife closer to Catherine's throat; she was still screaming, her arms and legs jerking up and down. Mae froze in place, eyes wide.

"Here's the computer; I want you to tell, Annie, you've changed your mind and we've sorted things out," Mae held out her arms with her palms up, a sign of surrender.

"Please, you don't want to hurt her; you'd be guaranteed to go to jail. Besides, she's your own daughter," Mae's eyes were desperate. Anthony smiled.

"Is she, though? You know I have my doubts about that.

How sure are you I won't slit her throat? Are you prepared to try me?" Mae wasn't sure. It was possible he could do it. The frustration of the situation was making her tremble. She'd come so close; why didn't she just leave whilst he slept? Broken a window or something and run to a neighbour. She could have fought him in the courts instead of going through this now. But she knew what the courts were like, they would have allowed him access, and they would never have been free from him. *Why couldn't he just let them be?*

Rage built up within her, and a fiery heat started to build up in her gut. It was a familiar sensation, and she'd felt it before a long, long time ago. It was something she fought to forget—the feeling scared her, but she couldn't control it; she no longer had command of her body, the fire did. Mae screamed and grabbed at her scalp as she felt her head start to burn, then her arms, legs, torso, and chest. Anthony's eyes dilated as he took in the spectacle; Mae's eyes were glowing, and they were bloodshot. She then had a moment of stillness as she let her arms drop to her sides. She focused on Anthony's feet, and they immediately combust into flames, moving quickly up his legs. He leapt up from the bed. Mae immediately saw her chance and grabbed Catherine. As Anthony dived to the floor and started rolling around, she picked up Toby's Car seat and ran from the bedroom. Hurriedly she looked behind her and saw Anthony was still on the ground; the fire was no longer just spreading on him. It transferred to the bed sheets, then to the curtains.

Mae ran with the children down the stairs. Soon after, Anthony was at the top of the stairs, his back ablaze and his legs charred. As she looked up at him, it was like she was looking at the devil in the depths of hell. In a fit of rage, he slipped on the steps and slid down toward her. The force of the fall was putting out the fire on his back. Mae quickly moved out of the way as Anthony crashed into the wall at the bottom of the stairs. He was motionless and lying on his front; *was he dead?* She wondered. Mae approached him slowly. The fire took hold at the top of the stairs and made its way down the bannister; Mae needed to be quick. She crouched, still holding Catherine in her left arm. She rooted around in his burnt tattered pockets, then success. She'd found the key, and she pulled it free from the back pocket of his jeans. Mae flinched; the keys were red hot, and she dropped them. Anthony turned and grabbed Mae's throat, pulling her towards his face, his rancid breath making her gag.

"You'll pay for this; I will find you and those kids, and I'll gut them whilst you watch," Anthony croaked. Mae wrenched herself free, horrified by his threat and grabbed the key, wincing at the heat, but she kept hold of them this time. Mae grabbed Toby's car seat and unlocked the front door; she dashed outside and slammed the door behind her. Perhaps the fire would kill him.

There was already a collection of neighbours on the pavement by the house, and Mae ran toward them all. Smoke was streaming from the bedroom window, filling the sky and blocking the sun from view. The front door suddenly burst open, and Anthony fell over the threshold and crashed onto the front lawn. The flames were visible from the open door, and the fire engulfed the entrance hall; he'd got out just in time. Mae ran to the nearest neighbour; her name was Ellen.

"Help me please," Mae never properly met her, but she often saw her walking past the house with her little Yorkshire

Terrier.

"He hurt me and tried to hurt the twins. I told him I was leaving him, so he set the house on fire trying to kill us all." Mae was manic; her emotions were genuine even though her story was not. Ellen tried to calm her and told her to come to her bungalow, where they could call the police. Anthony was still on the lawn; he wasn't moving, but he was alive; Mae could hear his groans.

The ambulance and police arrived shortly after. Anthony was taken away in an ambulance. The police interviewed Mae in Ellen's home, where Mae forged her story. There was no doubt the police believed her; the emailed video would also back up her story. The officer advised her they would interview Anthony when he was able and they'd let her know how they were going to proceed. Once the police left, Mae called her dad on Ellen's phone.

"Hey, dad, I've left him. Please could you come and get us?"

* * *

Anthony awoke in the hospital. An oxygen mask covered his nose and mouth. He reached up to pull off the mask, but his hands wouldn't move; they were cuffed to the bed. He looked around the hospital ward, and a police officer was standing by the door. He'd forgotten for a moment what happened. He paused for thought, then he remembered. He remembered Mae's glowing eyes, the intense look on her face as his feet went up in flames. He couldn't understand— things like that didn't happen in real life, and why hadn't she done it before? Then he realised something; she'd beaten him, and she got away. Anthony grew angry, but then his thoughts clouded as

32

pain took over, his whole body burned. He began to scream, and he shook his hands, the metal of the cuffs clanging against the bars of the bed. His outburst was a mix of agony and rage. He wanted the pain to stop, and he wanted Mae to pay. Nurses rushed over and pumped his line with Morphine, and the pain quickly eased away as his mind began to drift into sleep. The last thing he thought before closing his eyes was made of pure vengeance. *When she least expects it, I will destroy her.*

Chapter 2

Anthony spent three weeks in the hospital having his burns treated. His legs were the worst, being badly scarred after suffering third-degree burns. He had second-degree burns on his back, and it was an excruciating few weeks.

As soon as Anthony was discharged from the hospital, he was remanded in custody by the police, pending trial. He was arrested for attempted murder. He'd told the police he didn't start the fire, yet he didn't tell them what really happened either. He told them the injuries to Mae's face and the video were all fabricated, which was true and that she started the fire, but more conventionally.

The case went to court, and even Anthony's solicitor told him to plead guilty; he said the sentence might be reduced if he saved the court's time on a lengthy trial. The evidence was stacked up against him. There was the video, statements from the hospital staff, and even a statement from his mother. He didn't need the solicitor to tell him a jury would most definitely find him guilty. He was over six feet tall, stocky, had a grade one haircut and a deep scar on his face just beneath his eye. He looked like a thug. On the basis the victims were twin babies and a young woman who'd been reported to be a timid, oppressed and fearful girl, he didn't stand a chance. Anthony was an intelligent man, so he took his solicitor's advice and pleaded guilty.

Before sentencing, Anthony underwent a psychological evaluation. This was quite typical in this situation— it was alleged he'd started the fire intending to kill himself and his family, so there was an assumption that he was disturbed. The evaluation revealed he had a borderline personality disorder. The solicitor was particularly interested in the critical aspects of his condition, mainly that subjects were unstable emotionally and often took actions without thinking through the consequences. This was going to be the mitigating circumstance that would reduce his sentence. The diagnosis made sense to Anthony. He'd always struggled with his emotions since he was a child. He was always getting into fights with very little consideration as to what could happen after the fact. Anthony was no stranger to a police cell.

Anthony found it very difficult talking to the psychiatrist about his past, but his solicitor insisted it was essential to be fully honest. Without a psychological issue, he'd be looking at a lot longer in prison. Against his better judgement, he opened up about everything.

* * *

Anthony's early years were okay. His mother was single; she never married and had no contact with his father. Anthony didn't even know who his father was or what his name was; his mother refused to tell him. Initially, he was brought up by his grandparents— they were strict but fair. It was when his grandparents died that the trouble started. His mother was taking care of him alone, and she didn't know how to be a mother. She fed and clothed him, but that was about it— there was no emotional support or any shows of love and affection.

Anthony was a lonely boy growing up; he played by himself in his room. His mum liked to keep him out of sight and out of mind. His uncles would occasionally come over to see his mum, and if she needed to go out, she sometimes asked them to keep an eye on him. One Uncle, Jacob, was much like his late grandparents. He had his own children; he was stern and severe, but this didn't bother Anthony in the slightest. He would take Jacob over Uncle David any day.

Uncle David lived alone and had no children. Anthony could remember that he recalled him as friendly on the first visit, unlike his other family members. He interacted with Anthony, played with his toys and even play-wrestled with him. He was about eight years old then, and Uncle David was his favourite. He loved him like a father and looked forward to his visits.

When Anthony was ten years old, these feelings changed. Uncle David started to ask Anthony to do things Anthony did not want to do; he asked him to feel him in places where no child should be touching an adult man. Uncle David told Anthony that this was what happened when you loved somebody, but it had to be a secret. He told him if he said anything to anyone that he would end up in a children's home all by himself, he wouldn't love him anymore. Anthony wasn't a massive fan of his home or his mother, but it was all he had; so, he said nothing.

The abuse got worse over the years and became more regular and more painful. Anthony felt he had to tell someone— he didn't want to do it anymore, even if it meant that he had to go away.

One evening following his uncle's last visit, Anthony told his mother. He explained what his uncle was doing and how long he'd been doing it, and he asked her for help. She slapped him in the face and called him a filthy liar in response, and she demanded he never speak about it to anyone ever again. He was then sent to his room without dinner, and she didn't talk to him for weeks. When she did start talking to him again, it wasn't a meaningful conversation— she didn't ask him about his day at school or ask him where he'd been with his friends. He could be out all day, and she didn't care. She barked out orders like, *"Tidy your room; dinner's ready; Do your homework."* The only good thing that came out of telling his mum about Uncle David was that he never saw him again. He didn't know why— had she told him not to come over anymore? Did she tell Uncle David that he'd told her and he chose not to come over? Either way, it didn't matter to Anthony; he wouldn't be abused by him any longer.

When Anthony was a teenager, he became paranoid of any overly attentive or friendly men. He stayed clear of them and was quick to lash out at anyone who got close. He got along better with women, and this remained the case throughout his adult life.

* * *

When he sat down and spoke to the psychiatrist, who was a female, Anthony realised he had deep emotional problems that he didn't even know he had, yet he couldn't see how his treatment of Mae was wrong. He still stood by everything he did.

He remembered when they first met. He was a security guard, and Mae was a shop assistant in a discount retail store. The moment he saw her, he was besotted. She had dark shoulder-length hair, blue eyes and fair skin. She wasn't particularly slim but had nice feminine curves. She had a shyness he found attractive; she was a genteel girl. He was still with his partner at the time, Sarah, with whom he had two children, but things weren't good between them. She had a big mouth on her, and she didn't fall into line. Her family was constantly getting involved with their lives, and she refused to move away to get some distance from them. He'd already decided his time with Sarah was over; he was merely waiting for someone else to move on to first. He didn't like being on his own.

Initially, he made a point of just befriending Mae; he paid her compliments, helped her with heavy lifting, and he was a perfect gentleman. The more time he spent with her, the more he felt they were made for each other. Mae wasn't like Sarah; she wasn't loud and didn't have a foul mouth. She spoke politely and softly, and she had a gentle character. After a week of working with her, he asked her on a date. He'd told her he was single— Anthony didn't see it as a lie because depending on how their date went, he soon would be.

Their evening went well. Anthony collected Mae from her home and took her to a quiet country pub. She was receptive to his attentions, and he asked her about her life. She was bullied as a child, her parents were divorced, and she had a brother. She had low self-confidence, but she was pretty; she didn't know she was, which suited Anthony fine. The last thing he wanted from a girl was someone who walked around flaunting herself, thinking she was god's gift to men. He didn't think confidence was an attractive trait in a woman. She was also just twenty years old at the time. He was thirteen years her senior, and she came across as naïve and vulnerable. He liked her. There was just one disappointment at the end of the evening— she had sex with him, and anyone that has sex on a first date had questionable morals, in his opinion, but it wasn't a deal-breaker. It was just something he wanted to keep an eye on.

A few days later, he ended his relationship with Sarah and asked Mae if she wanted a romantic weekend in Cornwall. She agreed, and they left on a Friday night. They had an amazing time; they drank, played pool and did some sightseeing. On the Sunday afternoon they agreed to bunk off work and stay another night in Cornwall. It was then he demonstrated how spontaneous he could be. He asked her if she wanted them to move in together, and not just move in but to move from Gloucestershire to Cornwall. He was sure she felt swept off her feet, and she jumped at the chance. The same day they looked for houses for rent and found one that looked suitable. Mae called her dad and he agreed to put up a deposit, so they quit their jobs over the phone and began job hunting. He loved how she agreed with everything he wanted; all she seemed to want to do was to please him. She was definitely the woman for him. Within three months they were married and she was pregnant. He told her he wanted to look after her, and said that she didn't need a job and that she was his wife and he wanted her to look after the home. All of this was true, he considered himself a traditional type of man, but he was mainly concerned that another man would take her from him. She was perfect and he couldn't bear the thought of someone else taking her away from him. He knew the wedding ring wouldn't give her protection, it meant nothing. He knew what men were like— they were horny bastards with no respect.

Everything was going great for a while; he was due to go for an interview for a job, but something bothered him about Mae. Every day they spent together, he kept thinking, *she's too good to be true, she's too perfect.* There had to be something wrong, and he endeavoured to find out what it was. One evening he asked her how many men she'd slept with. She didn't like the question. She said she had three serious relationships. Anthony wasn't happy with that; a girl like her was bound to have had more partnerships than that. She was lying. They had a huge row, the biggest they ever had since they'd been together. He was persistent, and he wouldn't let it drop. The argument lasted for two days. Mae finally admitted she had two one-night stands when she was eighteen. So there it was; that's why she had sex with him on the first night. It was because she was a slut. He was angry she'd allowed him to put her on that pedestal for so long. From then on, he knew he couldn't trust her, and he had to keep her close just in case she was tempted to whore around. He took her phone, and he stayed with her twenty-four-seven. He cancelled the job interview, and they continued to live on benefits and by bouncing cheques.

The time came when they couldn't afford the rent anymore. They rented their home on the basis they'd both be working, so they were forced to abandon the house and headed back to Gloucestershire to move in with his mother.

Anthony had kept his word—he took care of Mae, and she didn't have to do anything. All he wanted in return was respect. He couldn't abide any kind of disrespect, and he made sure she knew it. Now here he was, accused by her and the nurses of cruelty and abuse when all he did was keep her safe from perverts and from herself. If it weren't for him, she would have ended up as someone's whore. He kept her respectable, and she knew where she stood. He was in charge, and she just needed to do as she was told. But then those babies came along, and they were the biggest mistake. Perhaps it was the time in hospital that changed her, or maybe a doctor tried to have her away, giving her ideas. Whatever it was, he knew he shouldn't have let her stay there. It was strange how it was their first night ever apart, and then she came back with an attitude. Then the next thing he knew, she was doing some crazy voodoo shit, and he ended up in court for something he didn't do. He could only hope the judge would take mercy on him.

After the evaluation, the judge was made aware of the psychological result and diagnosis. The judge had minimal sympathy for him after he'd seen the statement from his wife. All the judge could see was a cold, cruel bully who deserved to be punished, but he needed to take his disorder into account. Anthony was sentenced to nine years in prison for the attempted murder of his wife and two children, serving no less than five years. He was also ordered to undergo therapy with a psychiatrist throughout his sentence. The solicitor tried to convince Anthony that it was a positive result and could have been much worse. Anthony couldn't see it that way.

* * *

The years came and went, and Anthony ensured he carried out his sentence without hassle. His presence tended to keep other inmates away from him. There was something about his face that told people to *fuck off, or else.* Based on good behaviour, Anthony was released on parole after serving six years. It could have been earlier, but his psychiatrist had concerns. Apparently, he lacked remorse, which was an essential aspect of rehabilitation into society. However, once he knew this was holding up his release, he made sure to show remorse in his following sessions. He was eventually released on the provision he continued his psychiatric treatment.

For the whole time he was incarcerated, he tried to think of ways to make Mae pay. Anthony knew the children were the key—they were the trigger for her strange fiery-eyed episode. He was sure that if it weren't for them, she would never have left. She may have tried to, but he would've been able to make her stay. Those kids needed to be out of the picture for good.

Chapter 3

<u>**28th May 2010**</u>

"Mummy..." Catherine looked up at her mother with her mouth full of cereal. Milk was spilling out the corners of her mouth as she tried to speak. Mae was washing up from the previous evening's dinner.

"Yes, sweetie?" Mae looked around at her daughter and screwed up her face. "Cat. I've told you so many times, don't speak with your mouth full; you're dribbling your cereal down your school cardigan." Mae grabbed a cloth from the back of the sink and manically mopped off as much as she could before the chocolate colouring stained yet another cardigan. In the meantime, Cat swallowed her mouthful.

"Mummy, I don't want to go to school today." Cat placed her spoon back into her cereal bowl and looked down into her lap.

"Oh sweetie, why not?" Mae took a seat next to her and stroked her long strawberry blonde ponytail.

"Other girls are mean to me," Mae sighed. This was the third school in the last year, and in all of them, Cat seemed to struggle to make friends. Mae hated to move them around. Perhaps if she could stay in a school for longer than six months, she'd be able to allow other kids to get to know her properly. She was the sweetest, most sensitive girl, but unfortunately, it was necessary to move.

Ever since she left Anthony, she was always on edge, even more so now that he was out of prison. Mae remembered getting the call last year telling her he'd been released. She was horrified. She'd been living near her mum in Gloucester. It was handy because her mum was able to pick the children up after school, allowing her to save money on after school clubs. Mae was afraid he would easily find them there, Anthony knew where her mum lived. So she packed their things and moved into the neighbouring town of Churchdown. She decided to switch schools as well. Her mum's house was close to the school, and if he was watching her mum, he might see the children.

Six months into being at the new house, Mae was spooked. She was receiving withheld calls to her home phone, and every time she answered, no one spoke on the other end. It was just silence, but that wasn't all. When she slept, she felt as though she was being watched. One night she opened her eyes, and she was sure she saw the silhouette of a man standing in front of her bed, but when she turned the light on, he was gone. It got to the point that she couldn't sleep anymore, and she was always exhausted, so it was time to move again. This time she moved further afield— it was a forty-five-minute drive from Gloucester. They arrived at another new house and school in Swindon. So far, nothing weird had happened, and it seemed safe, but Mae doubted this feeling would last long, not when she knew he was out there somewhere. Mae hoped that someday Cat would understand why the moves were necessary.

Toby seemed to do fine at school; he seemed pretty popular with the other little ones. Although Mae didn't think he cared, he was quite happy with his own company either way. Mae turned in her seat to face Toby.

"Toby, do you look after your sister at school?" Mae asked. Toby already finished his cereal and had started to read his book. He was so far ahead of the other children his age when it came to reading, and he liked to write and create his own stories. At seven years old, he had quite the mature head on him. He considered himself the man of the family, and he was always very helpful to his mother. However, Cat irritated him; she always wanted to play silly games, but he wasn't interested. He would rather read quietly to himself.

"No, he doesn't," Cat said, pouting. "He tells me to go away when he's with his friends." Toby rolled his eyes.

"She's so annoying, though; my friends laugh at me if I let her play with us." Mae collected the twins' bowls and ditched them in the sink.

"Honey, she is your sister. More importantly, your twin sister, you two, are supposed to have a special bond that no one else can break, not even your friends. Now, I want you to look out for her. If you see other kids bullying her, you need to protect her; that's what siblings do. We all need to look after each other, okay?" Instead of agreeing, Toby just got down from the table with a huff. "Good, now both of you get your shoes on. It's time for school." Mae clicked her fingers rapidly, and they did as they were told.

The school was only a ten-minute walk from the house, which was why Mae took the house in the first place. They moved in just after Christmas, so the children joined their new school halfway through the year. Mae knew it wasn't ideal, but she had no other choice.

When Mae returned home from dropping the children off, she let out a sigh of relief. She had the day off from work as it was her birthday. She didn't feel it necessary to have the day off, but her work did it for all employees. Mae was a bartender for around three years before she moved onto call centres. She was now working in an office doing administration, but she only did it to pay the bills and rent. Mae was a creative soul; she enjoyed art, photography, and she loved to write. She always thought this was where Toby got his love of books and reading from. She read to both Cat and Toby every night since they were out of the hospital. Cat lost interest quite quickly, but Toby was always engrossed in the story and the characters. She had no luck finding a job within writing or publishing, and she didn't have any experience or qualifications in that field. She hoped one day she'd get to do what she loved, but right now, she needed to be responsible.

For her birthday, she was planning on making a special dinner for the three of them. There was going to be a more significant celebration with the rest of her family that weekend. Today was Wednesday, which was a rubbish day for a party. She would make their favourite—pizza, but she would make everything from scratch, including the base. Feeling motivated, Mae made a list of the ingredients and got into her white SUV, which she adored. She only had it for a couple of months, and it was the newest car she'd ever owned— she needed to get a loan to buy it. She only passed her test five years ago, and from then, she'd been driving small second-hand cars that were cheap to insure. After all these years and moving onto a job with better pay, her life finally came together, and she decided to treat herself. Mae put the key in the ignition and pulled off down the street.

* * *

He watched from his car as Mae drove down the street. He'd been parked on the opposite side of the road and saw her leave with the children earlier on, but he dared not emerge then as he knew she wouldn't be long— twenty minutes at the most. He needed longer. After he saw her come back from school, he'd decided to bide his time. It was clear she wasn't going to work today as she would usually have left at eight-forty-five; that's what happened the last few days anyway.

As soon as he saw her car disappear around the corner, he got out. He was dressed in dark clothing and wore a sweatshirt, the hood drawn up as he ventured across the road and down the driveway. The street was deserted, and driveways were empty. Most people who worked already left their homes for the day. There was a passageway down the side of the drive, going to the rear of the house. He was met with a large wooden gate blocking the way to the garden. It was secured with a padlock, but he already knew about this and was well prepared. He took the large rucksack from his shoulders and removed some bolt croppers. They made easy work of breaking the padlock. He entered the garden and closed the gate behind him. He proceeded to the glass-paned back door and quickly picked the lock open expertly. He could have smashed the glass, but he didn't want anyone suspecting he'd been there. He slipped into the house, taking his rucksack with him.

Twenty-five minutes passed, and he re-emerged from the back of the house, leaving the house the same way he entered.

His rucksack became noticeably less bulky. He replaced the broken padlock with a new one— this one he had the key for, allowing easier access later. He jogged to the car, threw the rucksack in the boot and climbed back into the driver's seat. He drove around the corner and out of sight of the house. Now, all he needed to do was wait.

* * *

After Mae returned from the shop, she prepared the dinner. She made a huge mess trying to make a pizza base, but she was happy with the result. Finally, she cleaned up, then made herself comfortable in front of the TV before she had to go and pick up Cat and Toby. Exhausted after her pizza making efforts, she managed to fall asleep. When she awoke, she opened her eyes slowly, rolled over onto her side and looked at her phone for the time. Shocked, she bolted upright; it was two-forty-five. She was going to be late fetching the kids! In a hurry, she grabbed her shoes and rushed out the door, practically jogging to the school.

When Mae arrived, Cat and Toby were the only children left to be collected. That was embarrassing; it wasn't the first time it happened either.

"I'm so sorry I'm late," said Mae breathlessly. The teacher, Mr Roberts, didn't look put out; if anything, his whole demeanour oozed with sympathy; Mae hated that. Because it was only her and the children, people looked at her with pity. *Poor girl, having to bring up twins alone; poor girl, living alone; poor girl, she must be so lonely; poor girl for this and that.* She knew they thought it— she had an uncanny ability to sense people's feelings, and she'd been feeling this particular one for the past seven years. She was a different person all those years ago; timid, scared, naïve and vulnerable, but she has come a long way since then. Now she was strong, independent and perfectly capable of looking after herself and her children. Now sympathy was merely insulting.

"No worries, Mae, we know it must be difficult juggling life and the kids all by yourself. We are here to support you." Mae wanted to roll her eyes, but she knew Mr Roberts meant well.

"Thank you, Mr Roberts; I do appreciate your understanding. Come on then, children. I have a surprise for you when we get home." As she hurried them away, she could sense Mr Roberts behind her, and she guaranteed he was watching her walk away with that solemn look on his face. Mae looked over her shoulder, and sure enough, she was right. She smiled and waved and watched as he waved back. She turned around, then felt it was now perfectly safe to roll her eyes. They had a slow walk back home; it was such a lovely day, the sun was out, and it was hot. It was the beginning of June, after all.

They enjoyed their special dinner; home-made pepperoni pizza and cola was quite the treat. Mae usually liked to eat healthy as best as she could, but she occasionally allowed a little bit of junk food for these special occasions. On the basis Mae had no partner to buy gifts on the children's behalf, she didn't receive any presents from them, but they did make her an extra special card. Cat was the artistic one, and she drew a flower and decorated it with glitter and paint. Toby did the writing part, sharing the most beautiful poem inside.

To our mum, who loves us the most,
It's your birthday today, sorry we couldn't be by the coast,
If I could get you a gift,

It would give you a great lift,
You deserve the world for being the best,
So I will provide you with the universe and the rest.
We love you, Mum x

The poem brought tears to Mae's eyes. Toby could be sensitive when he wanted to be. She gave the children extra kisses that night; they'd both been so well behaved. She followed the usual routine of tucking them in and telling them a story. They both slept in the same room at the moment, and she knew they'd be needing their own rooms when they were older, but she could only afford a two-bedroom house for the time being.

"Night, night, my babies," she whispered.

"Mummy. I'm not a baby," said Toby. His voice was weary and didn't at all sound annoyed.

"Yes, well, you're MY babies. Thank you for a lovely day." Mae blew them kisses from the doorway. Toby and Cat spoke in stereo.

"Love you, mummy."

Despite Mae's nap earlier, she felt exhausted, but she wasn't ready to go to bed yet. It was nine-thirty, she didn't typically let the kids stay up this late, especially on a school night, but it was a special occasion. Mae poured herself a glass of cider. She didn't like wine, and wine didn't like her, and she'd always enjoyed the cold, crisp, fresh flavour of sparkling cider. It was so refreshing, especially on such a warm evening. She gulped down half a glass in less than a minute, at which point she decided to grab another bottle from the fridge. This one wasn't going to last long. She took her spoils into the living room and turned on the television. Channel surfing didn't produce anything interesting, so she decided to watch her favourite box-set. She managed to get to the third episode before falling asleep halfway through. She didn't notice the shadowed figure watching her through the window.

It was just past midnight when the smoke started to trail through the hallways of the house. It was like a fine mist setting in, it hung in the air, and it flowed past several smoke detectors, but they all remained silent. The children's bedroom door was ajar. Mae kept it open slightly to allow light from the hall to enter the room. Cat hated the dark, always had done since she was small. Cat always insisted she needed to be able to see and the door needed to remain open. Unfortunately, in this case, it allowed the smoke to flow into the room unhindered. Cat was the closest to the door, and she was the first to begin coughing in her sleep.

The smoke continued through the house and was then followed by flames. The fire started in the kitchen. Mae had closed the living room door; apart from the smoke seeping underneath it, the fire bypassed her. But it spread quickly down the hall and to the stairs. The fumes filled the children's bedroom before the fire arrived, although half of the house was now ablaze. Toby managed to cough himself awake, and as he opened his eyes, he could see the tendrils of smoke moving through the beam of light from the hallway.

"Mum!" Toby leapt from his bed; his cough was now hacking. He struggled to breathe as the air got thinner, and he rushed over to Cat's bed. She was choking but wasn't waking up. Toby slid open the bedroom window at the front of the house. He grabbed Cat and tried to lift her, but she was too heavy. She was a dead weight. He shook her shoulders to try and wake her, and then her eyes blinked open then shut again.

He managed to lift her torso into a sitting position, and her head lolled forward. He smacked her cheeks, and she flinched; she was semi-conscious, and he shouted at her to get up, but she wasn't responding. He put her arm behind his neck and tried to heave her up, and she finally responded and helped herself to stand. She half walked and was half dragged to the open window where he rested the top half of her body on the windowsill. She held herself up and gasped for air.

Toby called from the window, "Help, fire. Somebody help us." A few people were already standing outside their houses, gaping as flames and smoke engulfed the house. Some people were on their phones, and Toby hoped they were calling the fire brigade. When the residents saw the two children at the window, they were horrified. There was a man from across the street who quickly approached the house. Toby saw him talking to the others, and they were shaking their heads at him and trying to pull him away from the burning house. It was then the man attempted to break down the front door. The door gave in immediately, but the moment the clean oxygen-filled air entered the doorway, flames erupted and blasted out from the house. The man was thrown backwards from the force, and he lay on the pavement as other residents ran to his aid. They dragged him away from the blaze.

* * *

Mae awoke as she heard shattering glass, and she bolted upright on the sofa; the television was still on. Her immediate thought was that the noise came from there, but she soon realised this was not the case as her eyes started to sting, and she felt a burning at the back of her throat as she inhaled the polluted air. Mae felt sick, there was a fire, and her next thought was of the children. She sprinted to the living room door, but she didn't have to touch it to know that fire was beyond it— she could feel the heat radiating several feet away. She needed to get to the children, but the hall wasn't an option unless she wanted to die immediately. She needed to be practical, and she'd be no good to the children if she were dead. The living room was at the back of the house, and there was a small lean-to on the side of the house whose roof was below the children's window. The problem was, she always kept that window locked with the fear that the children might climb out of it or someone could climb in. This now posed a problem. She decided to deal with that when she got there. First, she needed to get out of the living room.

It was getting more and more difficult to breathe. Mae grabbed the side table that was housing her glass of cider; The golden liquid soaked into the carpet as the glass shattered. She stood before the living room window. It was double glazed, but she heard once that it was more likely to break if you impact the window in the corner. Mae stepped back and swung the table into the bottom left corner of the window. Nothing. Not even a mark. She needed to hit it with more force. She swung again, and this time a crack formed in the corner. Heaving the table over her head, she did it again, and this time the table managed to penetrate the glass. It shattered into what looked like tiny diamonds, and they promptly showered over the lawn. Mae hopped through the opening and sprinted around to the side of the house. It was still warm outside, and all Mae was wearing was a thin nightshirt and women's boxer shorts. The only things protecting her feet were some non-slip bed socks. Glass already penetrated those, and every footfall stung.

* * *

Toby darted to the bedroom door and closed it. He grabbed the duvet off of his bed and pushed it under the door to stop the smoke from pouring in. He could hear the crackle of flames; they were close, and he was sure there was no way to get down the stairs. He went back to Cat to check on her. She seemed to be more lucid now, but she was shaking.

"Toby. Are we going to die?" Tears were streaming down Cat's face, she watched all the bystanders out in the street, as well as the injured man who attempted a rescue. Their faces said it all— the look of hopelessness and fear. Cat recognised some of them. One was the next-door neighbour who occasionally babysat them when their mum had to work. She was crying, and someone was holding her as her shoulders shook. *She thinks we're going to die.* Another was the old man who lived opposite them. Sometimes, when they played on their bikes at the front of the house, he would come out and give them ice lollies. He was a widower, and he liked telling them stories about his late wife. He now looked very distressed, pacing back and forth. He was one of the ones who had a phone to his ear. *He thinks we're going to die.*

"We're not going to die, Kitty-Cat." Toby hadn't called her that in ages. Before he'd become mature beyond his years, they had nicknames for each other. She called him Toby-Woby. She'd stopped calling him that after she said it at school in front of his friends. He didn't speak to her for a week, and all the boys in the class would go around calling him Toby-Woby. Some boys still did, and he was not impressed. Toby went over to Cat's bed and grabbed her favourite stuffed toy, Mr Bear.

"We can't die because someone needs to look after this guy." He handed her Mr Bear, and she took it thankfully and hugged him tightly. Toby scoured the room, looking for something heavy. He knew his mum locked the other window, and he also knew this would be the best window to escape from. It was getting hard to see in the room— the smoke was so thick, it hung in front of them like an impenetrable curtain. Then he remembered last Christmas, his grandad gave him a paperweight. It was transparent but had swirls of colour in the middle, almost like a still lava lamp effect. It was on his desk, and he liked to look at it when he was sat writing his stories. Out of desperation, he grabbed the orb-like ornament. With as much power as he could muster, he threw it at the window. In an instant, it sailed through the air and burst through the glass.

* * *

Mae ran around the house and reached the lean-to. It was used as a utility room and had a low roof and a small window. She heaved herself up onto the window ledge and grabbed the guttering. It didn't feel very secure and wouldn't hold her weight for long. She quickly grappled for the roof. It was made of felt material and was abrasive; it hurt her fingers. As she grabbed hold, she pulled her legs up behind her, grazing them trying to drag them up onto the roof. It was a small roof, no more than three metres wide and a metre deep. The moment she got up on her feet, she immediately ducked as she saw what looked like a clear ball smashing through the glass. She shielded her head with her hands as the ball soared over her and to the ground. She looked back at the window and saw Toby looking down at her, his face sooty with streaks under his eyes where his tears cleansed his skin.

"Mummy. Help us," yelled Toby.

"It's okay, baby, you need to be quick, you need to get out here. Where's Cat?" Mae's voice was urgent; she knew there wouldn't be much time.

"She's by the other window. I'll go get her."

"No baby come back— Toby was gone, and Mae peered through the window. She could see Toby next to Cat on the other side of the room, but just as she was about to call out to them, the bedroom door exploded open, and flames filled the doorway. Mae instinctively ducked again, and when she went back to the window, Cat was screaming. It was strange; it was almost as if the fire had a path around the room. Flames coursed in front of Mae just below the window, blocking their escape route. There was no way she would remain outside whilst her children were still in there, so she dived through the window and through the flames. They licked at her skin, and she could smell her hairs burn. She landed heavily on the floor, dislocating her shoulder, and she screamed in pain.

Toby and Cat ran to her, and the three of them sat on the floor in the middle of the room surrounded by the fire; it reminded Mae of the day she escaped Anthony, back then she had a way out, she couldn't see one here, not this time. The beds and the plush toys that scattered them had gone up, and every possible exit was now obstructed. Mae bundled the children onto her lap and hugged them tightly, ignoring the pain in her shoulder. She could hear sirens in the distance, but she was sure they couldn't arrive in time. They were all coughing uncontrollably. The flames were so tall they were burning the ceiling. It was now on fire, and debris began to fall on them. Mae looked above her, and as the roof was about to collapse completely, she accepted the inevitable. She dived to the ground, the children beneath her as she tried to protect them.

Mae closed her eyes, and in her children's ears, she whispered, "we're going to be okay, don't be scared. Mummy's here."

Chapter 4

The cooker was broken again; it was the third time in two months. The problem was, the landlord hired useless mates to fix these things when what he should be doing was calling out a professional. But then again, the cooker was over a decade old, it had grease encrusted knobs, and he'd never been able to see through the oven door glass it was so caked in burnt, god-knows-what. It was probably cheaper to just buy a new one. Anthony kicked the oven door in irritation, and it swung back open; the damn thing just wouldn't close. It appeared the dinner he was planning on eating, that he prepared himself, a sausage casserole, was now going to be replaced with beans on toast, again.

Anthony had been in the flat since he left prison a year ago. It was indeed a dump. The flat was situated above a convenience shop in Newent, Gloucestershire. The rent was cheap, and it was private; it was either rent the most affordable flat he could find or rent a room within a house for the exact same cost but in a better area. On the basis he was no social butterfly, he went with the grotty flat. It was in serious need of decoration; wallpaper was peeling off the walls, large areas of black mould were present in most corners of every room, and the carpet was threadbare. He considered decorating it, but it would be like polishing a turd. He couldn't see the point. The property came furnished, but the quality of the furniture and appliances matched the wallpaper. He hated it. He asked his mum if he could move back in with her, but disappointed by his past, she told him she was disowning him. Apparently, she was embarrassed to be related to him, and she refused to see him again. It was harsh, but Anthony expected nothing less from her; she would never win the Mother of the Year Award.

Anthony sat on the sofa where the stuffing was forcing its way out of the arms. He placed his plate of beans on toast on his lap and began to eat; he'd been looking forward to the sausage casserole. He intended on it being a celebratory dinner. Anthony's boss at the haulage company was finally giving him a pay-rise. Shortly after his release from prison, he landed a job as an HGV driver; he'd done driving before. It did usually pay well, but because he was on parole, the boss would only give him the job if he accepted a reduced wage. According to him, he was a risk. Anthony agreed; he knew it would be difficult getting a job of any worth after serving a prison sentence. It was yet another thing to thank that bitch for. Because of her, he was working a shitty paid job and living in squalor.

As he looked at his meal for one, he was reminded as to how alone he was. He was rarely without a girlfriend, partner or wife. It wasn't like he needed someone to take care of him, he could take care of himself, but he preferred to be tended to. Mae was good at that.

During Anthony's residence in prison, Mae was all he thought about. He wanted vengeance. His heart was full of hate. Nobody ever got the better of him, ever. He took it upon himself to find out Mae's whereabouts. He had a friend on the outside keeping tabs on her. His name was Daryl, and they'd been friends since they were boys at school. Daryl was a hopeless case; he was an alcoholic and a drug addict. Daryl didn't have any family, so Anthony was all he had; they were like brothers. Anthony called him from prison. He knew Mae would have gone straight to her mum's house because she lived alone, and her mum had the most space. So he asked Daryl to keep track of her whilst he was gone and in return, he'd buy him a good supply of cigarettes when he got out. Daryl was quite happy to help.

On his release, Anthony had to be careful what he did. There was a restraining order on him; he wasn't to get within a hundred yards of Mae and the children. Daryl informed him she'd moved to Churchdown. He wanted to see her; despite the hatred he had for her, he was curious to know if she'd changed at all. He couldn't chance it yet, though. He decided to play with her a bit. Daryl agreed to break into Mae's house for him; he needed Daryl to carry out a task.

The house wasn't difficult to get into; the locks were very basic, and he could pick the lock with ease to gain access. Daryl found himself in a small hallway. The floor was a mess with children's wellington boots, shoes and toys scattered around. He accidentally stood on a doll, and a high-pitched wailing came out of the tiny speaker on the dolls back. Daryl jumped back and looked around himself; no one seemed to be close by. He relaxed his shoulders and closed the door behind him, and continued into the snug living room. Anthony gave him instructions to call him from Mae's house phone. This was all he had to do. He pulled out the piece of paper with Anthony's number on it, and he picked up the receiver with a gloved hand and called him.

"Hey mate, has the number come up?" Daryl asked.

"Yeah, mate, it has, thanks. Now get out of there quick before anyone sees you," replied Anthony. The line immediately died.

Daryl put the phone down and went for the door but then hesitated. The addict in him wanted to know if there was anything worth stealing. He slightly opened the front door and glanced outside. The coast was still clear. He turned and went for the stairs. He entered the master bedroom and rooted around in the dresser drawers. Compared to the downstairs, this room was tidy. He was careful not to disturb anything too much. He pulled out some underwear. Even though they weren't lacy or sparse of material and were pretty basic briefs, he found himself becoming aroused. He raised the garment to his face and sniffed, his erection pushed against his grime smeared jeans, he inhaled deeply and grinned, he quickly shoved the knickers into his pocket, he would utilise those for his own purposes later, Anthony need not know. He continued to search for something of value. He checked his watch; he'd been there for fifteen minutes, and it was time to leave. She didn't seem to have anything that was worth much. He used the toilet before he went, leaving the seat up, and he exited the property without detection.

Once Anthony had the phone number, he began the mind games. He started by calling her around three times a week. Sometimes there was no answer, but when she did answer, he remained silent.

"Hello?" she would say. She would repeat it several times. After the first few calls, she started to add more words. "Who is this?" Then, "I don't know who you are, but this has to stop."

Then she stopped answering the phone completely. When that happened, it frustrated him. He realised that he looked forward to hearing her voice. He was no longer using the calls with the intent to harass her but to hear her, the way she was breathless sometimes; he wondered what she'd been doing beforehand, perhaps she just got out of the bath and rushed to the phone, he would imagine her standing there wrapped in a towel. Sometimes she would sound tired. He wondered if it was because she'd been asleep or just had a busy day. He knew he'd overdone the calls, but it became an addiction, and now, thanks to his greed, he had to think of another way of satisfying his obsession. A restraining order or not, he needed to see her.

One late night, he drove to Mae's house. It was the beginning of December, so it was cold. He wore a thick coat with a scarf and some gloves, ready for a cold night outside. He parked his car around the corner of her house, which was a cul-de-sac, all curtains were drawn, and there was no sign of any nosey neighbours. Anthony got out of his car and walked the rest of the way. He could see his breath in the air. Anthony was breathing rapidly, primarily due to excitement. He wore dark clothing and tried to avoid the street lights. No gate or wall was blocking off the back of the house, so he slinked around the back without hindrance. Most of the rooms were dark; the only one showing any light was the room furthest away. The light was dim; it may have been a night light, and he assumed this was the children's room. It was two in the morning, so nobody should be awake. He'd asked Daryl to go on a reconnaissance mission before his visit; he'd reported there was a small conservatory at the back of the house. Anthony stepped up onto the ledge near the windows and scrambled onto the glassed roof. It was only a short way to the apex of the conservatory, so he could clamber over the top quite easily. He was then directly under the window of what he hoped was Mae's room. He peered over the ledge and could see her bed; it was dark in there, but he could see the more minor details when his eyes adjusted. Mae was facing the window, her eyes shut. He squinted and noticed that her hair was relatively light. It was dark when they were together, so she must have dyed it. Her lips were slightly parted, and he could see the duvet rising up and down with her breathing, occasionally she twitched; she must have been dreaming. He watched her for an hour. Then she rolled over, and all he could see was the back of her head. What pleased him about this whole exercise was that she was alone. She hadn't replaced him yet, but she could if she wanted to; he'd agreed to the divorce. The psychiatrist in prison told him if he didn't agree to the divorce, he would never be able to move on. Anthony thought that was bollocks; he only agreed because he didn't want the hassle, and he didn't want anything slowing down his release.

Anthony returned home. He felt exhilarated. Seeing her reignited his passion for her, and he wanted her back more than ever, but he didn't know how. He went back to her house a further four times. On every occasion, she was alone. He wished he'd done this in the summer; he may have got to see more, with it being so cold she was constantly huddled inside a thick duvet. The last time he visited, he made a foolish mistake. He'd arrived sooner, wanting to spend more time with her. She seemed to be in a lighter sleep because she was fidgeting around a lot. Perhaps she'd gone to bed quite late that night. Then her eyes appeared to blink open for a moment; he ducked down under the window immediately, then light flooded out into the night sky. She must've turned her light on. He couldn't risk being seen, so he slid down the glass quickly and landed heavily on the ground, and his knee twisted. He wanted to shout out from the pain but resisted. He got up quickly and limped back to his car.

Shortly after the botched visit, Daryl told Anthony he'd seen the movers outside her house. *Shit,* he thought. He hadn't been arrested, so he assumed she didn't see him for sure, but she must have smelled a rat which put her into flight mode. He could've kicked himself; it was the greed again. His hunger for being near her was getting out of control.

It was hard to find out where she went after that; the last time, Daryl followed her. He tried this time as well, but he only had enough fuel in his car to travel a few miles. She'd gone onto the motorway, and she'd travelled so far that Daryl had to pull over into the services; his fuel was about to run out. Anthony was nothing but persistent; there was no restraining order on her family. Mae's mum didn't drive, so it was pointless watching her, so instead, he watched her dad's house. Anthony ensured he had a full tank of petrol and followed her father everywhere. There were lots of wasted journeys. Trips to town, the supermarket and on one occasion, he'd ended up at the hospital. He didn't know why and he didn't care. Finally, after tailing him for over two weeks, he went to visit his daughter. He now knew where she was; she'd moved to Swindon.

Snapping out of his silent reflection, Anthony finished up his meagre dinner and ditched his plate in the sink with the others; it was starting to look like the leaning tower of Pisa in there. He was exhausted. He'd recently come back from a night away in the lorry. He'd gone to Scotland. Even though it was a long drive, he loved those trips. The company paid for his dinner and breakfast, and he got to park up in quiet and secluded areas. He spent his evenings staring up at the clear unpolluted skies and watching the stars. He was due to complete another overnighter in a couple of days. He was looking forward to it, a couple of days away from this shit-hole he called home.

He collapsed back on the sofa to watch TV when there was a sudden knocking on the door. He looked at his watch; it was just past nine o'clock at night. Anthony frowned. "Who the fuck?" He whispered. He went to the door. He didn't have a peephole, so he had no choice but to open it. Two police officers were standing there; one was a man and the other a woman. He didn't open the door fully.

"What the fuck do you want?" he demanded.

"We have a few questions we would like to ask you, sir. Please may we come in?" the female officer asked.

"No, you fucking can't; I ain't done nothing, so you can just go away and leave me the hell alone." Anthony went to close the door when the male officer put his foot in the gap. Anthony looked down at the officer's foot and started chewing the inside of his cheek.

"We can discuss it here, or we can discuss it at the station. It's up to you, Mr Newton," replied the male officer. The female officer stepped forward and put her hand in the door, making eye contact with Anthony.

"At this stage, we just have some questions, Mr Newton, that's all. Please don't make it more difficult than it needs to be." Her voice was soft and kind, just like Mae's. He released the door but stood in front of it with his arms crossed.

"I'll let you in after you've told me what this is about." Anthony narrowed his eyes, his heart beating hard in his chest.

"It concerns a house fire in Swindon in the early hours of this morning. We need to ask you where you were last night and this morning, Mr Newton."

Chapter 5

The fire service had been fighting the fire for several hours, and there shouldn't have been any survivors. There were still flames licking the outside of the door when the firefighters entered the children's bedroom. Nothing could have prepared them for what they saw.

Sat untouched in the middle of the bedroom were three figures tightly intertwined in a huddle, embers glowing in a perfectly formed circle around them. None of them moved until a firefighter tentatively approached them and touched Mae's shoulder. Mae flinched to his touch; she was holding her children tightly, and she felt like she'd been in a trance. It only felt like five minutes ago that she leapt into the room, grabbed her children and reserved herself to the idea they were about to die. When she opened her eyes and looked up to see the startled, pale firefighter, who looked like he'd just seen a ghost, Mae wondered if she were a ghost herself. She took in her surroundings. Mae suddenly realised she felt boiling, and she was sweating. She looked above her and could see the night sky and the stars; the roof was gone. She was scared for the children; were they okay? She had one child per arm, and she shook them. They both looked up at her, tears streaming down their faces.

"My God, are you okay?" asked Mae. She pulled around Cat's hair looking for injuries and did the same with Toby. Cat looked up at her mother and whispered in response.

"Mummy." Cat's eyes were wide. "I saw the roof falling, and I didn't want it to kill us. I was so scared. I concentrated hard on it as it fell and shouted in my head, STOP," Cat hesitated, and Mae rubbed her back.

"It's okay, baby. What is it?"

"And I stopped it. I watched as it just stayed there over us; it was floating. Is that possible mummy, did I do that?" Cat's eyes were imploring. Toby looked at his sister wide-eyed, then he began to whisper too.

"Mum, bits of fire were coming down, and it burnt my arm." Toby lifted his arm to show his mum like he needed to prove he was telling the truth. "It was coming down on you and Cat too, and I didn't want it hurting either of you, so I concentrated hard like Cat said she did, then it started to come down like it was falling on an umbrella. It was sliding over us and landed on the ground, see," Toby gestured to the ring of embers around them. "It's like a circle, and none got in. Is that possible too, was that me, did I do that?"

Mae hugged her children tightly; she would speak to them about this later. They saved her and each other. She had no idea they were born with such gifts, although she didn't know why she was surprised; they were HER children after all. Part of her was relieved because if they didn't have these gifts, they would all be dead now, but the other part of her was afraid. What could they be capable of as they grow up? After the incident with Bobby all those years ago, she tried to forget about what she could do, and she fought to keep it hidden. Now she couldn't control it; it came when she was at her most vulnerable when she's afraid for someone she loves. It never happened when she was fearful for herself. To have this power at the height of such strong emotions, there's no telling what mayhem she could cause. Perhaps she should have taken the time to hone and control her ability. Mae decided then that her children should learn to control what they could do. For their sakes, but no one could know. The firefighter cleared his throat.

"Are you all okay?" he asked.

Mae forgot he was there. She smiled.

"Yes. Yes, we are."

All of a sudden, to Mae's surprise, both of her children gasped and grabbed hold of their feet. They were bare-footed as they'd been in bed when the fire started.

"What's wrong?" asked Mae. She inspected Cat's foot first.

"The side of my heel is stinging, mummy," The birthmark she and her father had noticed when the children were born was now different. The triangle that was there previously, now had a horizontal line going through it, and it was bright red. She then took a look at Toby's foot and his, too; the inverted triangle also had a bright red horizontal line going through it. Mae blinked repeatedly. This was more than just a weird twin thing.

The police told Mae that the Fire Report showed the fire had been caused by faulty wiring. Mae knew differently; this fire was no accident. Anthony had to be behind it, and she told the police as such. The police went to see Anthony after she told them of her suspicions. They came back to her saying that he was in Scotland for work on the night in question. His Transport Manager confirmed this and the tachograph information from the lorry supported what Anthony had told them. He had a solid alibi. Mae knew Anthony wasn't stupid; he left prison a year ago, and he would know if anything happened to them, he would be the prime suspect. She wondered if he had someone do it for him. Whoever was responsible for that fire, she was damn sure Anthony would have been the brains behind it. The police were happy to put it all down as an unfortunate accident, but Mae wasn't going to sweep it under the carpet as such. Besides, the cause of the fire wasn't the only thing to think about. She checked the smoke detectors the previous week, and they were all working, but the alarms did not go off that night, and the fire spread so quickly, she was confident an accelerant must have been used.

The landlord was held liable for the fire. Unfortunately for him, he failed to show proof of a wiring test by a registered electrician within the last five years. The previous test was carried out eight years ago, so it was deemed as negligence on his part. Despite Mae suspecting the wiring had little to do with the fire, the police encouraged her to claim against the landlord for compensation. The police and the fire service believed the fire to be caused by the negligence of the landlord. Who was she to argue?

The landlord did not dispute the claim. The insurance company made an offer Mae could not refuse; they were offered £600,000. This was to pay for everything they lost within their home and the trauma caused to them. The compensation also covered the minor injuries to Mae and the children. Everyone had superficial burns, but Mae sprained her wrist as well as dislocating her shoulder.

Mae treated this money as a lifeline to change her and the children's lives forever. She needed to do something drastic that wouldn't just affect her and the kids but also the rest of her family. They needed to move away, far away, and couldn't tell anyone where they were going. The family weren't happy. Her dad offered the spare room in his home, but Mae didn't want to put more of her family at risk. Her mum cried, her brother looked shocked, and her friend Annie had no words. They eventually accepted Mae's choice and just hoped this separation wouldn't be forever. Mae promised to keep in touch by Skype.

Mae reverted to her maiden name, Reynolds, following her surprisingly easy divorce, but Cat and Toby still had their father's name of Newton. She decided to have another name change for all of them. She thought long and hard, then finally settled on Phoenix; she felt it to be fitting. They did not perish after the terrible fire, and from that fire, they rose from the ashes and started again, just like the mythical Phoenix of legends.

The children were happy to move away but not so glad to leave their extended family. Mae didn't tell them she thought it was their father who started the fire, so unlike her, they had no fear of what would happen as far as he was concerned, but they were still shaken up. This wasn't just because of the near-death experience but more to do with their discoveries about themselves. Mae knew how they felt.

The move went well. Mae found the most beautiful detached barn conversion in Broughton-in-Furness, Cumbria. It was just what she was after; it was a good four hours away from Anthony. It was remote and private. It wasn't a house you'd just stumble upon by accident. It was a large house, more extensive than what they needed, but Mae wanted to get the most for her Pound Sterling. The house cost five-hundred and twenty-thousand pounds, leaving Mae with a decent amount of money left from her pay-out for furniture and anything else they might need.

The children were enrolled into the local school less than a mile away. They seemed to be getting on okay there. Cat made a close friend on her first day; it shocked Mae that she befriended a boy. She used to be such a girly girl, the boy's name was Jake; he was a sweet kid. On the other hand, Toby was a little slow to make friends, which was surprising; he seemed to retreat inward and had little interest in socialising. Toby made a couple of good friends eventually, but he was nowhere near as popular as he used to be. It was like he was trying to disappear. Both of the children changed so much. Mae hoped that they would recover.

Chapter 6

<u>**10 Years Later.**</u>

I t was Mae's thirty-ninth birthday— also the tenth anniversary of the fire that changed their lives. Mae decided it was finally time to get her whole family together to celebrate; her mother, father, brother, and her best friend, Annie. She was ready to move on, and it was time for the paranoia to stop. It had been ten years; undoubtedly, any fixations her ex-husband may have had should be gone by now. Even though she was confident he would have given up, she wasn't going to be complacent. Mae hoped she was making the right decision. They couldn't live like this forever, and she refused to.

Mae gave each family member the rendezvous location by text and arranged to meet everyone simultaneously. The meeting point was almost an hour away from home; she'd decided a service station would be an excellent place to meet. From there, they would travel in convoy to the house.

Mae got there over an hour early and sat in her car, waiting and watching. If she saw Anthony show up, she'd be calling the police immediately. Cat and Toby wanted to come with her for protection, just in case, but she didn't want to put her children in a position where they'd be at risk; she knew terrible things could happen when her protective, untrained instincts kicked in.

After half an hour, she saw her dad arrive. He parked up in his car, and she noticed he still had the same Audi that he had since 2008. She could see Freya in her sunglasses in the front passenger seat and Darren, her brother, slumped in the backseat.

Mae didn't go to greet them yet; she wanted to watch everyone arrive so she could see if anyone was followed. People may think this was all over the top, but ensuring her family stayed safe was necessary. They'd been doing this too long to risk it all now without caution. At the same time, she wanted to get as close to an everyday life as possible. She missed her family. They hadn't seen Cat and Toby in real life since they were seven; they'd only seen them grow through photographs and Skype. Mae knew Cat and Toby longed to see their Nan and grandad again. Cat especially couldn't wait to see her grandad; they were incredibly close in the early years.

Next to arrive was Annie; she was married, but she chose to come without her husband. He had strange shifts, and he had to work early in the morning. Mae asked Annie if she wanted to stay over, and she'd agreed. Annie wasn't alone; she had her two children, Molly, who was soon to be seven and Milo, who was just three years old. She also brought her chocolate Labrador, Steve, affectionately known as Stevie. Mae missed Annie so much; she wanted to run over to her and give her a huge hug, but she wanted to wait for her mother to show. As usual, she was late; she was reliant on her man-friend, Alan. Her husband died several years ago, and she'd been single ever since. She had a few male friends that were happy to help her out. Her mum asked Mae if he was welcome at the party, but Mae didn't know him, so she was unsure. She didn't want to say no because her dad was there with his wife. It seemed pretty mean to expect her mum to be there alone. She quizzed her mum about her friend, and by the time she was finished, she knew his life story. She was satisfied he probably had no relationship with Anthony, so he could come.

Mae waited a few minutes after their arrival; it didn't appear like anyone was followed. Cars were going in and out in a constant stream; none of the drivers looked at all familiar. They all assembled outside the entrance of the services, chatting to each other. Mae approached them cautiously, and as they caught sight of her, she smiled widely.

It was quite the reunion, and they all took turns hugging Mae and gushing about how well she looked. Her mum cried, and her dad tried not to. Everyone changed so much. Annie's children were a delight; they were a handful but a breath of fresh air. Milo blew raspberries as Mae tried to introduce herself, making her laugh and Molly smiled sweetly at her and held her hand as she went around her other loved ones. Stevie was leaping around, licking everyone. Once everyone was all hugged out, Mae asked them to go to their cars and get ready for the trip back to her home. She wanted to get them back as soon as possible so she could start to relax; being out in the open like this made her anxious.

* * *

Cat and Toby just finished putting up the gazebo in the back garden. Their mum already prepared all the food, and it was up to Cat and Toby to decorate and lay everything out nicely. They had the help of Jake, Cat's best friend.

"So why haven't you seen your family for so long, Cat?" Jake hadn't been told about their troubled past. Toby and Cat were given strict instructions from a young age that no one in their new life was to know anything. Cat knew this question was coming, and she had a pre-prepared lie all lined up.

"I'm not overly sure. There was some massive family feud years ago; mum doesn't talk about it. Apparently, it's taken years to get everyone back together again, so this is a first in a decade." Cat thought the less detail she had to remember, the better. Her mum always told her to plead ignorance; not knowing was almost like not lying. This was the story of her life.

"Well… I'm glad I could be part of it. What I mean is, I'm honoured." He took Cat's hand and smiled. Cat stood back and looked at Toby, pulling a face.

"Honestly, buddy, honoured is a bit over the top for our lowly family. Just wait until you meet Nan; she'll soon bring you back down to earth," laughed Toby.

"Trust me, Jake, we're far from the royal family," replied Cat. She shook her hand loose from Jake's grip. Both she and her brother laughed. Jake's face flushed with embarrassment. He wanted to say he was joking, but that wasn't true; he did feel honoured to be meeting her family. It made him wonder if Cat was perhaps warming toward the idea of him becoming her boyfriend; why else would she ask him around to meet the family? Either that or he was being used as an event hand for convenience. He was hoping for the first option but thought the latter was more likely.

Everything was finally set up. A banner hanging from the

front of the gazebo said, "Happy Birthday!" and balloons were scattered randomly, tied to chairs and tables. Some were released loose, and they kissed the ceiling of the gazebo. Picnic tables were covered with plates of food, and it looked as if there was enough to feed a small army. There was also plenty of alcohol. After admiring her hard work, Cat ran inside and up the stairs to get changed. She'd been wearing old jeans and a cami top, but she had a dress all picked out. Toby was already dressed in his buttoned shirt and skinny blue jeans. That was dressed up by his standards; his style was usually a hoodie, holey jeans and trainers.

"So, Jake, when are you going to ask my sister out? You've been friends for what? Ten years? That's a long crush, buddy." Jake blushed, clearing his throat as he stammered.

"N-n-no, we're just friends. It's not like that." Toby smacked Jake on the back. Toby was about a foot taller than Jake; this wasn't because Jake was particularly short; it was that Toby was quite tall. Jake stumbled forward.

"Keep telling yourself that, buddy." Said Toby; he turned away.

Jake and Toby weren't close friends, but they got on well. Toby secretly rooted for Jake; he was a good guy, and Toby knew he would treat his sister like a princess. But to be honest, Jake was a bit of a limp lettuce, which was probably why Cat never looked at him that way. Toby didn't have a girlfriend—or a boyfriend if he'd been that way inclined. The girls in school were of little interest to him; he thought of them as silly and immature. Even at seventeen, he was older than his years. Despite being popular in his early years, he wasn't anymore. He distanced himself from people, almost invisible and purposely kept a low profile.

Jake and Toby stayed outside and cracked open a couple of lagers. Cat was trotting down the stairs when she heard a car horn blowing; she screeched in excitement.

"They're here. Toby, they're here." Cat swung the front door open and ran out onto their six-car sized, gravel driveway. All the cars pulled up one after the other. It was another hug-fest as they all got out of their vehicles, and it all started again when Toby came out. Jake was sitting on the step in the doorway watching them, specifically Cat. He'd never seen her smile as much as she was right now. He rarely saw Cat in a dress and with her hair down, but he wished she did it more often. She usually wore her hair up in a messy bun, wore no make-up – not that she needed it and wore either tracksuit bottoms or leggings. She had a beautiful figure but was reluctant to reveal it until today. She was wearing a pretty floral summer dress, it cut in at her petite waist; her strawberry blonde hair cascaded halfway down her bareback over the spaghetti straps that criss-crossed down her spine. She looked beautiful. When she was standing next to her mum, they looked remarkably similar; the same high cheekbones and the same small pointy noses, but Cat's lips were fuller, and she was also slightly taller than Mae. He couldn't get over how happy she seemed; she quite often had an air of sadness about her. If she laughed, she would suddenly stop; it was like she felt guilty for having a good time. Jake wondered where this came from. This was part of what added to the attraction—there was a mystery that hid behind those eyes.

Cat started to wave at Jake enthusiastically; she was beaming, her eyes alight with joy. Jake waved back, wondering what got her so excited. He then heard someone behind him; he looked up and back over his shoulder. Jake felt foolish. Cat wasn't waving at him; she was waving at the guy standing behind him, who was now waving back. Jake recognised him. *What the hell is Archie Brook doing here?*

"Come on, babe. I want you to meet my grandad." *Babe? And what the hell were you doing inside the house?*

"Out the way, limp dick," Archie growled as he barged his way past Jake, nearly knocking him off the step. *Asshole* thought Jake. Everyone knew Archie; to the girls, he was the hot, bad boy. To guys, he was a total shithead. The only guys who thought differently were the like-minded ones who hung around with him. Archie was a dick to teachers at school as well, and he picked on the kids who were smaller than him. Archie never really bothered Jake because he would tower over Archie even though he was skinny and tall. Jake was too much of a risk to him because he would stand his ground. Archie preferred to pick on the guys who would collapse into the foetal position begging not to be hit.

It was nice to see how much effort Archie made to meet Cat's family; he wore ripped jeans and a ragged grey hoodie, even the hood was up. It was a gorgeous sunny day, so Archie must've been boiling. Jake watched as the walking Adonis strutted towards Cat. As they met down the driveway, Cat wrapped her arms around his neck and planted a massive kiss on his lips. Jake didn't understand how he didn't know about this. He and Cat were best friends; she told him everything, which included who the flavour of the month was, but she'd never even mentioned Archie before, ever. Jake couldn't bear to watch any longer, so he went inside. He decided to make himself useful and load the dishwasher.

Toby was also surprised to see who Cat was kissing. She never did have great taste in guys, which was partly why he wished Jake would get his finger out of his ass. Toby didn't know Archie personally; they didn't mix in the same circles. They did, however, play some sports together: football and rugby. Archie played dirty and didn't give a damn who got hurt. He liked to win, no matter what it took, and Toby didn't like him.

The family and Archie made their way through the house and into the back garden. Mae took one relative at a time on a tour of the place whilst the rest drank and ate. Music was playing softly in the background. They didn't need to worry about neighbours when it came to noise, the closest house was half a mile away, and the family home was reasonably isolated and situated at the end of a private road. Mae liked it that way; there was no reason why anyone would need to walk past the house, but if they did, Mae would know something was up.

Cat took on the role of child entertainer for the afternoon; she'd been playing tag with Molly and Milo for half an hour. In the meantime, Archie was slumped into a chair next to the drinks table. There were four empties next to him. He watched Cat running around; he didn't look at her in the same way as Jake did; he ogled her hungrily and licked his lips,

"Hey, Cat. I think it's about time you came over here and played with me." Cat turned and giggled as she trotted to him and sat in his lap. Jake was watching it all from the kitchen window. He sighed. It was time for him to go home; he was surplus to requirements. He lived in the village, which was a couple of miles away, and he felt the walk would do him good. Jake marched through the front door. As he began down the driveway, he saw Darren, Cat's uncle. He was drinking a bottle of lager up against a car. It was a silver Audi, the vehicle

Cat's grandad had gotten out of. Jake approached him,

"Hi, you're Darren, aren't you? Cat's Uncle," said Jake. Darren nodded slowly.

"Have you had enough of us already?" Darren asked flatly; he wasn't smiling. Jake laughed awkwardly.

"No, no, you guys are great; it's the non-relative I can't take anymore of," Jake replied.

"The guy who looks at my niece like she's a porn star?" replied Darren. Now he smiled. Jake smirked.

"Yep, that's the one. Cat deserves better than him. He's an utter dick. Pardon my French." Jake cleared his throat nervously.

"No worries, I had harsher words in mind; a fuckwit, lowlife twat." Jake liked Cat's uncle; they seemed to be on the same page. They then spent another minute or so coming up with different varieties of vulgar insults.

"So, does she know?" Asked Darren as he took another swig of beer. Jake furrowed his brow.

"Know what?"

"That you're totally in love with her?" Jake swallowed his beer quickly. *Was it that obvious?* He wondered.

"Probably, everyone else seems to know. As far as she's concerned, we're just friends. I can't see she'll ever consider me as anything more." Now he was saying this out loud, he only just started to realise how unlikely he and Cat were.

"She's out of my league." Jake looked down at his feet, then drank more beer. Darren patted Jake's shoulder.

"Pretty girls will always be bad news; you think you're out of their league? Take a look at me; they're out of my division. A good-looking girl would never look in my direction." Darren laughed, but it was apparent there was some bitterness there.

Jake thought it was slightly unfair; Darren may not have the looks of a model, but he was an intelligent guy. Not all girls or women were so superficial. Darren continued, "I mean, look at my sister. When she became a teenager, guys flocked to her. Did she choose the nice guy with a brain? Or did she opt for the guy who was buff and had an attitude? She had the pick of the bunch, and where did that leave her? She ends up with a nasty guy who tried to kill her and her babies." Darren shook his head in disapproval. Jake gawked in response.

"A guy tried to kill Mae, Cat and Toby?" Darren wasn't aware Jake didn't know. He saw his mistake immediately.

"Shit. Cat obviously didn't tell you. Forget I said anything." Darren drank the last of his bottle and started back to the house. Jake wasn't prepared to let Darren walk away on that bombshell. He knew Cat would never tell him; they'd been friends for years, and if she were going to tell him, she would've done it already. Jake grabbed Darren's arm before he could walk away. With a pleading look, he managed to convince Darren to tell him everything. He was outside with Darren for almost an hour talking. He was told how Mae was going to leave her husband and he'd tried to burn down the house with them in it when the twins were just babies. He then went on to tell him about the second fire and it was believed that her husband was responsible, but it was never proven. Jake finally realised where Cat's melancholy came from. She was traumatised. To a certain extent, Jake knew how she felt; he, too, had been through a lot when he was young.

It was just before he'd met Cat in primary school. His mum just picked him up from school; she'd been at work, she worked part-time as a cashier at the bank. When they arrived back home, his dad should've been there; he'd been unemployed after being laid off at a car manufacturing company. Until he found another job, he was playing house-husband. For the previous two weeks, he would have the dinner on the table as soon as they got in. Jake could smell Spaghetti Bolognese, or Spag Bol as they called it; it was his favourite. There was also the faint waft of garlic; he'd put garlic bread in the oven too. Jake called out to his dad, but there was no answer. Jake won a prize for a story he'd written at school that day and was keen to show him. He went to find him, but he was nowhere to be found in the house.

His dad had a large shed in the garden; it was more of a workshop, where he did woodwork, which was Jake's next port of call. The light was on, so he was confident he was in there. He pushed the shed door open and stepped inside. He found his dad but not how he expected to see him. His dad was swinging by the neck from the ceiling's apex, attached by some old blue rope. His dad often used this rope to tether down his car boot when he was carting around planks of wood that hung out the back. His dad's eyes were wide open, and Jake was sure his dad was looking at him. Jake was convinced he was still alive, and he tried to lift his legs to give the rope some slack, but he was too heavy. He yelled out for his mum, and when she arrived in the doorway, she screamed and broke down on the floor.

The emergency services eventually arrived; the neighbour called them; they heard the screams and hopped the fence in the garden to find out what was going on. His father was quickly taken away, and little was said to Jake afterwards, not by his mother or anyone.

Things got worse after the funeral; it was almost like

he'd lost both parents. His mother turned to alcohol. She later found out she was pregnant. They'd conceived Jake's little sister just two months before his dad died. She drank throughout the pregnancy. Fortunately, his sister Jennifer, who was now ten years old, was born without any alcohol-related problems, but Jake brought her up. Most of the time, his mum was sleeping, and if she wasn't sleeping, she was out of her face. Life was tough. Cat knew what happened to his dad, and she'd been supportive and helped him with Jennifer. He just wished she trusted him enough to tell him about her past. He was disappointed.

It was getting dark; it was around eight o'clock in the evening, and Jake needed to get home to give his sister her dinner and put her to bed. He said his goodbyes to Darren and went on his way.

* * *

The garden party was thinning by ten-thirty. Mae's Mum and her "friend" already left, and her dad, wife, and brother were just going. Annie was in the house putting her children to bed whilst Mae said goodbye. She hugged her dad and wished them a safe trip. She then approached Darren.

"It was nice to see you, even though I didn't see you much today. Hiding away as usual?" said Mae with a smile.

"You know what I'm like around crowds, even when it is my own family. I don't like it much." Darren looked around the estate, taking in the big house, the vast grounds and the trees which were all of Mae's property. "You fell on your feet again, I see. I hope you appreciate it all."

"Of course I do. I don't take anything for granted these

days." Mae gave her brother an awkward hug. They never had the "huggy" relationship that some siblings have. He got into the back of their dad's car and strapped himself in; he waved as they drove out from the driveway. Mae watched as the cars disappeared down the track.

Mae went back into the house. As she walked into the living room, Cat and Archie were getting a little too steamy on the sofa for Mae's liking. Cat may have been seventeen years old, but she was pretty sure her daughter was still a virgin, and she'd rather not watch her lose it on her new three-week-old sofa. Mae cleared her throat as indiscreetly as she possibly could. Cat removed herself from between Archie's legs and corrected her dress which was currently leaving nothing to the imagination.

"Mum, some privacy would be nice," said Cat.

"Some self-control would be nice too. Annie's upstairs, and she'll be back down in a minute. I think it's time for Archie to leave." Mae turned her gaze from Cat to Archie. "It was nice to meet you, Archie, but it's late."

Archie was clearly drunk, and as he stumbled up from the sofa, Mae looked away as she saw a bulge protruding from the crotch of his jeans. *Nice,* she thought; she rolled her eyes.

"Mum, can't he stay the night? As you said, it is late, and his house is three miles away." Mae shook her head frantically.

"Not a chance Cat, I barely know this boy. Besides, I think the fresh air might do him good." Cat glared at her mum.

"But mum, it's dark. What if something happens to him?" Mae glanced at Archie's groin again; the bulge was still there.

"He's a big boy Cat, and I'm sure he'll be fine. Come on, Archie, I'll see you out."

Cat smacked her hands on the sofa cushions in frustration,

and she stormed from the room and stomped up the stairs, presumably going to her room. Mae's assumption was confirmed when she heard the door slam, echoing through the house.

Mae escorted Archie out, and he stopped in the doorway. He thanked her for the lovely day, and he kissed her on the cheek. He then kissed her again, but this time his lips were closer to the corner of her mouth. *Randy sod,* Mae thought. Mae turned her head and manually turned Archie around, and gave him a gentle push toward the exit.

"Off you go, Casanova." Mae laughed to herself. Archie stumbled away into the darkness. She was sure he'd be alright; she was confident he'd been in worse states before and been farther away from home.

Mae went back into the house. Annie was sitting in an armchair, a glass of wine in hand; she smiled at Mae.

"Teenagers…" laughed Annie. Mae sniggered back.

"You have it all to come," said Mae. Annie grimaced with the thought, but at least she had a while yet.

Annie was very sensible. She married her school boyfriend, got her education and a fantastic career as a teacher. Only after she achieved that did she decide to start a family. Mae was proud of her friend. Mae only really got this far through luck and her uncanny ability to start fires by accident. Things could have been a lot different. Annie's life wasn't perfect, she had issues just like the next person, but she seemed happy. Mae and Annie spent the night reminiscing. They didn't hear a peep from Cat or Toby. Cat was sulking and was no longer talking to her mother, and Toby, well, he'd had a skin full. He went off to bed quite early, but not before spending an hour vomiting into the toilet. He was going to be feeling rough in the morning.

* * *

The house had gone quiet. Cat was still awake; she heard her mum and Annie going up to bed just after midnight. Cat was lying in her bed awake listening to music; she was still angry. She hated how her mum treated her like a defenceless child when they all knew she was far from vulnerable. She had a power, an ability that she spent many a night perfecting and tonight was no different. The whole room was full of floating objects. When she started, she could only move one or two items simultaneously, and even then, she had to concentrate; it was hard. But now, there didn't seem to be a limit to what or how much she could move, and it was easy. The problem with practising whilst angry was, Cat tended to damage things. On this occasion, she aimed her frustrations at her pillow. Feathers were everywhere; Cat sighed. One day, she would prove to her mother that she didn't need anyone's protection. She mentally dared her estranged father to try and hurt her or her family. She stripped open another pillow with the scissors as she wondered what her father was doing right now.

Chapter 7

When the police first told Anthony about the fire in Swindon, he assumed Mae and the twins had perished. It turned out they hadn't. Anthony didn't know how he felt about that. He didn't care about the kids; but Mae was different. If Mae died, then she would have gotten her comeuppance, but on the other hand, he would never have been able seen her again; he wasn't okay with that. He was glad she was still alive.

Anthony assumed correctly that Mae would be returning to her mother's house. She was there for about four months, and Anthony kept close tabs on her. If it wasn't him watching the house, then it was Daryl. One Thursday evening at about nine-thirty, Anthony called it a night and went back home. He was starting work early in the morning, and he struggled to get up, whether he went to bed early or not. Daryl said he'd go around to watch Mae the following morning. Most of Anthony's money was going to Daryl at the moment; he was paying him with a packet of cigarettes per day to stake out the house. It was setting him back sixty pounds a week, but he wasn't going to stop until he knew what Mae's next move was.

Anthony received a call from Daryl that morning. He said

Mae's car was gone and that he'd arrived at her mum's house at eight. Anthony didn't overthink it; she might have a new job or had an appointment to attend, so he wasn't concerned. He told Daryl to go back home. Anthony would be there at six, so she should be back by then.

When he arrived, her car was still missing. Now he was worried. Where had she been all day? After a few hours of watching, he saw little activity. He saw the silhouette of her mother, Samantha, walk past the windows, but no sign of small people. Wherever Mae was, the children were with her. He stayed longer than he usually did. He needed to be up early again for work, but he couldn't leave yet. He wanted to see Mae come home before he left.

It was midnight, and there was no sign of her. Perhaps they'd gone on holiday, there's no way she could have moved to a new house between his leaving last night and Daryl's arrival this morning. He gave it a few days, but when she didn't show up again, he had enough. He needed to know what was going on. There was no reasoning going on in his head. He was frustrated, and he couldn't control his urge to get answers. He stepped out of his old faded red Vauxhall. He marched up to the front door. There was a doorbell, but he ignored it and hammered on the wooden panel. There was a square hole with a window in the door at head height, but he stepped to the side of it so that Samantha wouldn't be able to see him. She opened the door. Before she even realised who it was, he barged the door open and forced his way into the house. She stumbled back, eyes wide and trembling.

"Where is she? Where's Mae?" Anthony demanded. He towered over Samantha at nearly two heads taller than her. His face was glowing crimson; he was chewing his cheek and shaking with his fists clenched. Samantha's frightened eyes hardened.

"She's gone," she yelled. "And it's thanks to you that no one will probably ever see her again. It's your fault that I won't see my grandchildren grow up." Tears streamed down Samantha's face. Anthony stepped back, attempting to calm himself.

"What do you mean?" he asked. He'd levelled his voice slightly; he was frightening her, but he needed this information.

"She has moved away; the children have gone with her. No one in the family knows where she is, and we will never know. She's afraid of you finding her. The fire was the final straw. She was afraid, and she feels that the only way she and the children could move on safely is if she disappeared. So that's what she's done; they have disappeared. You will never find her." Anthony backed up and sank into an armchair as he stared down at the floor. He wondered if Samantha was telling the truth. He was convinced that Mae probably moved, but had she gone without telling her family where she was going? The anguish on Samantha's face told him that it was true.

"She really didn't tell anyone?" He didn't look up as he spoke; he just needed to clarify that point.

"Not a soul. I hope you're satisfied. Not only did you ruin her life, but you've ruined ours too. I want you to leave now." Samantha wiped her face dry and widened the already open door. Anthony wasn't going to push it any further with her. He believed what she said, and he needed to consider his next steps. He left the house and sat in his car. He punched the door panel, slapped his steering wheel, and kicked the bottom of the footwell. He growled to himself.

"Fuckin', fuckin', bitch. You fuckin' bitch whore twat!" He

rested his head on the wheel, and he sobbed.

Anthony spent six months looking for Mae. He continued to watch Samantha just in case she was lying—he doubted she was. He also followed her dad. This didn't achieve anything. Anthony went as far as to hire a private detective. He didn't come cheap. He told him his ex-wife took his children, and he was playing the doting father wanting to find them. This also turned up nothing. Mae had disappeared off the face of the earth, and he didn't have any idea how to find her.

* * *

Over the following nine and a half years, Anthony never forgot about Mae, but as he'd done all he could to find her, he chose to move on. He had several relationships. Most of them were short. He got out of his flat and moved in with the first girl, Celia. She was younger than him, ten years his junior. She wasn't the prettiest girl, but Anthony wasn't ashamed to be seen with her. Upon first meeting, she was like Mae in that she seemed to have low self-esteem. As he got to know her better, some qualities arose that he wasn't keen on. She wanted to know where he was all the time, and when he was out, she was calling him constantly. When he got home, she would bombard him with questions. She would then break down in tears, asking him if he was going to leave her. She was so clingy and suffocating he couldn't cope with it anymore. He stayed with Celia while looking for someone else; she was surprisingly good in the bedroom department. Besides, he was living in her house. If he moved out, he'd have nowhere to go.

Anthony finished with Celia just before their year's anniversary of the first meeting; she didn't take it well. There were lots of tears, and she even threatened to slit her wrists. Anthony told her to do whatever she wanted as he didn't care. He walked out of the door whilst she was holding a small kitchen knife over her wrists. She screamed when he closed the door behind him. As he walked away to his car, he wondered if she was lying on the floor in a pool of her blood. The thought made him smile.

As sadistic as he was, Anthony could be charming when he applied himself, and he didn't have any trouble luring another woman into his company. The next girl he was with was Charlotte, and he arrived at her house promptly. They'd met in the local pub. She worked behind the bar; a little overweight but she had a pretty face. She was always very attentive when he walked into the pub every Thursday night. He never once took Celia there, so Charlotte didn't know that she even existed. They flirted with each other often, and one night after the pub closed, Anthony waited outside for her, and they kissed. Charlotte seemed to lose control, and they'd ended up having sex in the car park on some grass behind the cars. This told Anthony that she, like Mae, was a bit of a whore, but he was keen to get away from Celia, and Charlotte was eager.

Charlotte lived in a council house. She had two young children aged two and four. They had the same father who was out of the picture, so she was very much on her own. Anthony stayed with Charlotte for about three years—she was what he considered a long-term investment. Over those three years, he kept her in line. He took her phone from her, and she was forbidden to see her family. He told her that he believed her family had a problem with him and they were trying to turn her against him, which made her angry. To his joy, she fell out with them, and they barely talked anymore. When there was ever any talk of her leaving him, he manipulated her by telling her that he was the only person who could ever care for her. He told her she was too fat and ugly to get anybody else and she would be lonely and sad for the rest of her life if she ever left him. Charlotte believed it for a while.

The relationship was over when Charlotte found out her mother was dying of cancer. She wanted to see her, and Anthony told her that she couldn't. They got into a huge row, and even her children witnessed it. Anthony lost his temper and attacked Charlotte with a pair of scissors. Thankfully she wasn't seriously injured; there were some cuts to her abdomen and her forearms. Anthony agreed to let her leave but on the basis that she told no one about the attack. He said to her that if he even sees the police, he will find her and cut up her face because it was the only attribute going for her. He would also go after the children. Charlotte ran from the house terrified, and she never looked back. They had made the tenancy joint soon after Anthony moved in, so he could stay there. He never heard from Charlotte again, and he never received a visit from the police.

The rest of Anthony's relationships lasted anywhere from three months to a year. He didn't have any interest in getting into anything too committed; things always seemed to go wrong, and he didn't want to end up in prison again.

Whilst Mae was celebrating her birthday with her family for the first time, Anthony enjoyed a casual relationship with Tina. Anthony still lived in Charlotte's old house; it was too good of a set-up to give up. Tina came round every other night; they'd have sex, then she would go home. Anthony found this lifestyle befitting to him. He didn't have any affection for Tina. She wasn't particularly good looking, but she fulfilled a need they both had.

Tina just left; it was about nine-thirty at night, and he was smoking a cigarette whilst laying in bed. He took a swig from a can of lager and switched on the television. He was watching the news when his phone started to ring. He assumed it was Tina; perhaps she'd left her knickers behind again. He looked at the display, and it showed the number as withheld. Anthony answered the phone.

"Hello?"

"Hi, is this Anthony Newton?" The voice was deep, and it didn't sound natural.

"Depends who's asking." Anthony's voice was disinterested; he was sure it was a telemarketer.

"I have five words for you, Mr Newton. I. Know. Where. Mae. Is. Do I have your attention?" The profound words were self-assured. Anthony sat upright in his bed, took a deep drag from his cigarette and exhaled. Smoke plumed above his head.

"You better not be fucking with me, pal," Anthony growled.

"I assure you, I am not fucking with you. I know where she is, and I will tell you what I know."

"What's the catch, pal? You want money? If you do, I ain't got none." Anthony stubbed out his cigarette in an already overflowing ashtray on the bedside table.

"Of course, I want something in return, but it's not money. Let's meet, and I will tell you exactly what I want." Anthony was unsure, but he agreed to meet up with the guy that same night.

* * *

They met in a supermarket car park. It was two in the morning. The car park was empty apart from the odd car dotted here and there, probably supermarket employees working the night shift. The mysterious caller concealed his face with a scarf. It looked strange as the air was mild. They talked under a street light; the conversation was short. They ended the meeting with a handshake, and Anthony put a piece of paper in his pocket.

Anthony arrived back home. He couldn't stop smiling. He grabbed himself a beer from the fridge and downed it in one, then he took another and sat on the sofa. He pulled the paper from his jeans and looked at it. It was Mae's address. Not only did he know where she was, but he also had her new name. Mae Phoenix.

Chapter 8

Toby pulled himself away from the party. He'd just been drinking brandy with his grandfather, his grandfather being a seasoned brandy drinker, was ready for another, but Toby had to decline; the last one didn't seem to sit well in his stomach. Toby was feeling light-headed and stumbled as he walked. He glanced over at Cat and Archie. Cat was sitting on Archie's lap, and his hands were moving up her leg under her dress. Toby growled to himself.

"You keep your fucking hands off my sister, you—" he was about to approach them when his stomach gurgled; he put his hand to his mouth and tasted something acidic come up his throat. He would have to deal with Archie some other time. Toby ran for the house. He managed to make it to the bathroom just in time.

Toby thought he'd been vomiting forever; just when he thought he'd finished, he heaved again. After half an hour of crouching next to the toilet and producing nothing more, he decided that he was probably okay for a while. Toby dragged his feet towards his bedroom. There was a bottle of water on his bedside table; he downed it one. He couldn't understand why the water tasted of brandy. Wiping his mouth with the back of his hand, Toby laid down and stared at the ceiling.

He laughed at himself. The last thing he'd expected to do this afternoon was to become ridiculously drunk; he was against this party from day one. He thought back to the conversation they'd had.

"Toby, what the hell are you saying? You don't want to see nan and grandad?" screamed Cat, sounding betrayed.

"Of course I do; I've missed them just as much as you have." He sighed, "I'm just concerned, okay. We've been here for ten years; we've got friends and a semblance of a normal life. I don't want to have to move again; I'm happy here."

"Exactly. It's been ten years. Do you think our dad, who didn't give a shit about us when we were born, is still waiting around for us to pop up?" Cat placed her hands on her hips. "I'm quite sure he would've moved on to his next victim by now, ruining their life. If we continue to live like this, he's won." There was a moment of silent tension in the room.

"She's right," said Mae. Those words surprised both Cat and Toby. They stared at her wide-eyed. "I'm still going to be cautious; I'm not taking this decision lightly. But we can't keep living like this. You guys are seventeen now. Your nan, grandad, and uncle have missed out on so much, nearly all your childhood. I refuse to allow Anthony to take anymore from us. He has likely forgotten about us by now. I mean, who would wait around for a decade?" Toby chuckled, but there was no smile on his face.

"A psycho would wait, and let's face it, he was one hell of a basket case." Said Toby, then he sighed; this party was going to happen whether he wanted it to or not. "Fine, but I'm going to be looking out. There is no way that I'm going to be able to relax until they're all gone."

And now, here he was, watching the room spin out of

control. He couldn't watch it any longer, so he closed his eyes. He didn't want to be the buzz-kill of the family, but knowing what they'd run away from made him feel responsible; he would protect the family. Toby trusted no one. He did wonder what he would be like now had his mum not told them about their dad. She'd told both of them that they only moved away from nan and grandad for her job. As the years passed, they kept asking more and more questions about why they couldn't go and visit their grandparents and why their grandparents weren't coming to see them. They had Skype, but it wasn't the same. Their mum came clean on the day that Cat broke into tears.

"Don't they love us? Did we do something wrong?" Cat sobbed. They were eleven years old and only just started senior school. Cat was having a tough time. She was being bullied and was struggling to make friends, her frame of mind suggested that everyone hated her. Toby still remembered the conversation six years ago.

"Children, I need to tell you something," she sat them down on the sofa and covered them all - including herself with a blanket. They sat either side of her, and she put her arms around them. Two pairs of innocent, anxious eyes looked up at her. "We didn't move here for my job. I lied to you, and I'm really sorry," the twins looked across Mae and gazed at each other. They turned their eyes back to their mother. "We left because your father was a nasty man." Mae took a deep breath. "Before you were born, your dad was very cruel to me. I was afraid to leave him because I thought he'd hurt me. When you children came along, I was even more afraid that he might hurt you because he said he would do horrible things if I tried to get away. So I had a plan." Mae continued to tell them the story from the beginning. All the way up to the final fire that revealed their abilities. Now they understood why they had to run away.

The truth, however, was damaging for both of them. From that day forward, Toby struggled to relax. He suffered from extreme anxiety; he had nightmares and night terrors. Many a night, Toby would awake suddenly with his bedclothes damp with sweat. He'd be breathless and shaking; the dreams were so vivid, it felt like he was there. He didn't scream anymore; he taught himself not to because it frightened his mum. There was a time that she said she would take him to see a child psychologist, but he didn't want to go. Mental health expert or not, he wouldn't trust them. So he told his mum he was no longer having the dreams. The trust issues didn't stop there. Toby was suspicious of most people. Even the everyday man on the street could be a potential killer or maniac. Toby became quite obsessed with the psychology of serial killers and the like. Even the lovely, widowed lady down the road could be a murderer; perhaps she'd killed her husband. You could never really know someone. This was his life now; anxiety and suspicion.

Cat, on the other hand, became angry and rebellious. Toby failed to make Cat see the danger. She had a powerful ability, and she knew it. His sister decided that no one would ever try to hurt her again; if they tried, she would make them wish they hadn't. This concerned both him and their mum; she was a loose cannon and they were always on edge.

Toby's thoughts of what could have been slowly drifted away. He rolled over onto his side and fell into a restless sleep.

* * *

The dream started as they often did – with fire. Flames were everywhere. The smoke was thicker than fog; Toby tried to see through the haze but couldn't see anything. He closed his eyes and tried to listen. There was screaming in the distance, he moved towards the sound, and the screaming became louder. There were many voices in the room, but he was unable to identify them. It was so cavernous, everything echoed. He then recognised that he was in an old building without any rooms; it was one large expanse of space. The smoke was beginning to clear, and he could see figures moving around. He tried to concentrate on what was going on; distracted, he wasn't watching where he was walking, and he tripped. Toby looked down and saw a body; blood was pooling and spreading out on the ground. He was unable to see who it was; the air was still too thick. It was usually at this point where he awoke, but this time the dream continued.

There was a sudden cry of anguish; it was Cat. Toby ran forward blindly, but it was like running in mud. He was desperate to help her, but he couldn't move anywhere near fast enough. Then he was blocked by a tall, dark figure. He looked up, the person was over six feet, and all he could see was the flicker of fire reflected in the whites of the man's eyes. Toby tried to push by him, but he was an unmovable barrier. Hands grabbed Toby's wrists, and he screamed at the man to let him go. All the man did was laugh. Toby was physically powerful, it was one of the many abilities he had as well as his defensive, protective bubble, but now he was powerless.

Cat's cries became louder and became more hopeless. Toby made one final effort to release himself from this stranger. He managed to yank a hand free, and he went for the eyes. Toby sank his thumb and forefinger into the stranger's head and felt the eyes pop. Hot blood cascaded down his arm. Toby withdrew his hand, but the man was still laughing. The empty sockets in his face were spurting fresh blood. The man drew up his free hand; the other still held on to Toby tightly. He then placed his open hand on his face and abruptly tore off his skin. Under the skin was the face of Toby's mother. The black, empty sockets were now filled with a red glow.

Toby screamed for the first time in years. Nobody heard him.

Chapter 9

After Mae's party, Annie decided to prolong her stay; it was half-term at school anyway, and she loved Mae's surroundings. It was almost like a holiday from the hustle and bustle of home. It was Mae who asked her to stay. It was the first time she'd had a proper friend over since they moved here. She wasn't quite ready to go back to the solitude she'd grown so used to. Mae was generally comfortable with her own company, and given a choice, she'd gladly live this way for the majority of her life, but she would love the freedom to be able to have friends and family around if she wanted. For the last ten years, she felt she had no choice but to keep people away. Mae hoped someday that would change. The party was the first step in getting to that point.

Mae never had another relationship since Anthony. She'd been out on dates, but nothing ever became serious. Some of the guys were a definite no for her; they were apparent players. Others seemed to be genuinely lovely and could make someone a great partner. However, she remembered having those same thoughts about Anthony when they first met. Mae couldn't bring herself to allow another man into their lives. She didn't want to be the vulnerable woman again, and she couldn't risk her children. Mae decided she couldn't trust her judgment when it came to men, so she was better off alone.

Cat had been moping for a couple of days, Mae scarcely saw her, but when she did, they barely spoke. Cat seemed to be spending a lot of time with her new boyfriend recently. Mae really could see herself in Cat, and that wasn't necessarily a good thing. Mae knew Archie was not a good choice, but he would have been Mae's choice at Cat's age. Mae knew better now; this type of guy was bad news, and it left her with a lifetime of fear and looking over her shoulder, as well as two children without a father. She'd hoped Cat would've learnt from Mae's mistakes, but she knew from experience that very few children learned from their parents. Mae tried to keep her opinion of Archie to herself, but she would keep an eye on him, and rightly or wrongly, she asked Toby to keep an eye on them also; he wasn't too impressed.

"Mum, you do realise that if Cat found out, she would be beyond pissed!" said Toby sceptically.

"I'm not asking you to follow her around or anything. I need you to keep your ear to the ground. Kids talk, especially boys who want to brag about their new girlfriend." Mae looked at her son with pleading eyes. Toby understood where his mum was coming from; the idea of Archie being with his sister made him cringe, but Cat was a headstrong girl— she'd do what she wanted to do. Even if he did have information to give to his mother, he doubted either of them would be able to do anything about it.

"Fine, I'll keep my eyes and ears open." Said Toby; he walked away, shaking his head.

* * *

The next day, Mae found herself alone in the house for a couple of hours in the afternoon. Annie took her children out to explore the town, and she then promised to take them to the park. Cat and Toby were out as well, so Mae took that time to have a nap. It had been a busy few days. It didn't help that she and Annie spent the last two evenings staying up late drinking, which didn't do her any favours in the sleeping department. Mae turned on the television and found an old film. It was the standard type of film you'd see on the television in the middle of the afternoon; it featured a helpless woman waiting to be rescued by a big, tough man. The days before feminism showed women as strong, independent, and able to look after themselves. Mae couldn't be bothered to search for anything else, so she just left it on. Despite being warm outside, she covered herself with a small blanket; the windows were open slightly in the lounge, so it was just to keep the draft off. Mae fell asleep. She'd left her phone on the coffee table in case Annie called. She'd told her that if she got lost, not to hesitate to give her a call; she thought receiving a call would be doubtful, but you never know.

Mae awoke thirty minutes later, and she felt cold; she could feel goosebumps popping up over her legs. Mae still had her eyes shut—she wanted to sleep more and didn't want to let the light in, or she'd never get back to sleep. Mae felt around for the blanket; she only had it waist-high in the first place; she'd been wearing shorts, so she only wanted to cover her legs. She couldn't feel it. Mae's bottom was up against the back of the sofa, and she moved her hand around toward the back but still couldn't feel it anywhere. Mae huffed; it probably fell onto the floor. She opened her eyes and reached to the floor, but there was no blanket; it was gone. Now that her eyes were open, she had a better look around herself. *Where the hell did that go?* Mae sat up, then looked over at the neighbouring chair. Nicely folded over the back of it was her blanket—someone must have come in and put it there. Perhaps it did fall on the floor, and they just put it away tidily.

"Hey, Cat, Toby, Annie? Which one of you is home?" Mae yelled; she listened for a response. Nothing. Mae tried again. "Hello? Who's home?" Mae was still for almost a minute, and there was a noise in the Kitchen — a chinking noise. Mae jumped up and swiftly crossed the hall and into the kitchen. The kitchen was large and modern. The floor was covered with grey marble effect tiles, and the walls were painted white with a strip of lilac mosaics. There was an island in the centre which housed the sink. The kitchen was empty, but she could still hear the noise—it was louder now. She walked around the island, and on the floor was her good furry friend Casey. He was her Maine Coon cat; she got him when they moved in. There was no need for a man in her life when she had such an amazing companion. He was an affectionate boy. When he saw her, he weaved around her legs, purring and chirping. He wore a collar with a metal identity tag attached to a tracker; the fastener on the collar became undone, and the tag was hitting against the floor whilst he walked around. Mae picked him up and stroked his head, refastened the collar, kissed him on the head, and put him back on the floor. Unless Casey learned how to fold blankets, there must be someone else in the house. It was probably Cat or Toby; they more than likely had their earphones in and couldn't hear her calling. She checked both their rooms and the rest of the house—no one was in. Then Mae noticed the back door was wide open, it swayed slightly in the light breeze. Casey was a house-cat, so they weren't in the habit of leaving doors open in this house. She wondered if whoever it was had gone outside. She stepped out of the house barefoot, closing the door behind her, but there was no one out there.

Mae was feeling anxious now, someone had been in the house, and she needed to find out who. Mae went back to the sofa, reached toward the coffee table for her phone, but it was gone. Mae looked on the floor, but it wasn't there. She searched everywhere in the lounge. Mae was sure it was on the table before she went to sleep. If this was one of the kid's ideas of a wind-up, she wasn't laughing. Mae rushed into the kitchen. There was an archway leading to the dining room, and as she ran through, she saw right in the middle of the dining table, her phone. Mae grabbed the phone hurriedly. First, she called Cat; she was in town with Archie. She said she hadn't been home all day and then impolitely told her mother to go away and to leave her alone—she still wasn't talking to her. Then she called Toby; he was at a friend's house playing Xbox. He said he hadn't been home either, and he asked her what was wrong, but she hung up the phone. Lastly, she called Annie; Annie was at the park with the children. Annie detected the panic in Mae's voice and said she'd come back straight away.

Mae was convinced someone had been in the house—there was no other way to explain it, but *why?* She wondered, *what was the point?* It's not like she could call the police and say, "Someone came into my house, tidied my blanket, and put my phone on the dining table." It would sound absurd. Even to Mae, it seemed ridiculous. She decided she wouldn't call the police, but she would put her family on alert.

When Annie returned, Mae told her what happened. Annie

was sceptical that anything was wrong. She thought Mae just misremembered the events before sleeping; this would seem like a very fair assumption to anyone from the outside looking in, and Mae could see why Annie thought that way, but she knew something wasn't right.

Toby returned home before Cat, and when he came into the house, Mae instructed him to be available as soon as Cat returned, as they needed to have a family meeting.

"A family meeting. Really? What is it this time? Has Cat messed up again?" It was usually Cat's antics which triggered a family meeting.

Mae shook her head, trying to forget the past. "No, nothing like that Toby, we'll discuss it as soon as Cat returns."

Several hours later, Cat arrived home. She was immediately met by Mae standing in the hall, she had her hands on her hips and her mouth set in a line.

"Where have you been? I've been so worried. Why weren't you answering my calls?" When Cat didn't return by nine o'clock, Mae bombarded Cat's phone with voicemails, demanding her to come home and to call her back, none of which had a response. Mae was pacing whilst she waited, wondering if Cat's lack of communication was related to her mysterious housekeeper that afternoon. She was literally worried sick; she'd been nauseous for the past two hours.

"Mum, I'm seventeen; you don't need to know my every movement every second of the day," Cat spoke in a matter-of-fact tone as if she were talking to someone stupid. She stood in front of her mother with her arms crossed and looking away.

"If you were just a normal seventeen-year-old, that would be true to a certain extent. But you're not normal; we're not normal. We are in hiding, and we are in danger." Tears started to well up in Mae's eyes. "I just need you to let me know where you are honey, if you're going to be late, tell me. That's all I ask." Cat's eyes softened. She uncrossed her arms—she didn't like to see her mum upset.

"Mum, we're not in danger, we've been here for ten years, and we've been fine; there has to come a time when we start living a normal life." Cat moved closer to Mae and took hold of both her hands. "We can't stay here together forever. One day I want to get a career, move away and live a life of my own. That day is coming, and it's coming soon." Mae bowed her head; she knew this was going to happen someday, but now was not the time to discuss this. They were still in danger.

"I understand, honey, I do, and one day I'm sure you can have that life, but we are still in danger. When Toby came home earlier, I told him we needed to have a family meeting. We've been waiting for you so we can start." Cat rolled her eyes and let go of Mae's hands.

"Mum—" Cat interrupted. Mae put her index finger to her mouth. Cat stopped talking.

"Something happened today, and I need to speak to both of you." Mae turned and called up the stairs to Toby. Toby appeared after a minute then stomped down the stairs, rubbing the back of his neck as he stared at Cat. She looked back at him and folded her arms again. She turned away from him, avoiding eye contact; she could tell he was angry with her.

"Where have you been? Mum's been worried and even more than usual. She seems to feel the need to talk to us about something. I wanted to get it over with, but you decide to drag your ass in at eleven o'clock at night, making us all wait.

I've never known anyone as selfish as you." Toby was now in Cat's face. Cat wasn't fazed.

"Give it a rest Toby, we all know the sun shines out of your ass; he who can do no wrong, why don't you just get a life," said Cat moving even closer. Mae stood between them.

"Calm it down, you two." Mae turned to face Toby. "Toby, I have already spoken to your sister about how late she is. I don't need you to fight my battles." Mae now turned to Cat. "Cat, the sun does not shine out of your brother's ass, he has his faults too, but he has got a point. You have been very selfish lately." Cat was about to interject, but Mae interrupted her. "You're like me when I was your age. You're headstrong, and you don't see it as selfish, but please work on that for me. Especially after what I'm about to tell you."

Mae took Toby and Cat into the living room where she told them about her afternoon, the back door being left open, the blanket being moved, and her phone being taken to the dining table. Cat put her head into her hands, and Toby scratched the back of his neck, shaking his head.

"Mum," said Toby. "You're getting yourself worked up because you forgot to shut the door, and you have a lapse in memory of using the blanket and where you put your phone?" Mae expected this from Annie, but she thought her children would take her concerns more seriously.

"I did not forget anything; I know for certain the door was closed, the phone was on the coffee table and that I used the blanket; I'm not senile, you know."

"Mum, it's been a hectic few days. You've been anxious, and I know you haven't been sleeping well. I hear you get up in the night," said Cat. She was right. From the moment Mae started planning the party with her family, she'd had several sleepless

109

nights. It didn't stop after the party either; her dreams were frightening, she couldn't remember the last time she could sleep without consuming copious amounts of alcohol. Mae was the first to admit she was tired but not to the point where it would affect her mental competency.

"I did not imagine this." Mae stood, putting her hands on her hips. "Someone was in this house today, and they were doing it to mess with me. He didn't do enough for me to call the police, but he did enough to get under my skin." Toby looked up at his mum but remained seated.

"He? You think it was our dad, don't you?" asked Toby. Mae sat back down, chewing her nails, and Mae nodded.

"I think he's found us. The party was a mistake. I should have listened to you, Toby, and I should never have done it. I just thought if nothing happened after ten years that he'd given up—that he wasn't even looking, I thought we could move on. I was wrong." Mae was looking into nothing, lost in her thoughts. Cat and Toby shared a look. Concerned, Cat mouthed to Toby: *What do we do?* Toby grimaced. *I don't know.* Cat made circles with her index finger by her temple, but Toby glared and narrowed his eyes at her. Cat smiled then rolled her eyes. *No sense of humour,* she thought.

"Mum." Mae didn't seem to hear him, so Toby repeated himself. "Mum." Mae gave Toby a pained stare.

"Yes?" Toby hated seeing her like this. They'd all been doing so well till this point. His mum was getting less and less anxious, and he could almost physically see her letting go of the past. Just this one single day seemed to have undone ten years of hard work. He wasn't going to make fun of her—he was going to try and help her.

"No, you were right. I was wrong. The party needed to

happen, and we do need to move on. I do believe that someone came in the house and did something." Mae beamed at her son; she knew she could rely on him. Cat's head whipped around, and she frowned at her brother. She rubbed her forehead and wondered where he was going with this. She waited for him to continue. "But, it doesn't mean it was dad. I don't think we should be jumping to conclusions. Perhaps it was just some kids who came by and wanted to mess around and play a joke on you." Cat sighed in relief; she wasn't going to be the only sane person in the household after all. Mae's shoulders slumped, and she nodded. She couldn't imagine who else would want to come into their house and move some random items, but she understood why Toby didn't want to jump the gun. Toby continued, "So from now on, we're just going to be a little more careful. We make sure everything is locked when leaving the house or when we're alone, be more aware of anyone hanging around near the house, and Cat—he looked at his sister, his jaw firm, "—please make life a little easier for mum and let her know if you're going to be late and where you are. Keep your phone on and answer it." Cat frowned.

"Whatever. If we're done, I'm going to bed. Is that okay, sir?" Cat replied. Sarcasm was the family's favourite form of communication.

"You're dismissed, Kitty Cat." They saluted each other. Mae laughed; she loved her kids so much. She reached over to her son and hugged him tightly.

When Mae was on her way to the bedroom, Annie met her on the landing. She'd gone to her room when Cat arrived to give them privacy. She hoped that the kids were able to talk some sense into her friend.

"Did everything go okay?" asked Annie. Mae yawned and nodded.

"It was fine, we're not going to go nuts about this now, but we're going to be more careful. When you go out, and you're leaving the place empty, please, can you make sure that everything has been locked up before you go?"

"Of course," Annie replied. She was pleased to see Mae calmer than she was earlier.

"I'm exhausted. I'm going to bed. Casey, come here." Casey sat on the top stair with his back leg up in the air, licking his thigh. Excited, he looked up and then trotted to Mae's side. She picked him up and kissed him on the head, carrying him to her bedroom. "Goodnight, Annie." Annie smiled after her.

* * *

Annie sat on the end of her bed. She always called her husband before going to sleep. She reached over to her bedside table to grab her phone, but it wasn't there. Annie looked around herself on the bed, then on the floor, but she couldn't see it anywhere. The children were on airbeds on the floor. There was another bedroom for them too, but she preferred to keep them close. She searched around their beds, but she couldn't find the phone anywhere. She only had the phone five minutes ago. She was browsing Facebook when she heard Mae coming up the stairs, and she was sure she left it on the bedside table. Annie was getting concerned—*had Mae been right*? Annie wandered into the en-suite bathroom, and there it was on the toilet lid. There was no way she'd put it there. She hadn't stepped foot in the bathroom. She suddenly got goosebumps on her arms. Annie was then startled by movement in the corner of the bathroom—the shower curtain moved. Annie froze in place. She was holding her breath as she looked around the room for a weapon. She was defenceless. Suddenly a blur shot out from the curtain and jumped up at her, licking her face. Annie started to laugh.

"Stevie. You naughty boy. You scared mummy. Are you playing hide and seek with my phone as well now?" She spoke to him in a baby-talk manner. She wandered back into the bedroom, shaking her head. Mae's anxiety was infectious.

'It was hot, and Annie had the window open. She pulled the window just ajar and locked it in place as she then settled into bed to call her husband.

As the window closed, the dark figure pressed himself up against the wall. He was perched on top of the porch; the front door was directly below Annie's room. He only just made it out. He knew how risky his actions were, especially with a dog in the room, but he couldn't resist. Unless it was possible to lick someone to death, the dog was no problem. Phase one was complete.

Chapter 10

Half term was over. Annie had gone home, and the house was back to normal. Toby and Cat were returning to school, and Mae was going back to work. Despite it being a June summer's day, the sky was grey and oppressing, threatening a storm.

Cat hadn't seen Jake since the party. It was strange, he always called if they hadn't met up, but she'd not heard from him at all. She heard a knock at the door, and she smiled. He didn't disappear off the face of the earth after all. Cat opened the front door. She was back in her usual clothing, pale stone-washed skinny jeans, a black t-shirt featuring a pentagon, and her hair was up in a messy bun. Jake stood before her in his favourite, black, Game of Thrones T-shirt. It was clear why they were friends. He was looking at the floor as he shifted his weight back and forth on each leg. Cat squished her eyebrows together and smiled at him; he looked up at her.

"Hey Jake, you okay?" asked Cat. Jake cleared his throat.

"Is it okay I'm here? I didn't know if you'd be going into school with your boyfriend or not." Cat wondered what Jake was thinking; they always went to school together.

"Of course, Jake! Archie may be my boyfriend, but you're still my best friend." Cat playfully shoved Jake's shoulder.

"Silly!" Jake's face turned the colour of a tomato, and he laughed. Cat stepped out and double-locked the door. She was taking the safety thing seriously like Toby asked—he who must be obeyed. She still thought it was all a load of bullshit, but anything for a quiet life.

Cat grabbed Jake's arm and threaded her arm through. Jake acted strangely; he stammered as he spoke, so he was nervous or uptight about something. The way he talked about Archie earlier made her suspect it had to be something to do with him. Cat had dated a couple of boys before, and Jake didn't act this way with them. Archie wasn't any different, except in her eyes anyway. To her, Archie was unique. He was exciting—he made her heart race in anticipation. When they kissed, she felt like she needed to be even closer to him. She could never feel that way about Jake. Cat wasn't blind, she knew he wanted more than friendship, but she didn't see him in that way. He had a cute face, beautiful blue eyes, and short, curly dark hair, and he had the sweetest personality. The way he took care of his sister made her heart melt, but he might as well be a brother to her. She didn't feel the flutter in her stomach, no ache in her groin after each touch, or the yearning to be with him every moment of the day.

They made small talk on the way to school, and Cat mentioned how her mum was becoming neurotic about safety and how she thought someone had been in the house. She realised her mistake as soon as she said it.

"Why would she think someone would go into the house and just move stuff around?" Jake knew precisely why she would be worried about such a thing, especially with their history, which he only recently learned about from Uncle Darren. He did wonder if the question would give Cat the nudge to confide in him. It didn't.

"Oh. Um. I don't know. She's always been a little paranoid. I don't know why." She once again used ignorance. The conversation fell flat after that. Cat casually changed the subject to something less personal relating to her English assignment.

Cat didn't want to tell Jake about the past; despite being best friends, there were just some things she didn't want to revisit. She was always itching to tell people about her abilities—it was what made her special and different. She didn't want to be known as the poor girl who didn't know her father because he was a nasty piece of work, who tried to kill her and her family and that she was in hiding. Cat didn't want pity; she merely wanted to forget. They had a new life, and she wanted to start living it, if only her mother would let her. Cat did feel wrong about not being completely honest with Jake, especially after he told her about his dad committing suicide. It was the perfect cue for her to voice her life history in return for his trust, but she couldn't do it,

They approached the school gates, and Cat's heart quickened. She began to grow hot all over her body, and she felt a flutter in the pit of her stomach. Stood beside the gate with a sexy, crooked smile stood Archie. She noticed how the girls looked at him as they passed by, but he only had eyes for one person. Cat immediately released Jake's arm and ran to him. It was like a romantic comedy where you saw the girl run to the boy in slow motion, and the boy would grab the girl's waist and lift her, then she would wrap her legs around his body, and they would kiss tenderly. In this case, it was the same, except the kiss was more urgent and hard rather than tender. Jake stood still. He flinched away from the scene unfolding before him. He felt like there was a void inside of him that just grew ten-fold. He yearned for that contact so much, and he couldn't think of anyone less deserving of those affections than Archie. Jake walked past them like they weren't there.

Cat unwrapped herself from Archie. She didn't want to, but class started in five minutes, and she needed to compose herself. Her cheeks and lips felt as though they were on fire. She was sure it was visible too.

"You got any plans after school?" Archie's voice was deep and hoarse, and Cat struggled to think clearly.

"Er. No, I don't think so, but I can't be late; my mum's freaking out. I got a bollocking last night when I came in late." Cat rolled her eyes, and Archie smiled down at her. He was a fair few inches taller than Cat.

"Well. I'll try not to keep you too late, babe. It's just I found a place, a nice place where we can be alone to… you know, have some privacy?" *This is it,* Cat thought excitedly; she would lose her virginity on this very day. They'd talked about making love before, but Cat insisted she didn't want to do it in the backseat of a car, not in her house and not in a dank outhouse of some kind or, at worst, in a back alley. She wanted her first time to be beautiful and memorable—special. He agreed to wait until such a time and place.

"Really? Where?" Cat's body started to tingle and ache in anticipation.

"It's a surprise. I'll meet you here after school." Archie delicately lifted her chin and touched her top lip softly with his mouth. He lightly licked it with the very end of his tongue. Cat wanted more as she lifted herself on tiptoes, but Archie stepped back and grinned a cheeky grin. He winked at her and walked away briskly, leaving Cat staring after him like an abandoned child. The school bell rang. Cat snapped out of her lusty revelry, and she ran to her class.

Cat found it difficult to concentrate all day; she found herself slipping into a daydream, imagining what her first time would be like, but by lunchtime, she was nervous. The excitement and warmth was great until she realised that she had no idea what she was supposed to do when the moment came. She imagined that most girls would speak to their best friend about this, but she knew that wasn't an option for her. She wondered whether she should talk to Amber, but they weren't close enough; they spoke about music, films, and who was hot, who was not. But the emotional stuff was shared with Jake. He was always there when she needed a hug after a fight with her mum. He was there to talk to when she was feeling down, and he was a shoulder to cry on when she split up with her boyfriend. There haven't been many relationships, only two, but to her, they were the boys she was going to marry. When Cat loved, she loved hard. She would just have to figure it out for herself. If all else failed, there was always Google.

"Did you want me to come round later and help you with the English assignment?" asked Jake as he shoved a corner of a ham sandwich into his mouth. Cat didn't answer. She was pushing her salad around with her fork and staring down at her plate. "Cat? Hell-ooo." He clicked his fingers in her face.

"Hmm?" She looked up and blinked.

"Are you okay? You seem a bit distracted." He looked into her eyes to see if he could visually identify what was wrong.

"I'm fine; I just have a few things on my mind, that's all. Nothing for you to worry about. You know, girl stuff." Said Cat. Jake cracked up laughing,

"If you think saying 'girl stuff' is going to stop my inquiries, you're seriously mistaken." He raised his eyebrows and crossed his arms on the table in front of him. "I'm not like normal guys that get freaked out by that kind of stuff. Remember, I buy my mum's tampons. My sister is asking me about bras even though she is still way too young. I take my mum for her smear tests and—" He hesitated before saying the next thing; he went from an upbeat mood and a mocking face to a more pained expression. "I've had to put my mum in the shower on more than one occasion when she's had a few too many, or she's had an... accident." Cat should've known better than to put him off the scent that way, she knew what he's had to do for his mum, and he didn't shy away from women's problems.

"I know. I'm sorry. I just don't want to talk about it. Not right now anyway, but thanks for asking." Cat reached over and squeezed his hand. "So, what were you saying?" Jake repeated his initial question.

"Oh, I'm busy today. I'm meeting Archie after school. Maybe tomorrow? Would that be okay?" Jake took his hand away from Cat's. He couldn't hide his disappointment. "Do you have a problem with Archie, Jake? You've been weird about him ever since the party. You disappeared, and I didn't hear from you for days until this morning." Jake put down his half-eaten sandwich.

"Now that you bring it up," Jake leaned back in his seat. He wondered how to phrase this, but there wasn't a nicer way to put it. "He's an asshole Cat. What the fuck are you doing with this guy? You're the last person I thought would go with a guy just because of good looks and muscles." Cat stood up from her seat rigidly. *Where the hell did that come from?* She wondered. Her nostrils flared; she ground her teeth and tried to speak calmly.

"To be perfectly honest, Jake, it's none of your fucking business. He is actually a really good guy. He puts across a tough persona because it's expected of him. He has to deal with a lot. I know him, and you don't." She paused momentarily. "Why am I explaining myself to you?"

"Because you know just as well as I do that being with him makes absolutely no sense, especially when it's you. You're better than that. You can do a lot better than him," Jake countered. Cat narrowed her eyes at him.

"I can do better, can I? Would you be better for me, Jake? Is that it?" Jake looked down at his hands. He could feel his face getting extremely hot all of a sudden. "Let's face it, Jake. You're just jealous," Jake stood up as well now, and the students in the lunch hall were all staring at them both.

"You're right, Cat. I am jealous, but that isn't the reason why I'm questioning your reasons. This whole room knows Archie is a dick. Everyone except you. He's a thug, Cat, a bully. But hey, if he gets you going, you carry on." Jake pushed his lunch box into his backpack and marched away. Cat was speechless; they'd never fallen out like this before. People were still staring, and she collected her things and went outside, her eyes filled with tears.

Did Jake think she was that superficial? It seemed evident that he did. When she first met Archie, she did think he was brash and what people may consider to be an asshole, but he seemed to see something in her. He saw something no one else saw, and in turn, she saw something in him.

They met at a party. Cat had planned to go with Jake, but he needed to stay home with his sister. His mum wasn't available. This was Jake's language, for his mum was pissed as a fart and was in no shape to be left with his seven-year-old sister. Cat went anyway; she went with Amber in the end, although she barely saw her for most of the party. Cat was sat alone with her drink, regretting that she bothered coming at all, especially when she knew her mum would go nuts when she didn't come home by nine o'clock. She was about to call it a night when Archie approached her.

Archie swaggered over, exuding confidence. Initially, Cat wasn't impressed. She knew what he was like. She saw him as a guy who had the pick of the girls; he would bed them then move on, and he had quite the reputation. It took a couple of hours of coaxing, she was suspicious of his motives, but she finally agreed to dance with him. She thought his perseverance deserved some kind of reward. By this point, she was already getting quite drunk. By the end of the evening, she could barely walk. Archie offered to take her home, and she accepted. She was astonished he didn't try anything. He took her to the front door. He thanked her for a great evening and asked if they could meet up again. She agreed. It was then that he gave her the lightest kiss, and that was all. It was at that moment that he won her over. They met up the following evening for a proper date. Since then, they'd become closer and closer. Archie was a good guy in her eyes. No one else's opinion mattered; not her mum's, Jake's, or her brother's. She knew Toby disapproved too; he was glaring at Archie all through the family party. Cat dried her tears and decided to hell with them all.

After school, as promised, Archie was standing by the gate. Cat tried not to look at the materialistic side of him, but she couldn't help it. He was tall and dark, and his eyes were the darkest brown. He was wearing his sports kit, and his t-shirt hugged his frame. She could see every contour of his body which admittedly consisted of a considerable amount of muscle. Cat wasn't ashamed, it wasn't just his body she was attracted to as Jake suggested, but there was no harm in appreciating it. She hugged him tightly, and they kissed for a long time before Archie gently released himself from Cat's grip.

"Shall we go somewhere more private?" Archie whispered in her ear. His breath tickled, and she trembled. Cat could feel her pulse quicken in response. All of her worries drifted away. She wanted to go with him to a private place. She wanted to be close to him, and she needed to be with him. She couldn't think of a better way to spend her afternoon. They interlinked their fingers as they joined hands and strolled off down the street.

A disappointed Jake watched from a distance as they walked away together. He gritted his teeth and clenched his fists. He vowed that if Archie ever hurt her, he'd be sorry.

* * *

It was a nice walk. They hiked up a small hill and into a wooded area. The blissful sun was beating down on them but was then blocked as they entered the trees. They trekked deeper into the woods. Archie was pulling her through the foliage by her hand. Cat stopped. Archie turned to her to see what the delay was.

"Are you okay? Why have you stopped? Are you tired?" Cat turned her head from side to side and glanced at her surroundings. They'd been walking for about forty-five minutes. They were far away from anything familiar and were completely off the beaten track. She took her mobile phone out of her pocket—there was no reception. If they, or she, got into any trouble, they were a long way from help. She failed to understand where they could be going. All she could see were trees, and there was no way she would be performing any sexual activities in the undergrowth by a tree.

"I'm fine. I'm just a little concerned about where we're going. You said you found somewhere that would give us privacy. I accept that in the middle of the woods is technically private, I can't imagine there's anyone out here, but I was kind of expecting somewhere undercover?" Archie released Cat's hand and put his hands on his hips.

"Do you really think I was going to get my way with you out here?" He raised his arms. "As I said, it's a surprise, it will be undercover, and it will be really romantic. Trust me." He held his hand out for her to take. She took it and allowed him to lead her deeper into the woods. She trusted him.

It was starting to feel a bit chilly. Cat hoped it wasn't going to be any further; she still needed to make it home without being late. They walked a further five minutes, and Cat could hear something—it sounded like water.

They emerged from the treeline, and in front of them was a small valley covered with rocks, grass, and pretty meadow flowers, creating sprinklings of purple, white and yellow across the amazing landscape. Within the valley was a beautiful waterfall and the crystal blue water crashed down into a small lake. Bright sunlight burst out from behind a large grey cloud, there was enough blue sky for the sun to stay out for a little longer until the vast black cloud in the near distance would cover it once again. She'd lived here for ten years and had no idea this was here. Archie helped Cat down into the valley and to the edge of the lake.

"This way." Archie led her toward the waterfall itself. The water fell over an overhang like it was flowing over the top of an umbrella. A small cavern was behind the water canopy, roughly six square metres in floor space and around eight feet high. It wasn't just any ordinary cavern. Besides the stalactites and the stalagmites that grew from the floor and ceiling, Archie decorated it with soft furnishings. Sheer fabrics hung from the walls, cushions, and pillows littered the floor, and it was lit by battery-powered fairy lights wrapped around the rock formations. Cat walked into the middle of the makeshift room, sat on one of the pillows, and sank into it. It seemed that underneath there were several airbeds. It was indeed beautiful, cosy, and overwhelmingly romantic, especially when she looked towards the cave's opening and saw the waterfall's curtain shimmering in the sunlight. Archie went into one of the corners and switched on a small stereo, and slow music played softly in the background. Cat turned to him. She was beaming and started to feel the all too familiar flutter in her stomach.

"Oh Archie, this is perfect. How long have you known about this place?" Archie strutted towards Cat, removed his t-shirt revealing his perfectly formed torso, and threw his shirt onto the floor.

"I've been coming here since I was about ten years old. I ran away from home after a fight with my dad. I found this place. I was probably here for two nights until I ran out of food. I missed my mum too, so I went back home. After that, it became a den I would play in. As I got older, it was where I came to think and hang out. You're the only person I've ever brought here, and this is the first time I tried out my interior decorating skills. I wanted it to look nice for you." Archie closed the distance between them as he spoke, and he took Cat's hands and pulled her up into a standing position. He hugged her close against his bare chest. Cat wrapped her arms around his waist and buried her face into his neck under his chin. She inhaled him; he smelt of masculinity—a salty mix of sweat and deodorant; it was an oddly pleasant smell.

He started to caress her skin under her shirt, beginning with her back. He lightly ran his nails down her spine; she shivered in response and began to kiss his neck. She was breathing heavily as desire flooded through her body. He moved his hand around to the front, where he cupped her breasts over her bra. He urgently lifted her shirt up and over her head. Archie fumbled with her bra strap and then expertly unclasped it with a single hand and threw it to the floor. Heat erupted in her groin. She wanted him so much; she wanted to be one with him, and she wanted to be as close to him as humanly possible.

He kissed up her neck and found her lips. Any tenderness that was there at the start was gone; it was now hunger which drove them on. She bit his lip; he groaned and kissed her harder. Her hands shakily moved to his shorts, and they quickly slipped down over his hips down to his ankles. He sighed and hastily unbuckled her belt and impatiently tugged at her jeans, but they were tight. He lifted her from under her arms, and she wrapped her legs around him as he carried her to a large pile of cushions. He gently laid her down, kissed down to her neck, then down to her belly button. She squirmed underneath him as her body prickled with electrifying energy. He grabbed her jeans and yanked them down her thighs, revealing plain white briefs. He kissed her thigh, and she whimpered. She submitted herself to him as he made his way down her legs, removing her jeans at the same time. They made love passionately and urgently.

When they were done, he collapsed on top of her, and they were both breathing heavily. Cat's eyes were closed, and she couldn't stop smiling. Archie looked at her; he twitched his lips to hide his satisfaction.

They'd been lying in the cushions for half an hour without saying a word. Cat laid with her head on his chest, just listening to his heartbeat as his chest rose and fell. His arm was draped over her back, and he lightly stroked her shoulder blade. Cat felt sleepy; she'd never felt so relaxed, and she couldn't imagine being anywhere else at that moment. Cat giggled.

"What's so funny?" His voice was gruff like he was dehydrated.

"I just find it funny how I was worried about this all day. I don't know what I was so stressed about." She took Archie's hand which rested on his stomach and kissed it. It was silent again for a few minutes. Cat thought there needed to be someone in her life who needed to know her through and through. She just allowed this guy to explore her body, and she'd never felt she could trust anyone more than she could trust him now. She decided to allow him to explore her mind too.

"Can I tell you a secret?" Archie stopped stroking, moved down the pillows, and made himself comfortable facing Cat. He put a hand under his cheek and placed a hand on her hip, his eyes glowing in anticipation.

"I'm going to tell you something, but I need to show you something first." Cat sat up, and Archie turned onto his back.

"You see those rocks over there?" She gestured to a pile of rocks near the cavern's opening.

"Uh... Those rocks? Yeah, what about them?"

"Just watch."

Archie watched the pile of nondescript stones which were lying on the ground with a furrowed brow. Cat concentrated on them, and just a moment later, one by one, the rocks rose from the ground and ascended into the air.

"What the..." Archie sat up straight. His eyes widened as he watched the spectacle before him, his mouth falling open. Cat glanced at him from the corner of her eye and smirked. Cat decided to show off a little, so she raised each stone to form a circle, then made the ring rotate. Archie rose from the bed. He was still naked as he moved toward the rocks. Cat broke the loop and made them into a snake-like form. The rock snake weaved around Archie's body; all his muscles tensed, including those delightful glutes. Cat chuckled as Archie flinched and winced any time the snake got too close. He turned to face Cat. He grinned widely, his eyes gleaming, and he laughed along with her and hooted with excitement. Many ideas flashed up in his head. The possibilities of what he was seeing were endless.

"Oh my god, Cat! This is fucking amazing." Cat allowed the stones to drop. "How do you do it?" Archie sat back down alongside her.

"I think I was born with it, but I didn't know I could do it until I was seven. My family and I suffered a bit of a trauma," Then that was it. Cat spent the next two hours telling Archie about her life, about her dad and how her mother was a secret pyro-kinesis expert, how Toby could move faster than the usual person and shield against harm.

It was dark by the time Cat finished her story. Archie's reaction was better than she'd hoped—she was worried he'd think she was a freak. On the contrary, he seemed keen and excited about her ability. Cat glanced at her watch.

"Shit. We have to go. It's nearly ten o'clock. I told mum I'd be back by ten." Cat bolted out of their cosy love nest and whipped her clothes back on. Archie stayed where he was and watched her. "What? Come on, get dressed." Archie held out a hand.

"I will once you give me one more kiss," he breathed. Cat wasn't about to refuse that. She took his hand, and he pulled her down, and ever so gently brushed her lips with his and whispered, "I love you." Cat pulled away, and her eyes widened. She was speechless. It was the first time a boy had ever uttered those words to her—she quite often used the words herself, but the sentiment was never returned. But here she was, hearing it from a guy's lips. She felt light-headed, her eyes teared up with joy, and she clutched his face and kissed him with as much passion as she could muster. In between breaths, she said,

"I love you too."

* * *

Cat was late coming home that evening—she walked in at eleven-thirty. Mae wasn't impressed, but Cat apologised immediately. She didn't pick a fight and didn't make a big deal out of her mum's rant—she wasn't really listening. Her mind was elsewhere. She remembered the kisses, the touches on her breast, the feeling she felt at that final moment, and then recalled the three words Archie muttered. She could feel her face flush. Her mum was finally coming to the end of her tirade.

"Mum, as I said, I'm sorry. It won't happen again. I'm tired, and I'm going to bed, we'll talk again in the morning if you like. I love you." She kissed her mum on the cheek and sleepily made her way up the stairs. Mae was taken aback by the whole thing. She touched her cheek where Cat kissed her—it was her first show of affection in years. Mae liked the new Cat but wondered where she'd come from. She was also quite suspicious as to what happened to the old Cat.

Chapter 11

Mae began to wonder if this whole blanket and phone thing was all in her head after all. Nothing had happened since, and it had been three days. Mae was working from home, which is where she preferred to be, so she could keep an eye on things. The idea of leaving the house empty felt like it would be just asking for trouble.

Mae was constantly on edge —every creak and squeak had her jumping out of her skin. It wasn't easy concentrating on her work. She would investigate nearly every noise, but there was never anything there.

The anxiety she was feeling took her back to the early days of their relocation. She remembered how she took sentry duty by the front window, looking out for anything suspicious. The children weren't allowed outside on their own for at least a year. Mae was convinced Anthony would find them no matter where they went. She seemed to believe that, like them, he was also superhuman, that he could follow their scent in some freakish way. However, the months passed, and she slowly allowed herself to loosen up a little, much to her children's relief. They still didn't have the freedom other kids in town did. They couldn't go any further than their grounds without Mae being with them; even on their own property, she needed to be able to see them from the window. It wasn't the same childhood she had; for this, she blamed Anthony; it was his fault that they had to have such a restrictive life.

Today Mae was a little more relaxed, and she conceded that she might have over-reacted. She was sitting in her dining room with her laptop. Mae had several places she liked to do her writing. There was a desk in her bedroom, but unfortunately, that room got full sunlight in the morning, so it was far too warm. There was a study in the house; it was more like a library—there wasn't room for much else apart from books. It was a little cramped. She also had a fabulous workshop in the garden, but she usually used this in the winter. It had a log burner and a comfy sofa, but much like her bedroom in the summer, it was far too hot, even with the windows open. The dining room was ideal; it was at the rear of the house, so it had shade from the sun up to late afternoon, and when she kept the rear door open slightly, a glorious draft would waft through, cooling her skin and stirring her hair off her neck.

Mae looked at her watch; it was ten-thirty in the morning. Looking over at Casey's food bowl, she noticed it was still full, and she wondered where he got to. She hadn't seen him all morning. It wasn't unusual for him to come to his food late in the morning. He always had dry food available, so he was never starving. She wasn't going to worry yet; he was probably napping in a laundry basket somewhere and getting his long fur over everything.

By lunchtime, she still hadn't seen Casey. Anxiety suddenly took over. Mae searched the house, checking cupboards, drawers, and wardrobes in every room. She couldn't find him, and she called out, but there was no response. Mae collected the remote for the pet tracker which was in the kitchen drawer. She switched it on. It was a skinny contraption—there were two rows of lights which went up the remote vertically. It could locate up to four trackers. She touched the first button that linked to Casey's tracker, and all the tiny bulbs lit up. The first few were red; the next few were amber, then the last ones were green. It beeped, then all the lights switched off; it meant that the tracker, having a range of one-hundred and twenty metres was undetectable. Mae took deep breaths to calm herself as she knew what this meant; Casey was not in the house. She took a bag of dry food from the cupboard and stepped outside; she closed the door behind her.

A lot of land came with the house—there was an acre of landscaped gardens and another acre of woods. The garden area had large flower beds and a pond half the size of an Olympic pool. Reeds and bushes surrounded it; she pushed the foliage and grass apart; a frog sprang out making Mae jump. Casey liked to sleep in these when she brought him out on the harness on a sunny day, but he wasn't there today. Mae spun around, holding out the remote, then one of the red lights flashed on with a single beep. She was now facing the woods and was finally in range of the tracker. She moved forward slowly. One by one, the lights lit up, and the beeps were regular and getting faster. Now she stood on the treeline of the woods, and she hesitated. The remote was going crazy; she rotated her body, then there it was; the grey collar was laying on the ground, and she could see the sun glinting off the name tag, but Casey was nowhere in sight.

Mae's mouth went dry. Casey was her companion. After she had the twins, they took up all her time as babies, but as they got older, they became more independent. As much as Mae would've liked to have found a human life partner, she couldn't risk it. Her safest option was to get a pet. Mae initially worked a nine to five job, so getting a dog wasn't feasible, and she'd decided on getting a cat instead. Casey changed her life. In the evenings, he would snuggle up to her whilst she watched the television. When she worked from home, he would sleep on her feet late morning and in the afternoon occasionally jump on her lap, wanting to play. In the mornings, he would nestle beside her on the bed, and he would chirp and purr sweetly as she stroked and tickled his chin. She missed him so much already, and seeing the collar on the ground gave her a sinking feeling, like she was never going to see him again. Mae tried to remain positive. Perhaps he'd wandered into the woods. There were no busy roads nearby, so he was probably fine.

Mae didn't like going into the woods; it felt unsafe. There were too many things to hide behind. Her arms and legs felt shaky, and she found herself holding her breath; she exhaled loudly, attempting to calm herself. She picked up the collar and gripped it tightly to her chest.

"Casey. Come on, baby, come home," she couldn't hide the trembling in her voice, and she shook the bag of food she'd carried out with her. There were noises everywhere—she was confident that squirrels and rodents probably resided in the woods, but her mind wouldn't allow her to believe that it was just wildlife. She'd only been walking through the trees for ten minutes, but it felt like an hour. The wood was getting denser, and Mae wanted to turn back—it was the height of the afternoon, and the sun was high in the sky, but she could feel the light fading. She was so sensitive to the noises around her; the rustle of the leaves, the snapping of twigs, and the fluttering of the wings of birds she'd disturbed. She wanted to turn around and go back to the house, but something was willing her forward. Finally, something caught Mae's eye over to her left.

There were scores of flying insects circling the base of a tree. Mae made her way toward it. She moved carefully, and her heartbeat started to race as she proceeded closer. She could see tufts of flesh on the mossy ground. Mae's breath caught in her throat, and she squeezed the collar in her hands. Mae swatted away the flies, and as they fled, Mae could see the flesh was furry. Mae heaved; she tried to steady herself as her head went light. Her vision became fuzzy; she needed to get away from the grizzly scene, she covered her mouth and ran. She darted through the trees, twigs whipping at her face and arms. The tears in her eyes made it hard to see where she was going, and she hoped she was heading in the right direction. It began to get brighter, and then she burst out from the trees onto her mown lawn. She vomited onto the grass, and she fell to her knees, sobbing 'till her chest hurt. Mae looked across her expansive garden and could see the house in the distance. It looked as though the back door was open. She could have sworn that she closed and locked the door when she left. She looked down at the collar which still sat in her palm, and she clenched her jaw. It was HIM who did this; *he's come back for me*, she thought. Mae sprinted across the lawn, taking out her phone as she went, dialling 999.

"Hello, emergency service operator, which service do you require?"

"Police." Mae was breathless, and she was panting hard.

"I will connect you now." The line rang again, and a male answered.

"You have reached the Cumbrian police; what is the nature of the crime?"

"I need to report an intruder in my house; they have taken my cat and killed him." Mae talked quickly, shivering; she tried to hold herself, to be still and coherent.

"Is the intruder in your house now?" the voice asked—it was calm and soothing.

"I…I…I don't know; maybe, he could be in the house now."

"We'll send someone your way now; please confirm your address?"

Mae told the officer her address, and he offered to stay on the line, but Mae said she had to get back to the house to search and secure it. The officer attempted to talk her out of it, he wanted her to stay where she was and wait for the police, but she hung up.

Mae stepped into her home cautiously. She quietly closed and locked the door behind her. She went room to room, securing the windows and closing the doors; she even looked under the beds. The house seemed clear. As far as she was concerned, the house was sealed tight now, and no one could enter without her knowing. Mae sat on the sofa, and she rested her elbows on her knees and chewed at her nails. Occasionally her eyes would dart to a window, but otherwise, she remained still.

Mae had been waiting twenty minutes since she made her emergency call, and she finally saw the police car roll up outside. She stood and jogged to the front door and opened it. Two police officers approached her. One of the officers was relatively young; he was pale-skinned with acne scars, and his face was severe and harsh. He identified himself as PC Harding. The other was an older man, perhaps in his early forties. He had dark brown eyes which went well with his golden-brown skin, and he introduced himself as PC Carrick. He was the one who spoke first.

"Ms Phoenix? You reported an intruder?" Mae nodded as she stood aside to allow them into her hall.

"I have secured the house, there doesn't appear to be anyone in here, but I think he might be in the woods behind the house."

"He? Did you see this man?" PC Harding replied. Mae lowered her head and replied in a careful voice.

"No, I didn't see him, but I know who it is." Mae showed the officers to the living room so she could explain. She gave a quick summary of her past, about Anthony and how her family had to change their identities to protect themselves. She then went on to talk about the previous week, then what happened today. PC Carrick seemed quite sympathetic to her story. Still, PC Harding only picked up on the immediate information, which consisted of items being moved around in the house last week, finding a furry bit of flesh by the tree in the woods and that her cat had been missing for just over 12 hours. He was not impressed.

"I'm sorry, Ms Phoenix, but you reported an intruder. We have arrived here to find no intruder in your house and that your cat is missing. You found some remains in the woods, which could easily be leftovers of a squirrel or something similar. I can't help but think that you're wasting our time. PC Carrick, I think we should go." Mae gaped at the officer in disbelief. He wasn't taking her seriously, even with the knowledge of her past. PC Carrick saw the expression on Mae's face. He could see she was scared; he did agree with his partner, this probably was a waste of time, but this woman needed someone to listen to her. She was clearly in need of help, she looked so vulnerable, and he wanted to assist her in any way he could.

"PC Harding, I think you should go back to the car and report back to base and tell them there doesn't seem to be a matter of urgency here." Mae shot him a look of disgust. "But... I'm going to go check it out, I could take a sample of the remains, and we could find out whether it is that of a cat or something wild?" Mae's shoulders relaxed. Even though the police weren't particularly concerned about her story, at least, they were going to look into it. Well, half of the police anyway. PC Harding turned on his heel and stomped to the car. Mae glowered after him; she didn't like him. After PC Harding left, Mae showed PC Carrick through the house and to the back door. As soon as they stepped out, Mae turned and locked the door. She didn't want anyone sneaking in whilst they were out, no matter how briefly. However, the lock didn't seem to stop him earlier.

"It's a lovely place you have here. Despite a bad start, it looks like you've done alright," said PC Carrick admiringly. Mae forced a smile.

"We're getting by. If it weren't for the insurance money, I don't know where we would be right now. The silver lining, I guess." They walked together making small talk, and they were nearing the wood's edge.

"So, it was through here?" PC Carrick pointed into the mass of trees. He pressed his lips together, removed his police cap and swept the sweat off his forehead. Mae nodded—she knew this was where she entered because it was where the grass was thinning. It was a regular trail used by the gardener; in the summer, he came a couple of times a month to control the trees and nettle growth. It got very overgrown and would spread into the garden. "Okay, you lead the way; I'm right behind you." Mae felt safer knowing he was there, and she moved faster and was less conscious of the noises than before. Mae knew they were close; she could hear the humming of the flies.

"Over there." Mae pointed to the base of the tree—it was hard to see anything with the number of insects moving around, but her gut tightened as the smell of rotting flesh wafted into her nose. She covered her mouth with her hand. PC Carrick approached the tree and swatted away the winged pests; he wrinkled his nose, the smell was putrid. Bile rose into his throat; he swallowed it back down. PC Carrick removed a pen and plastic bag from his pocket. Quite a few grizzly pieces were lying around, and he picked the smallest one and hooked the furry tissue with the nib of his pen. It was impossible to tell what colour the coat was due to the blood. He dropped it into the bag and sealed it. He continued to look around the surrounding area, then noticed a trail of blood on the dirt floor.

"Did you try following this?" asked PC Carrick. Mae shook her head. She didn't exactly hang around when she saw the gory scene; she didn't think to investigate further. Mae felt a bit silly for that; what if the trail led to a dead fox? She would've wholly wasted the police's time.

"I'm sorry, I panicked earlier; I should've checked." Mae lowered her head. "I was stupid. I just saw the fur and freaked out." PC Carrick put his hand on her shoulder, and Mae looked up at him.

"You're not stupid. From what you told me earlier, running back to the house sounds like the best move you could've made. Give yourself a break; with what you've been through,

I'm surprised you're still a fully functional human being as well as being a single mother. I'm going to see where this trail leads. Do you want to go back to the house? It may not be very pretty, and if it is Casey..." Mae gulped; she knew where he was going with this.

"If it is Casey, I need to be there to identify him. I'm coming with you, officer."

"Please, call me Isaac. Officer sounds far too formal" Mae nodded, the corner of her mouth twitched upward.

It was Mae's turn to follow. The drops of blood were getting harder to see, and they were getting smaller. Just when they thought they lost the trail, Mae shrieked and gestured toward a pile of rocks. A relatively large quantity of crimson liquid dribbled down the rocks and formed a puddle. There was no sign of a body. Isaac gestured to Mae to stay where she was, and he went over to investigate. After a few minutes of wandering around the site, he returned to Mae.

"There's no sign of a carcass. Whatever it was, it was probably caught and injured where you found some of the remains and was then carried over here where it was probably finished off then taken away. There are no bones here. There's nothing here to suggest what animal it was either. I'll get this sample sent off for you." Mae's eyes began to tear; she was sure it was Casey, he was still missing, and something had been killed on her land. She was convinced that Anthony found her and that he was punishing her, killing the things she loved, first Casey, then he will probably go after the twins.

"It's Anthony, he's found us—he's taunting me, he's telling me that he's here and that he's in charge. I need to get my family away from here." Mae's eyes were wide, she was starting to hyperventilate, and she felt sick again.

"Hey, hey!" Isaac held her firmly by her upper arms. She was slightly shorter than him, so he needed to duck his head to make eye contact. "Look at me." She still looked at the floor. "Look at me." He repeated. Mae finally looked up from under her lashes. "I need you to calm down. Breathe. Listen. I understand, I do, you went through a lot, and you're scared, but you need to look at this from a police officer's perspective. What we have here are a couple of situations which may or may not be linked. You're too close to see it. These two situations could be a mere coincidence. I'm not saying it is, you could be right, but we need more to go on. For starters, this may not be Casey. Can you at least wait for the test results before doing anything rash?" Mae turned her head to the side, contemplating. She was still trembling. Isaac was talking sense, and when you looked at things like that, her case was feeble. But she knew deep down something was very wrong; she couldn't explain the feeling; it felt like chills from deep within and it changed to a burning sensation behind her eyes.

"Okay. You're right; I'm overreacting. Maybe we should go back to the house." Isaac agreed, and he followed Mae back.

Mae unlocked the door, and they both stepped inside. As the door closed behind them, a figure in black stepped out of the tree line. He held a hunter's knife in his gloved hand, smeared with red. He wiped the blade clean with his other glove and slipped the knife into his belt. With a smirk, he slipped back into the trees and disappeared.

Chapter 12

Cat asked Toby if he wanted company walking to school this morning. This was odd as Cat usually walked to school with Jake. Toby would normally go alone; his friends lived quite far from the main town, so they got the bus. Toby didn't mind. He usually liked to use this time to put his music on full blast in his earphones and get lost in the screams and yowls of heavy metal. He was pretty old school with the bands he listened to, with Iron Maiden and Metallica being amongst his favourites. The other guys seemed to be more interested in rappers, but Toby didn't get it. Not to say it was terrible music, but he didn't understand what the artists were trying to achieve. It seemed to talk of gangs and gangsters, none of which Toby knew much about, especially when spending much of his life in the country.

Cat was unusually cheerful for a Wednesday morning. Toby was happy to have her walk with him on this occasion. It gave him a chance to get some information to give to his mum, a bit of intel. His mum seemed to have calmed down from Sunday, apart from the other night where Cat got her worried again by coming in late. Cat did apologise, which Toby was pleased to hear. He was still angry that she was late in the first place, especially when he specifically asked her to consider their mum after her anxiety attack. Toby loved his sister and understood why she acted the way she did, but she wasn't the only one who wanted freedom. The difference between him and Cat was that he wanted to have a 'normal' life—he wished he didn't have his abilities. Toby's bubble helped save their lives all those years ago, and for that, he was grateful, but it was a secret he felt he could never tell. He would have to spend his life lying to people, and he was confident that if someone knew what he could do, they would never look at him the same again. Even if people thought it was cool, he would still be a freak. Different. On the other hand, Cat was immensely proud of her gifts; she wanted the world to know and hated having to hide—he could appreciate her point of view too.

"You seem to be in a good mood today; anything you want to share?" Cat was looking at the floor. She had the strangest smile on her face, and her cheeks were flushed.

"You know, it's just a nice morning, and I'm happy," said Cat. It was evident to Toby she was hiding something. Toby raised an eyebrow.

"Happy?" He nudged her with his shoulder. "What could my moody sister possibly be happy about?" Cat nudged him back.

"Hey! I'm not moody. I'm just opinionated." They both laughed, and he was satisfied she wasn't going to tell him anything.

"Where's Jake this morning?" Cat's smile suddenly disappeared. "Uh-oh, no longer happy?" Cat stopped with her hands on her hips, facing up to her brother.

"Thanks for that. Do you have a problem with me being in a good mood?" Toby shot his arms up with his palms out.

"Hey! How was I to know that my question was going to ruin the good mood?" Cat let go of her hips and crossed her arms instead, swivelling on her one foot.

"Fair shout, I guess. We had a fight." Cat started to stride forward again; Toby resumed walking with her.

"What happened?" Toby wasn't smiling now. As much as he liked to wind up his sister, she was clearly upset by her row with Jake. Cat sighed.

"He has an issue with Archie."

"Ah…" Toby nodded knowingly. Cat shot a look at her brother and narrowed her eyes.

"You don't sound surprised." Stated Cat accusingly. Toby laughed.

"Well, duh. The guy's in love with you. Of course, he's not going to like your new boyfriend, especially when it's someone like Archie." Cat stopped again and looked at Toby with a pinched expression and once again changed her stance.

"So, you have a problem with him too?" Toby shook his head. He'd heard love is blind, but he thought his sister was above all that.

"Cat, he's a Doof Nugget," this was one of Toby's words he used as a child; he still enjoyed using it, even now at seventeen. "No one likes Archie. I don't think even Archie's friends like Archie." Cat stamped her foot and stomped ahead, leaving Toby standing in place. She looked over her shoulder and shouted,

"You're a Doof Nugget!" Toby sighed and shook his head. That went well. He ended up walking the rest of the way to school alone. He couldn't be bothered to catch up to Cat, and he didn't think she wanted him to.

It was a slow morning. Toby didn't have any issues with

school, but it bored him. He was a brilliant boy—he knew it, and his teachers knew it. Toby was known to correct teachers regularly. Some took it with a pinch of salt, and others took it as an insult, thinking he was too smart for his own good. He didn't go out of his way to embarrass people, but he did get a little satisfaction from it. School didn't seem to offer him any challenges. He couldn't wait to go to college. He wanted to study English Literature; he took after his mother—he loved books and not just reading them, he liked to write too. Some day he wanted to work in publishing, and for that, he wanted to go to London. He mentioned this to his mum once, and she wasn't happy. She said it was too far away and that they needed to stay together. He hoped that one day she would see that she needed to let him go—Cat too if they would have a semblance of a normal life. If their mum had it her way, both of them would still be living in her house at the age of forty.

Toby was on his way to the lunch room from English. His friends were in a different class—they worked with Bunsen burners and test tubes. They were science geeks, but they were cool ones. They weren't like the atypical nerds portrayed in American high school movies. Neither wore glasses, although one wore contacts, and they didn't have goofy teeth and acne. They looked like normal seventeen-year-olds, but they were smart.

Toby had his earphones in. This afternoon he was listening to "Bomber" by *Motorhead*, and as he plodded down the corridor nodding his head in time with the music, he walked past the gym. The door was slightly open, and he saw a flash of movement. Toby removed his earphones and heard the music of another band he liked. It was *Within Temptation*. It was a song from an old album, but he knew it well. "Dirty

Dancer". He stepped back and peered through the opening; there was just a single person inside. He recognised her, and she wasn't hard to miss. She had bright pink hair in bunches on either side of her head. It was quite a contrast against her russet brown skin. She was in the same year as him, but he didn't know her personally, not even her name, they didn't share any classes together.

She was a talented girl. She was dancing—it was a mix of ballet and modern dance. She was wearing all black workout clothes consisting of tight leggings and a sleeveless cropped top which hugged her petite figure. He watched her as she pirouetted on her toe and kicked out her leg straight up in the air. She then bent over backwards, touching the floor with her fingertips. She leapt into the air with no effort, and she danced toward the climbing apparatus fixed to the wall. Toby assumed she was using it as a partner. She grabbed a rung of the frame and leaned back with a hand to her forehead, and she then spun and perched a leg on a higher rung.

The dance was dramatic and beautiful, and he looked on, eyes wide. Suddenly feeling self-conscious, he glanced around him—no one else was in the corridor. He moved closer to the opening to get a better look. It now looked evident to any onlooker that he was spying. He leaned in slightly. The song was coming to an end, and she was getting ready for a big finale. She moved away from the frame and sprinted from the other side of the room, then did what appeared to be a gymnastic floor routine, cartwheeling and front flipping the whole length of the hall. She reached the frame again, leapt up into the air and landed on a high rung. Upon landing, she threw herself backwards in a backflip and landed softly on her feet. As the girl landed, Toby heard a snapping noise and a creak, and the music stopped.

The girl leaned forward and put her hands on her knees to catch her breath. She didn't hear or see the climbing frame coming loose from the wall. The top of the structure slowly moved further away from its attachments. Toby wanted to call out, but he knew that by the time he got the words out, the apparatus would have already come crashing down on top of her. Instead, he sprinted into the gym—it took less than a second to reach her, but it took him a split second to know he wouldn't be able to get her out of the way in time. Instead, Toby pushed her down to the floor. He made a bridge over her with his body and closed his eyes; he visualised the barrier in his head; it was a flexible bubble, and he imagined wrapping it around their bodies. Wooden pieces shattered around them. The girl underneath him was screaming, and she put her hands over her head in an attempt to protect herself. Then everything became still and quiet.

Toby opened his eyes. He felt no pain, but he checked himself anyway—not a scratch on him. He looked about himself, and just like the fire ten years ago, around them was a circle of clean, untouched hardwood floors. This was going to be difficult to explain. The girl was now lying in the foetal position, and her eyes were squeezed tightly shut. Toby touched her shoulder.

"Are you alright?" His voice was trembling—even though he knew he could protect them, it still shook him up. He'd only ever used the bubble in training, and it was strange to be using it whilst being in real danger . The girl slowly opened her eyes and peered up at him. She sat up quickly; she then saw the debris all over the floor.

"Holy fuck!" She stood up quickly. "W-w-what happened?

One minute I was standing here, and the next thing I know, you come from nowhere, and it sounds like a bomb has gone off." Toby looked at the floor, then to the wall where the frame had fallen from. On the wall was a sign:

<u>DANGER</u> – FRAME IS FAULTY – DO NOT USE.

He cleared his throat and pointed to the sign. The girl's mouth fell open,

"Shit. I didn't see that there," the girl said, laughing. Toby shook his head.

"Well, I'm glad you're okay; next time, be more careful." He turned on his heel to walk out.

"Wait!" she called, but he carried on walking. She ran up behind him and grabbed his arm.

"Just wait a minute. I have a question." Toby knew what was coming, and he tried to pull away.

"I've got to go. People are waiting for me." He yanked his arm free. The girl stood still and lifted her chin. Just before he reached the door, she called out again.

"Hey! I work for the school paper, you know. I'm Alison Jones." Toby froze—he'd heard that name before. Alison was quite the troublemaker. She'd been suspended from the school twice thanks to her outrageous so-called news articles, one of which was about a teacher's unsavoury relationship with a sixteen-year-old student. It turned out there was no proof, but because of the article, that particular teacher ended up having a hard time, not just from the students but teachers as well. A week after the publication, the teacher quit. Out of all the people he could have saved, it had to be her. He turned around, his shoulders sagged, and he sighed.

"What do you want?" he asked. Alison crossed her arms with a crooked smile.

"Don't get me wrong. I appreciate what you did. If it weren't for you, I could have been really badly hurt, maybe even killed. Thank god we'll never know. But my question is, how are you not hurt? And look!" She gestured to the clean circular spot on the floor. "What is that?" Toby bit his lip. He moved over to the wall next to the door and leaned up against it.

"What do you think happened?" He started to push a speck of dirt around the floor with his foot. He avoided eye contact.

"Well, I don't know, but if I were to put on my investigative hat, based on the evidence…" Alison wandered around the accident site like a crime scene investigator. "…I would suggest that you ran in extremely quickly, shielded me with your body and then took out an impenetrable umbrella which shielded us both from the extremely heavy climbing frame, which then broke to pieces around us," Toby smirked. "However, the problem with that theory is that no such umbrella exists, and if it did, where is it now?"

"Good theory, I will leave you with that. Let me know how you get on." Toby pushed himself away from the wall and went for the door. Alison called out again.

"I'll figure it out, you know!" This time Toby kept on moving—he didn't stop. *Shit.* He wasn't keen on the idea of telling his mum about this—he wouldn't hear the last of it. It was usually Cat who tended to risk their anonymity. He still had a clean record and wanted to keep it that way, although he'd never be able to take the moral high ground against Cat ever again. He wondered if Alison would let it go. He doubted it. It was a shame. Out of all the girls in this school, she was probably the coolest he'd ever met.

Toby arrived home before Cat. She would be a while, he saw her meet up with Archie at the school gates, and they'd wandered off in the wrong direction of home. He hoped she wouldn't be late again, he was worried about their mum. He was pretty sure she was on an emotional precipice—it wouldn't take much to knock her over, and Cat really wasn't helping matters. He came through the door and went straight to the dining room. It was what he always did. He was always starving after school, so he tended to raid the fridge before going up to his room to listen to his music. He made a bee-line for the refrigerator when he heard sniffing behind him. He looked around and saw his mum sitting at the dining table. Her head was in her hands with her back to him. He grabbed some leftover meat from yesterday's dinner and sat opposite his mum; there was a soggy tissue in her hands.

"Mum? What's wrong?" She put her head up, her eyes were red and puffy, and her nose was wet, as were her cheeks. She sniffed and wiped her nose with the tissue.

"Casey's missing. I think he's dead." She began to sob into her hands. Toby leaned back in his chair; he was about to take a bite of the cold ham but put it back down instead. Toby's eyes started to sting. He didn't have the closest relationship with Casey, but he'd been around since they moved there. He was part of the family. He did find that he yelled at Casey more than he was nice to him, but that was only because he was a pain in the ass. The other morning, it was about six o'clock, and out of nowhere, Casey pounced on his chest, winding him. He was a big cat. Casey then went on to attack any moving limb under the duvet. He arose that morning with scratches all over his legs and hands from where he tried to prise Casey off him. He then threw him on the floor and called him a little fucker. Casey also chewed several of his favourite CDs and soiled his clean clothes with his skiddy ass. But despite all this, he wouldn't want to be without him. He was like an annoying little brother.

"Oh my god, mum, what happened?" Toby shoved his chair closer to the table, he leaned across and took his mum's hands. Mae calmed her voice and sniffed again.

"He didn't come for his food this morning. I waited until lunchtime, and there was still no sign of him, so I went to look for him."

"What did you find, mum? What makes you think he's dead?" Toby squeezed her hands. He hated to think about what she could've found.

"After I couldn't find him in the main garden, I went into the woods. You know I hate going in there, but I was really worried." Toby knew his mum never went into the woods. She didn't mind him and Cat going in there as long as she could see them from the garden, but it made her feel unsafe. He wondered if it was a phobia of hers. Supposing it was a phobia, then she did well to go in there looking for Casey. Mae went on to tell him what she found.

"But you can't say for sure that it was him?" Toby held his breath, giving his mum a questionable gaze.

"Not for sure no, PC Carrick is running a test for me to find out what species the animal is, and I'll wait until I hear before I decide on anything." *Did she call the police?* Toby got up from his seat and stepped back. He stuttered as he couldn't find the right words.

"Why on earth did you call the police?! You don't call the police about a missing cat." Mae furrowed her brow; she scratched her temple.

"Toby. Don't you see? It's your father. He took Casey and killed him. He's getting back at me; it's only a matter of time until he comes after you and your sister. If the test shows the animal was a cat, then I don't doubt that it's Casey. If that's the case, we need to leave here. I need to keep you safe." Toby retook his seat and lowered his head onto the table. He spoke without lifting his head.

"Mum. This has to stop." He raised his head and looked into his mother's eyes. "I think you need to get help, mum. No one is after us. We are safe. I know Casey is missing, but that animal could've been anything. If it's Casey, maybe a fox did it, or some other predator, like an escaped dog or something, it does not mean dad is on the rampage. Do you realise how crazy you sound?" Mae rose from her chair; she bared her teeth at her son.

"I'm. Not. Crazy. You never knew your father, thank god. You don't remember him holding a knife up to your sister's throat, the way he would almost suffocate me, and you didn't see the look on his face when I got you two away from him. He's playing games; it's what he does. He probably wants everyone to think I'm crazy. He's manipulative and smart; even if you, your sister or the police don't see it, I do." Mae left the dining room with new tears in her eyes. Toby knew those tears weren't for Casey; those were because of him. Just as she left the room, the home phone rang. It was in the kitchen, and Toby answered. It was PC Carrick. He asked to speak with Mae, but Toby told him she was a bit upset now. He wondered if they gotten the test results back already.

"No, that's not why I'm calling; it will take a while for those to come back." Toby shifted his weight to his right foot and leaned on the worktop.

"Then what's this about?"

"Your mother told us about your family's past, which was

why I offered to run the test for her in the first place. We wouldn't normally do that. Your mother made it clear that she felt Anthony Newton, her ex-husband—"

"My father," Toby interrupted.

"Yes," PC Carrick continued. "She thought he was responsible for something that happened in the house the other day and that he took the cat." Toby nodded; he knew the officer couldn't hear him nodding, but he remained silent anyway. "Well, I took it upon myself to run some checks. There is no way that Mr Newton could've done any of those things—he has an alibi, a pretty strong one as well. On the day of the alleged intrusion, Mr Newton was arrested for antisocial behaviour, and at ten-thirty this morning, he was in court being sentenced. He was sentenced to fifty hours of community service. I seriously doubt he would have made the trip in the early hours of this morning to kidnap a cat." Toby exhaled in relief. He hoped that after hearing this, his mum would let go of this terrible paranoia.

"Thank you, officer. You've really helped us out, and I appreciate it. I'll tell her now. Thank you again."

Toby hung up the phone, and he went to the living room to find his mum standing next to the window. She was chewing her nails.

"Who was that on the phone?" asked Mae, her voice tired. Toby told her what PC Carrick said. Mae collapsed onto the sofa, where she pondered this for a few moments. She'd bitten her thumbnail down to the nail bed.

"Maybe he has an accomplice." There was no confidence in her words.

"Mum!" Toby threw his hands up in the air. "For fuck's sake!" Before he could carry on, the phone rang again. He shuffled to the kitchen for the second time in five minutes, and he snatched the phone off the counter and answered.

"Yes? Toby snapped. The voice on the other end of the phone introduced themselves. Toby closed his eyes. "I'm so sorry, Mrs Cresswell, it's all a bit strained here today. How can I help you?" Mrs Cresswell was their closest neighbour about a half-mile down the road. She was the nicest old lady, a widow. She was the one whose husband died last year, the potential serial killer in Toby's eyes. They'd all gone over to see her with food and treats, just to let her know that they were there if she needed them. After a short conversation, he hung up the phone, smiling. He went back to see his mum.

"Mum, that was Mrs Cresswell; she found Casey. He was in her shed." Mae leapt up from the sofa and hugged her son tightly.

"Oh my god! He's alive; he's okay." Toby hugged her back. Now was not the time to say I told you so. All he could think right now was that he needed to go and collect Casey. He would talk to his mum tomorrow, but in the meantime, he felt it wise to call PC Carrick back to let him know not to worry about the test. It was probably a squirrel who got on the wrong side of a fox.

Chapter 13

It was another sunny Saturday morning—it hadn't rained in weeks, the storm which threatened only the other day never came to anything. The air was thick and close; Cat mopped the sweat from her upper lip as she got herself ready; she was meeting Archie at lunchtime. They were spending the day together at the cavern and Cat couldn't wait. The last few days with him had been fantastic; it would be their third visit to the lusty grotto. Cat looked herself up and down in front of the mirror. She wore black lingerie, a lacy thong and an intricate bra that left nothing to the imagination, negating the whole reason for wearing a bra in the first place. She wanted to make an effort this time. The previous times they'd gone to the cavern was after school. The girls in PE may have questioned this type of underwear in the changing rooms, so she usually wore basic knickers and bras.

There was a knock on the bedroom door. Cat grabbed her jeans and pushed her legs through in one fluid motion.

"Just a second!" She tugged on a camisole; she was out of breath when she pulled the door open. It was Toby. She rolled her eyes and walked away from the door. Leaving it open, she plopped on the stool next to her dressing table and started to brush her hair. "What do you want?" She pouted. Toby entered the room with his hands in his pockets.

"We need to talk about mum," said Toby. Cat sighed and continued to pull the brush through the knots in her hair. She made eye contact with him in the mirror.

"Can't we talk about this later? I'm going out soon, and I need to get ready." Toby took his hands out of his pockets and rubbed his forehead.

"Christ sake Cat. That's what you said yesterday when I wanted to talk about this. It's important, and I'm worried about mum." Cat put down the brush and turned to face him.

"Toby. I'm concerned about mum too, but there's nothing we can do about it. Now that Casey's back, maybe she'll get better." Toby shook his head.

"I don't think so. Haven't you seen her lately? She's constantly on edge, flinching when there's a random noise. She's practically camped next to the window." Toby paced the room. "Casey hasn't seen the outdoors since he came back. I think mum's on the verge of a mental breakdown." Toby's eyes were stinging again, and he could feel his chin start to quiver, and he covered his face with his hands. Cat got up and rested her hand on his shoulder.

"Oh Toby, we've got through this before." She moved her hand from his shoulder to his upper arm, stroking. "It's not half as bad as when we were kids. Do you remember? Forget the cat; WE barely saw the outdoors; we had to beg her to let us out. Even when we were allowed, she was hovering over us the whole time. Mum's always been anxious, but like a lot of us, she has bad days. This is just one of those days—or in her case, a few days. As long as nothing else happens, she'll start to relax again." Toby wiped his eyes with the back of his hands.

"I hope you're right, Kitty Cat." They hugged, and before he let her go, he spoke quietly in her ear. "Are you off to see the Doof Nugget?" Cat clipped him around the back of the head. "Ow!" Cat was smiling—she'd forgiven him for what he said about Archie the other day. She knew this was Toby's way of lightening the mood and an attempt to cheer himself up.

"That's what you get. Now sod off and let me get ready." He laughed his way out of her room. Cat pushed the door shut with her foot. She sat back in front of the mirror, her eyes watery, and she dabbed at them with a tissue. It hurt her to see Toby so upset; he always seemed that little bit closer to their mum than she was. Cat was worried about her, but her mum was an adult and could take care of herself; it shouldn't be up to them to look after her. She was still bitter toward her, even though she'd joked about their childhood a moment ago. For her, those memories made her sad. They missed out on a lot when they were young because of her anxiety. Her mum's over-protective behaviour made her feel so confined. Now she was older, she did have more freedom, but it was too little too late.

Cat carefully applied her make-up, and she was good to go. Her phone vibrated; it was a text message. It was Archie saying that he was outside. Her stomach fluttered, and her face turned the lightest of pink through her make-up.

* * *

At the cavern, Cat's new black lingerie was cast away near the waterfall opening. Cat was lying under a white sheet, one leg dangling out from the cover. Her skin was glistening with sweat, and her hair was damp. Archie was lying behind her with no cover at all. He was naked with one arm wrapped around her waist and the other laid flat under her head, holding her hand. He was kissing the back of her neck and her eyes were closed, but she was smiling.

"That was amazing. I don't think I've ever felt this relaxed and happy," she sighed. It was the truth—she could lay there with him forever; she could think of nothing better. The way she felt when she was with him was incomparable to anything else. When they were apart, she longed to be with him, and when they were together, she couldn't stand to part from him. Her heart would race, and when he touched her, it was like electricity. He was stroking her stomach now, and it made her ache to be closer to him even though they were already as close as they could be. She thought she'd felt love before, but that was just a silly childish crush, which wasn't even love at all. This, indeed, was love that she was feeling right now, with some lust thrown in there as well.

"I'm glad you're happy," Archie replied as he nuzzled her neck. She pulled his arm up from her waist and kissed his hand. Archie took his hand away and lifted her chin, and kissed her roughly. This was different from the previous love-making; there was no tenderness, and she didn't particularly feel like it was making love at all. This was just having sex, but she liked it. There was something feral and raw about it. It took her ecstasy to a whole different level. She reached her climactic end, and to their shock, stones started to shower down from the ceiling. The cascade of water coming down over the opening of the cavern began to splatter inside. They then noticed several cushions were floating mid-air. Archie stood up, and Cat sat back onto her bottom. The stones stopped falling, and the water started to abide by gravity's law again as the cushions fell to the ground.

"What the fuck?" Archie was laughing. "I get the feeling that I definitely hit the spot that time!" Cat started to laugh too; she was worried he'd be afraid of what happened, but he loved it. He came over to sit next to her. "Now that was amazing!" He collapsed backwards on the cushions and put his hands behind his head, just staring at the ceiling, and Cat mirrored him. He then turned onto his side and propped his head up with a hand. He looked into Cat's eyes; he was grinning widely.

"Have you ever used your gift to, you know… get your own back?" Cat knitted her eyebrows together.

"What do you mean?" she asked.

"I dunno. For example, someone throws a ball at your head, and it hits you. When their back is turned, would you pick up a stone with your, you know…" he tapped her temple with a finger, "…then fling it at his head?" said Archie playfully. Cat giggled.

"Well. It is frowned upon by my family, but I've done *vengeful* things before. There was this time when my friend, Angela, was being bullied. The girl was a nasty piece of work. I'd had enough of seeing her make Angela cry day after day, so I took action. I confronted her and told her to leave Angela alone, but she just laughed in my face. It made me so angry, so I concentrated on her neck. I imagined my hands wrapping around her throat; as I did, she started to choke, people who walked past asked her what was wrong, but she couldn't speak. I remember staring deep into her eyes, she looked back at me, and I smiled; she knew, she knew that it was me doing this to her, a crowd had formed, everyone was panicking, and she was starting to lose consciousness. Then, I was busted. Toby came along and saw what was happening. He told me quietly in my ear to release her. He actually thought I was going to kill her."

"Weren't you? Deep down, do you think that was what you wanted?" asked Archie; he was smiling whilst asking the question.

"Of course not," Cat replied, "I just wanted her to know who she was messing with, and it worked. She went nowhere near Angela and me again. I'd love to do more with my ability, it would be nice to use it for good and help the oppressed, but I'm forbidden to use it at all. I mean, what good is having this if I can't use it?" Archie pondered this for a moment.

"Cat. Do you think you might be able to help me with something?" He spoke quietly and glanced up. Cat's forehead wrinkled, intrigued.

"What do you need help with, babe?" she asked. He cleared his throat.

"You know I told you about my dad; he's always going on at me, giving me a hard time?" Cat nodded; he'd briefly touched on his poor relationship with his parents. It didn't seem any worse than any other teenager/parent dynamics. "Well. I've had enough, and I'm fed up with it, Cat. I want you to help me make him stop." Cat took his hand and stroked it.

"What are you suggesting I do?" He stared down at the small void between them; he avoided eye contact as he spoke.

"I thought maybe you could come to my place—you can sit in my room whilst I go speak with my dad. It doesn't take much to set my dad off. If I bait him and he starts having a go, maybe you could make a few things happen. Slam some doors, shake some windows, blow a lightbulb or something, and I'll make him think it's coming from me. I want the same as you, to make the bully realise who they are messing with. I think it might shock him into leaving me alone in future." Cat listened to his suggestion, their eyes met, and Cat was grimacing. Archie continued his pitch. "I just want to scare him a bit."

"I don't know, Archie. Firstly, I don't know I can do it from another room—to be honest, I've never tried it. Secondly, I don't know that scaring your dad is the answer. Can't you just talk to him?" Archie let go of Cat's hand and turned away from her. Twenty seconds of silence passed.

"He hits me," Archie whispered. Cat gasped. She reached out to touch his shoulder, but he shrugged her off.

"I didn't know. I'm so sorry." Archie turned on his back and stared at the ceiling.

"I've never told anyone; you're the only one who knows. Not even my mum and brothers know about it. He only ever hits me when we're alone. He's careful about where he hits me; he makes sure it isn't visible when I'm clothed. He hates me, Cat. He wishes that he never had me." Cat moved in to hold him, and he didn't push her away this time. She rested her head on his chest. She was furious. Archie was right; his dad was a bully, he deserved everything coming to him, and she vowed to give his dad the fright of his life.

"Of course, I'll help you." He wrapped his arms around her and held her tight.

"Thank you. I love you so much." Cat closed her eyes and sighed deeply. There was no way she could let her family find out about this.

Cat wasn't late coming home, she could've stayed in the cavern the whole weekend quite happily, but she was taking Toby's concerns seriously. If her mum was on the edge, then she didn't want to be the one responsible for knocking her off it. She walked up the driveway, and as she approached the house, loitering outside was Jake. Cat was pleased to see him; she'd missed him, but as far as she was concerned, he was in the wrong, so she wasn't going to let him off that easily. She took a deep breath and pressed her lips together. They made eye contact. He beamed a huge smile, but Cat didn't reciprocate; the corners of his mouth dropped.

"Hi," said Jake. Cat ignored him. She stepped past him, removing her key from her pocket. "So, you are still mad at me." She continued to ignore him and put the key in the door. He lunged at her hand and pulled her away from the door. "Please, talk to me!" She snatched her hand back away from him.

"Why should I? I'm a shallow bitch remember?" she replied.

"Look. That's not what I said."

"It's what you implied." She smiled sarcastically.

"I'm sorry, okay. I miss you. You're right. I am jealous, you know I like you, and I suppose I always thought I might get a chance one day. I couldn't cope with the way that you were with Archie. I will be honest with you, though. I don't like him. But that's not your problem; it's mine." Cat sighed impatiently. "This last week, I've been thinking. I'm going to move on. You and I will always be friends, nothing more. I get that now. From now on, I'll be the best friend that you deserve." He stood back from her and allowed her access to the front door. She went back to the door and turned the key.

"C'mon then, are you coming in or what?" The corners of Cat's mouth tilted upward. Jake's eyes brightened, and he followed her into the house.

As Cat stepped through the door, she felt a sudden feeling of loss. It was great that Jake had finally let go of any possibilities between them—she always wished he would so they could have a more straightforward relationship—but she wasn't prepared for this feeling of disappointment. *Did I like him pining after me?* She wondered. She pushed those thoughts to the back of her mind. She now had a boyfriend whom she loved and a best friend she could rely on.

* * *

Toby was in for most of the afternoon—he was worried about leaving his mum on her own. She was usually busy on the weekend running errands, doing housework and pottering in the garden. But she'd stayed indoors despite the hot and sunny day wearing lounge-wear, which she generally reserved for bedtimes. She'd spent some time in the living room with Casey, but she couldn't keep still. She was up and down and in and out. In the end, she spent several hours sitting at the dining table gazing out the window toward the woods. Toby tried to talk to her.

"Mum, maybe you should get out of the house for a bit, get some fresh air." She shook her head and returned to sentry duty. Toby stood in her way; she tried to look around him, but he continued to block her view.

"Toby, get out of the way of the window." She swatted her hands at him.

"No, I won't. I want you to come away from the window," She frowned at him as he continued. "You need to get into some proper clothes and do your hair, have you even brushed it today?" Mae sat back and crossed her arms. She glared at him. "You need to snap out of it, and soon."

"Excuse me, but you're the child, and I'm the parent. All I'm doing is looking out for you and your sister; it's what a mother does. Now go do whatever it is that you do and leave me alone." Toby's shoulders sagged; he was getting nowhere.

"Fine, mum, whatever. For the record, what you're doing isn't protecting us; you're alienating us. Cat can't stand to be in the house with you, and I'm starting to feel the same way." Toby turned on his heel and stormed off.

* * *

During that evening, unbeknownst to the household, they were being watched. Alison furtively sneaked through the woods with her camera. It was about ten o'clock, and the sun had just set. Her palms were sweating. She didn't usually do things like this—not when it was a fellow student. She'd done it before with teachers and with town officials; they were ordinarily good to watch for a juicy story. She generally left students alone since they were her audience, and it was never a good idea to upset them. Toby wasn't just any ordinary student, however. She had no idea what happened in the gym earlier in the week, but she wanted to find out.

The last of the light was gone except for the light that formed rectangles on the lawn from inside. Alison jogged on tiptoe from the wood's edge to the darkest part of the house. She felt like a cat burglar—she wore black jeans, a black t-shirt and a black beanie hat, covering up the bright pink which would typically be visible a mile away. Alison arrived at the first lit window, crouched below it and carefully brought herself level with the windowsill. She peered inside. It must have been the dining room. She could see a large oak table in the centre of the room and four chairs positioned around it. There was an empty mug on it and a rather large cat; it caught sight of her, and she saw the cat hiss whilst revealing its incredibly sharp teeth. Alison quickly ducked down. Satisfied there was nothing to see here, she continued along the back of the house.

The next lit room was also vacant; it looked like a study. There was an open laptop which hosted a family photo screensaver. She recognised Toby; he stood next to his twin sister. She knew of Cat, and she was quite the school scandal recently. She was going out with bad boy Archie. Cat didn't look like the sort of girl he would normally go for—she'd seen her in school, and she wasn't part of the bitchy 'popular' cliques, which was Archie's usual hunting ground. There wasn't a virgin among those girls. Perhaps he fancied a change. The other woman in the picture must have been their mum—she was pretty, it wasn't surprising she had some good-looking kids. She had to admit though, her obsession with Toby wasn't solely to do with his intriguing secret; she could still remember his smell. It wasn't a deodorant smell or aftershave; it was his smell. She couldn't explain it, but it was so sweet.

The study door opened; Alison dropped to the floor. She slowly rose and peeked with one eye into the room but couldn't see anyone. She scanned the room—there was movement in her peripheral; she peered into the corner of the room to her right by the door. Someone was there.

Much like Alison, this stranger was dressed in black, and their back was to the window. *Who the fuck is that?* Alison thought. She moved to the other side of the window as the person moved away from the corner. They were ducking down, clearly not the behaviour of someone who lived there.

It was almost certainly an intruder. Alison grabbed her mobile phone and began to dial the local police station, but then she hesitated. How would she explain her presence there? Alison put her mobile away—she decided that if it looked like they were going to hurt someone, she would call the emergency services immediately.

Alison continued to watch as the person went through the drawers of the desk. Whatever it was they were after, they found. The intruder put something in their pocket. Alison hid again as the person turned around to go back out of the door. They slinked out unseen. Moments later, she heard the back door open—she pressed her back up against the wall tightly and she held her breath. The intruder ran across the lawn and darted into the woods, then disappeared. Alison's nerves were shot, her motivation for tonight's operation had dramatically waned, and she'd decided to try this again another day. She waited five minutes or so to allow the intruder a head start—she didn't fancy catching up with them. She took a deep breath then slipped back into the woods.

Alison came out of the woods onto a country road; it was where she'd entered. Quite a distance up the road sat a car. The interior light was on. Alison had the realisation that this could be the intruder. She squinted. She could only see a silhouette; it could be them. It looked as though they were on the phone. She turned off the flash on her camera, and she zoomed in as close as she could get and took a photo. She looked at the preview on the LCD display. She couldn't make out much, but she'd gotten the plate number thanks to the light over the registration plate. The car drove away, and she stayed still until it was out of sight. As soon as it was gone, she made her way home.

* * *

The man in black returned to his car. He was breathless. He was keen to get away from the house. He'd been in there so many times now; luck was bound to run out at some point. He made a call.

"Hi, mate. Yeah. Phase two is complete." He hung up the phone.

Chapter 14

Mae awoke early—it was Sunday, and she had no inclination to get out of bed. She didn't get to sleep until the very early hours. Toby's words were still ringing in her head. Was she alienating her children? All she wanted to do was keep them safe. She was the first to admit that the last ten years had been burdensome, that she'd been difficult to live with, but she did it for everyone's good. They'd changed their identities, and they needed to remain hidden. She was the person who achieved this haven for them, and they'd lived the last decade in relative safety. Nothing had happened throughout those years because she was careful. Mae didn't allow the children to go anywhere alone except for school; they weren't allowed to play in the street and weren't allowed to stay with friends; she needed to know precisely what they were doing at all times. This is what kept them safe.

Mae took a moment to remember her own childhood; it was hugely different from theirs. As a teenager, she could go into town with her friends as long as she was home before dark. She spent lots of nights at Annie's house. They had many laughs over the years, and they often wouldn't go to sleep until gone three in the morning. They would chat and scare each other to the point that they couldn't sleep. If more than two friends were sleeping over, they needed to stay awake for as long as possible because if you fell asleep first, you were subject to food art all over the face; it was hilarious, she laughed at the memory. Mae realised then just how much her children missed out on. Their childhood wasn't fun or memorable, and they wouldn't look back with a smile on their face like she did now.

She continued to drift in thought. Mae knew things had been moved around the house. She knew someone had been in there, but she jumped to the conclusion that Anthony was the culprit. What if someone was messing around; perhaps it was just some kid playing around harmlessly. Casey was found unharmed. Maybe he did just wander too far, and perhaps he did just get stuck in the neighbour's garden shed without the assistance of someone with sinister intentions. There was no solid proof that Anthony was involved in any of it; the guy had a rock-solid alibi. The more she thought about it, the more she felt like a fool.

Mae jumped up out of bed, did her hair and got dressed into a pair of jeans and a nice top. Mae spent the whole morning cleaning the house and doing the laundry—she'd fallen behind recently. At about ten-thirty, she made a cooked breakfast—she knew better than to do it earlier than that. When kids were teenagers, this was the general waking time. The bacon sizzled on the grill. Mae heard footsteps coming down the stairs; it was Toby.

"Morning!" Mae raised her spatula in greeting.

"Morning…" Toby's gaze was guarded as he went to the fridge to grab some orange juice. "What is this? An English breakfast? What's all this in aid of?" Mae pulled out a chair and gestured for him to sit.

"It is an apology," said Mae. Toby raised an eyebrow. Mae sat opposite him, "What you said last night…you're right. I've made things more difficult than they need to be. But I want you to know that this all changes from now." Toby smiled at his mother. "I'm going to the supermarket today to do some shopping. Do you need anything?" Toby shook his head.

"No thanks, mum, I'm good." He took a swig of his orange juice and put his glass down. "I want to apologise too. I know everything you've done, you've done it for us. It's been no picnic for you, has it?" Mae walked around the table and wrapped her arms around his shoulders, and hugged him tightly.

"Oh Toby, it's always been for you two, but it doesn't mean I went the right way about it."

Cat entered the room mid-embrace; she cleared her throat.

"Am I interrupting something?" Mae released her son and tackled Cat. She hugged her daughter. Cat's eyes were wide, and she held her arms up as if she were surrendering.

"Things are going to change, I promise." To Cat's relief, Mae released her. "Do you need anything from the supermarket? Anything you like. Ice cream, chocolate or booze. Archie can come 'round if you like. Does he drink lager or beer?" Cat stood back, looked over at Toby, back to her mum, then returned to Toby. He threw his arms up in the air.

"Err, thanks, mum; I'm sure that he likes lager, any will do. I'll ask him if he wants to come over."

"Great." Mae dished up their breakfast—she didn't make any for herself. She placed their plates in front of them then trotted out to get her car keys. "See you later, kids," she waved and vanished out the door.

"What the hell was that? Is she on drugs or something?" asked Cat. Toby shrugged his shoulders and tucked into his delicious breakfast.

* * *

Mae was feeling good; it was amazing how a positive outlook could change a mood. The local radio was on—they were playing oldies, and she remembered what oldies were when she was young. It was the likes of ABBA and The Carpenters, the type of music her mother listened to. Now it was Take That and Blur, the songs of her childhood. It was slightly depressing to think these songs were now considered old. However, it was impossible to feel glum when hearing "Tubthumping" by Chumbawamba. Mae was tapping the wheel and dancing in her seat, singing at the top of her lungs. It was like she'd set herself free. She pulled into the car park singing. "I get knocked down, but I get up again. You are never gonna keep me down!" she sang. She reversed into a parking space and switched off the engine. She felt wonderfully energised, and there was a spring in her step as she walked into the shop.

Mae had quite the shopping spree. She bought wine, lager, cider, Prosecco, pizza, sausage rolls, crisps, most products from the bakery and anything else considered junk food. Mae had a lot of making up to do, and nothing said sorry like a massive plate of carbohydrates and a crate of alcohol. She decided to spruce up her wardrobe, too, so she bought a few lovely dresses and treated herself to a fabulous pair of skinny jeans. This was going to be a new Mae, and this Mae needed a new look. She took her spoils to the car; she carried five large bags, and they were heavy; she heaved them into the boot. Mae was feeling good, and she couldn't wait to get back to start her new life—a life without fear.

The supermarket was five miles away from home. Mae drove about two. She stopped at some traffic lights at a busy crossroad and was still drumming on the steering wheel. Now they were playing "Livin' La Vida Loca" by Ricky Martin. Her light turned green. She was the second car from the front, and as the first car pulled off, Mae pulled off slowly after.

Mae was halfway through the intersection when she saw a large black car coming from her left from the corner of her eye—it looked like a Range Rover, but she didn't have much time to identify it for sure. The car wasn't slowing down; those lights should've been on red. Mae braked hard. She knew that if she continued, the other car would end up colliding right into the middle of her car. She stopped in the middle of the junction, hoping the driver would be able to manoeuvre around her, but they weren't changing their trajectory—they were coming straight for her. Mae strained to focus her eyes inside the vehicle. She couldn't see precise details of the driver, but a couple of things she *could* tell was that it was a man and he was smiling, possibly laughing. Mae braced herself for impact as the front of the Range Rover collided into the front left wing of her car. She was jolted to the side, throwing her head into her driver side window. She lost consciousness immediately, and the car spun around and was facing in the direction she'd come from. The vehicle that hit her failed to stop and left the scene.

When Mae opened her eyes, people were talking to her—she couldn't make out what they were saying; too many were speaking simultaneously, and it made her head hurt. She touched her temple. When she took her hand away, it was wet and covered in blood. Her eyesight was blurry, and her ears were ringing, but she could still hear the radio. The DJ was saying that he'd be back after the news. She couldn't hear the news reporter because all she could hear now were sirens. She felt dizzy, and she could see a person in green clothing coming toward her; it was a paramedic. Mae blacked out again.

When Mae awoke for the second time, her head felt like she'd just been hit with a hammer—it throbbed, and she moved her hand to feel what the damage was, but there was some resistance. She looked down at her hand and saw she was connected to a drip. Mae looked around the room, and she had the place to herself. She was unsure what happened—one minute, she was in the car, and the next, she was in the hospital. She tried to think of what happened in between. It took a good ten minutes, then she remembered. She'd been hit by another car; the driver was smiling, but she couldn't see who it was. He didn't try to avoid her, which told her only one thing. He'd hit her on purpose. A nurse strolled into her private room. She was quite a large lady, and she had the sweetest smile.

"Oh good, you're awake." The nurse looked at her drip and grabbed the clipboard which was hooked to the end of the bed. "How are you feeling?" Her accent was Irish. Mae shifted in the bed and winced.

"My head and side hurts." Mae's voice was hoarse and dry.

"I can give you something for that. I'll get the doctor to come in and have a chat with you. After that, do you feel up to seeing some visitors? It's the police, and they want to talk to you." Mae nodded. She was pretty happy with that; she needed to talk to them too.

The nurse syringed something into Mae's drip; it didn't take long for the pain to melt away. It made her sleepy as well. She felt like she'd drunk too many vodkas. The doctor came in soon after the nurse left.

Hello Ms Phoenix, it's great to see you awake. My name is Dr Griffins." He clicked the top of his pen and took her file. He wasn't the hot doctor you'd see in movies. He looked around fifty and had a bristly chin and bushy eyebrows. He was also very pale, and he looked ill. Mae found this strangely amusing.

"How long have I been unconscious?" she coughed. Dr Griffins passed her a small plastic cup of water; she sipped it and passed it back to him.

"You've been in the hospital for around eight hours. I understand you fell unconscious at the scene of the accident, so probably around nine hours in total." Nine hours! Mae lifted her head and tried to sit up.

"My kids are going to be worried; I have to go!" The doctor placed a hand on her shoulder and gently pushed her back down.

"Your children were notified, and they came in to see you when you were still sleeping, Toby, is it? He went home to bring you some of your things, and the other one went to the café to get herself a drink; they'll be back soon." Mae relaxed slightly. "Please, Ms Phoenix, you need to remain still; you're in no condition to be going anywhere right now. You have a concussion. We've done x-rays, and there doesn't seem to be any serious trauma to your head, but you do have two broken ribs on your right side." Mae could feel that one, the drugs were doing wonders for the pain, but there was still discomfort. "You also have a sprain to your right wrist; it's very bruised. Fortunately, you will be able to go home without further treatment, but we would like to keep you overnight just to monitor your head injury. You've had stitches, four in total." Mae touched her head, just above her right ear, she could feel the lumps of the thread. She felt sick, and heaved. The doctor reached for the cardboard fibre sick bowl and placed it under her chin. She didn't vomit much. It occurred to her she hadn't eaten today yet. Most of it was liquid and it tasted acidic.

"That'll be the concussion," declared the doctor. Mae nodded and gave him a sarcastic smile. "I'll leave you now so the police can talk to you. You need to rest, so not too long, okay?" Mae nodded again. She put the vomit bowl onto the bedside table.

It was PC Isaac Carrick who wandered into her room. Mae, all of a sudden, felt self-conscious. She looked over at her discarded bowl and prayed to God that it didn't smell too bad.

"Wow, that looks painful." Isaac took a seat next to her bed.

"No PC Harding today?" Mae's voice was a little slurred, and her sentence came out more like, "*No-Peasy-Harden-toody?*" It must have been the painkillers.

"He's here, and I asked him to wait outside. I didn't want to overwhelm you. We just have a few questions about the accident." Mae didn't even take a moment to pause.

"It was him; he tried to kill me. I saw the man's face as he hurtled toward me. He was laughing. He hit me on purpose." Isaac managed to understand somehow, but the words were again slurred and getting worse. "*It-shwas-im-h-tied-to-killme...*" Mae could hear her voice, and she knew how she must have sounded to him. Even to herself, it was like she was out of her mind. Isaac rubbed the small amount of stubble on his chin, and Mae could see the doubt on his face. "These drugs are making me sound crazy, but I'm not. This morning, I convinced myself, more like everyone else convinced me, that I might have been wrong before, so I let my guard down. I went out without a care in the world, and look what happened." She pointed to her injuries. Isaac shook his head.

"Mae, it was an accident. We initially investigated this as a hit and run, but the driver came forward a couple of hours ago. He said he was scared, but then he claimed you ran a red light, so he figured he didn't need to worry. Mae, he's saying it was your fault." Mae's eyes grew wide, her mouth fell open, and her face turned a shade of red.

"The fuck I did. It was a green light, and there were loads of people there. I'm sure someone will come forward to tell you that. I want to see him, the man who hit me." Isaac already foresaw she would want to see that. He took the copy of the man's driving license out of his pocket. He'd blacked out the name and details. He took the piece of paper out and showed it to Mae.

"Do you know this man?" Isaac asked. Mae studied the photograph, but she didn't know him from anywhere. It made no sense. The man she saw was laughing. Why would a perfect stranger take joy in hitting her car and risk killing her? .

"I don't know him, but it doesn't mean Anthony wasn't behind it. I bet he paid him, paid him to take the wrap. Shit, I'd probably agree to do it myself if someone were to pay me a few hundred quid." Mae's words were becoming even harder to understand, but Isaac got the gist. He sighed.

"So, you're telling me that your light was green?" asked

175

Isaac. Mae sat herself up straight.

"I even stopped because I could see him coming. I allowed him room to come around me because he was moving so fast, and I knew he would never be able to stop, but he made no attempt to miss me. He was laughing, and he hit me on purpose." Isaac made some notes in his notebook and got up from his seat.

"Okay, I'm going to go see if I can round up some witnesses, and I'll get back to you." Mae didn't respond. She knew he was just like everyone else; he thought she was nuts. "Hey. It's all going to be okay. I'm glad you weren't more seriously hurt. You were lucky." He took her hand and squeezed it gently. He lingered for a few seconds then left the room.

Mae already decided she wasn't going to lower her defences again. It's what kept them safe all these years. They'd overstayed their welcome in the small Cumbrian town. It was time to move on.

Not long after Isaac left, Mae's head was spinning, and the only way to stop it was to close her eyes; she fell asleep. She didn't know how long she'd been out for, but when she awoke, Cat was holding her right hand, and Toby held her left.

"Mum! Toby, she's awake." Toby gently squeezed her fingers and kissed them.

"Mum. We were so worried about you," said Toby.

"We came as soon as we could, but you were out of it," said Cat. Mae smiled at her children. Her head and ribs were excruciating again, but she didn't want more painkillers. There were serious things to talk about and she wanted to be taken seriously.

"I'm glad you're both here; I need to talk to you two about something important." They didn't say anything; they just stared at her waiting to hear what she wanted to say. They both still gripped her hands.

"When you get home, I'd rather it were sooner than later. I need you to pack up some clothes and anything else you might need." Cat and Toby released her hands.

"Wait. Why?" said Cat. Her brow was furrowed, and her eyes wary.

"We're leaving. I have to stay overnight, but I'll be discharging myself first thing in the morning, and when I get home, we're leaving this place straight away." The twins said nothing; they just stared at their mother, dumbfounded. "Shit, we're going to need a car; mine's all smashed up. Toby, I need you to hire a car. Just hire it for a week or so, to begin with. We can look to get another once we're settled. I was thinking Devon?"

Toby took several steps back, shaking his head.

"Unless you're suggesting we're going on holiday, which I seriously doubt you are, I'm not going to do anything of the sort. What's going on, mum? This morning you seemed like you sorted yourself out?" Cat walked around the bed to stand next to Toby. She was laughing and shaking her head.

"Let me guess," said Cat. She put a finger up to her temple. "You think this wasn't an accident. You think our estranged father came along and ran you off the road. Guess what? Wrong. You see, mum, we've already spoken to the police, and they said the driver came forward and it's not dad! It was just some random guy. For God's sake Mum, I'm sick of this bullshit. It was an accident, a fucking accident. Why can't you get that into your insane, stupid head?" Mae took a slow intake of breath; her eyes were wide in surprise. They'd fought many times in the past, but Cat had never spoken to her like that before. Mae looked to Toby for support, and for the first time, she didn't receive it.

"She's right mum; enough is enough. Years we've put up with this. Have you ever thought that perhaps you're not that special and dad forgot about you not long after we left? You've always told us that dad set the fire ten years ago, but it was never proven. We believed you because it's what you told us, except we weren't old enough to challenge you on it. I'm betting that he had nothing to do with it or anything else that has gone on. You've ruined our lives, mum, and you don't even see it." Mae tried to defend herself and explain, but Toby wouldn't let her. "No, mum. I don't want to hear it, I'm going home, and I will pack some things, but so that you know, I'm not going anywhere with you. I'm going to stay with a friend until I find something more permanent. Cat? Are you coming?" Cat was watching her mum. The more Toby spoke, the more deflated her mother looked; he was always the one standing up for her, but she'd lost him.

"I'll be there in a minute, you go; I'll meet you outside," replied Cat. Toby quickly left the room, and there were tears in his eyes. Cat stood back and stared at her mum in contempt.

"Well done, mother. The one who's always had your corner is angrier than I am. Don't get me wrong, I am annoyed with you, but no more than I usually am. You see, I always knew you were crazy and I got used to it. Toby had faith in you, and now you've shown him the truth. He sees the same as me now." Mae leaned forward with a pleading look in her eyes.

"Cat, please talk to him. I'm not crazy. We're in danger. We have to leave; I can't bear to lose you, either of you." Mae's voice was desperate, but Cat shook her head.

"You already have, mum." Cat turned and left the room; she

closed the door softly behind her. She whispered, "bye, mum." Through the door, she could hear her mum sobbing.

As Cat left the hospital, she saw Toby standing against the wall—he was pinching the top of his nose, and his eyes were closed. Cat stopped. She stepped back through the automatic doors, out of sight of Toby. She pulled out her mobile phone and searched for Archie's number. It rang, and Archie answered after three rings.

"Hey, babe. Change of plans tonight. I was thinking. You wanted me to do that favour for you? Well, tonight is as good a night as any."

Chapter 15

Cat and Toby pulled up to the house in a taxi. Toby paid the driver. They both got out and stood together on the driveway.

"So, are you staying here tonight?" asked Toby. Cat was kicking at a stone on the ground. Her head was down, and it remained there as she spoke.

"Probably, I might ask Archie to come around. Are you still going to one of your mates' houses?" She looked up whilst she asked the question. She didn't want him to see the dishonesty in her answer.

"Yeah, I've already spoken to Sean; he asked his parents, and they're happy for me to stay over for a little bit. I told a white lie; I told them mum would be in hospital for a while." Cat shrugged her shoulders.

"You could hardly tell them mum is a psycho. Don't worry, I understand." Toby reluctantly laughed. He wished he could be more like Cat. He was gutted about his mum, but Cat was taking it all in her stride. He wondered if she felt more but didn't show it; she wasn't the type who wore her heart on her sleeve.

"Well, I'm going to pack some clothes." Toby took out the house keys. Cat nodded and followed Toby in through the door.

* * *

The man dressed in black, hiding in the bushes near the front of the house, saw Toby and Cat go inside. He made a call.

"Hi. Yeah, they're both inside. No… I think she's in the hospital still. Okay yeah. We'll do it tonight." The man put the phone back in his pocket and continued to watch.

* * *

Toby didn't take long. Cat sat at the dining table as she watched him carry his holdall to the door. He approached Cat.

"What do you think is going to happen, Toby? What's going to happen to mum?" Toby collapsed into a seat next to Cat.

"Well. If she keeps talking utter madness, she'll end up in a psychiatric hospital if she's not careful. Either way, it's not our problem." Toby stared at his fingernails and picked at them. His face was sullen.

"Why now, Toby? After all these years, you stood by mum, stuck up for her; what's so different now?" Toby closed his eyes, reopened them, and met Cat's gaze, then sighed.

"I'm tired. This is the longest we've stayed anywhere. I've got friends; you've got the Doof Nugget and Jake, I think we're happy. I got used to mum's paranoia, but that was all it was, and I was able to talk sense into her. I understood her problems. She's been through a lot, and I sympathised. But now, it's like her brain has decided everyone is too happy; let's throw a spanner in the works and ruin it all. Well, I'm not prepared to let that happen. I think SHE thinks this ridiculous stuff is real; I don't think she's doing it on purpose. But it's her problem that she should get help for; we shouldn't have to suffer. So, I'm putting my foot down. We're not kids anymore; we can take care of ourselves." Cat nodded and took his hand. They held hands for about a minute. Cat's phone beeped; it was a text message from Archie:

I'M FIVE MINUTES AWAY, MEET ME AT THE END OF THE DRIVE XXX

"Anyway. Archie will be here in a minute, and I need to refresh my make-up." Cat stood up and pushed her chair under the table.

"Well, I'll be off then. Give the Doof Nugget my regards." He cringed, waiting for the swipe, but it never came. Instead, she came up behind him, wrapped her arms around his shoulders and squeezed. She softly pecked him on the cheek.

"Love you, Toby-Woby."

"Love you, Kitty-Cat." They both laughed. Toby got up and picked up his bag, and walked out the door. Cat watched him leave. She waited a few minutes then left the house herself.

Cat walked to the end of the drive; Archie was already there waiting.

"Are you ready for this?" asked Archie, a complex and determined look in his eyes.

"I guess." Her heart was beating hard, and her chest was hurting. If her mum and Toby found out about this, they'd go crazy. But as far as Cat was concerned, Toby has chosen to disconnect from the family unit. Her mum was so mad that she probably no longer cared, so why couldn't she help out the love of her life. Cat was dubious about the plan. But Archie said his dad was hitting him; which was unforgivable.

It was quite a long walk to Archie's house. Cat hadn't been there before. It was strange to think that the first time she goes to meet her boyfriend's parents was the day she would mentally scar them for life. Welcome to the family. Cat made assumptions about where Archie lived. She pictured a rough street with terraced houses, graffiti on the walls and youths standing on street corners. She was shocked when he pointed to his house.

The road was very upmarket—all the places had lovely gardens and paved driveways with garages. Parked outside the houses were Porsches, Mercedes, Audis and BMWs. There was the odd Ford and Skoda, but they were still relatively new looking and appeared to be second cars. Archie's house was detached—it was brick fronted with areas of cladding, creating a geometric pattern. There was a porch with a large black oak door, and he had a lovely landscaped front garden and a pretty multi-colour stone path leading up to the front door.

Archie put his key into the door and entered the large foyer area. It was very grand—the floor was a shiny black tile, the walls were brilliantly white, and there was a large staircase directly in front of the entrance. This too looked like solid oak stained very dark, but it looked modern and contemporary with the white background. Cat was gaping—she realised this, and she closed her mouth. Their houses probably had an equal value, but Cat's house had more of a rustic look. Archie's mum greeted them. She was a beautiful lady. She wore stylish, expensive clothes, sporting a white trouser suit. Her dark brown hair was swept into a high ponytail which draped over her right shoulder, hanging just over her breast.

"Hello Archie, and you must be Catherine?" Cat held out

her hand and smiled sweetly. Her voice trembled slightly. His mum came across as noticeably confident and somewhat intimidating.

"Please call me Cat." His mum took Cat's hand and shook it.

"My name's Sarah. You are quite the pretty little thing, aren't you?" Cat blushed. She was semi-aware that she wasn't unattractive, but hearing such a compliment from another woman was very flattering. Cat didn't respond; she just looked at the floor.

"Archie, my love, your father is going to be home late, so dinner will be a bit late too. We'll eat as soon as he comes in, okay?" Archie rolled his eyes; he gave Cat a pained look.

"Now, Archie, don't you get agitated. Your father works hard. He does it all for us; you should remember that." Archie took Cat's hand and practically dragged her up the stairs.

"Well, that's fucked it up." Archie slammed his cap on the bed and kicked his sideboard. His room was as she suspected. Posters of half-naked models littered the walls, and there were clothes all over the floor.

"What do you mean?" Cat scrunched up her eyebrows.

"Dad's late. The plan was to start something before dinner to be alone with him, but if we eat as soon as he comes back, we can't do it. It'll be too late for you to stick around after; he'll insist on giving you a ride home." Cat considered this for a moment.

"Why don't we do it over dinner then?" Archie looked at her like she was stupid.

"They're gonna see you're the one doing it, aren't they, and my mum will be there. I didn't really want to worry her; I get on alright with my mum."

"You've seen me in action; it's not like I go into a trance

or anything, they'll never know it's me, as long as you do something that makes it looks like it's coming from you. Just giving a look of anger will do the trick. As for your mum, nothing will be directed at her. Everything that happens could just be directed at your dad. Your dad would have probably told your mum anyway. To be honest, I think it'll be easier for me to "perform" whilst I'm in the room anyway." Archie pondered the idea. He would have to think of something terrible to bait his dad with, though. To get him to cause a scene in front of a guest, it would have to be. He was generally a pretty good host, and arguing with your son is not the done thing at dinner.

"Okay, we'll do it over dinner, but make sure it all stays away from my mum." Cat agreed. If she was in the room, she was pretty sure she could keep control much better than if she wasn't. She was nervous, though. Thanks to her mum forbidding the use of their abilities, she could only ever practice at a small scale, usually in her bedroom or out in the garden.

Whilst they waited for his dad to come home, they fooled around in Archie's bedroom. They didn't have complete sex, Cat knew she could never stay quiet, but they kissed and touched and everything else in between. They listened to music and chatted a little during intervals. It was coming on close to ten o'clock at night; Cat had never eaten later than nine. Archie told her their household was known to eat at eleven. His dad always insisted on eating dinner together, no matter how late it was. For Cat, this enforced the idea that his dad was a control freak. At ten-thirty, Archie's mum called up to them.

"Your dad's home and I'm dishing up dinner," Archie called

back down to let her know they were on their way. *Here goes nothing,* thought Cat. They entered the dining room together, holding hands. Once again, Cat couldn't help her mouth falling open again—it was beautiful. The dining room was the size of her living room. It was massive, and an elaborate chandelier hung from the ceiling, the crystals refracting the light around the room. The dining table was oak and was about twelve feet long. There were ten chairs spaced out equally, but there were four place settings tonight, and they were all put together at one end of the table. Archie's dad was already sitting down at the end. He stood up and greeted Cat with a smile.

"Hello Cat, I hope it's okay I call you that. Sarah said it was your preference." He held out his hand. Cat considered slapping his hand away and telling him to piss off with his fake niceties, but she thought better of it. She took his hand and nodded, confirming that Cat was fine. He didn't look like a typical abusive father. She'd seen a photo of her dad, and as soon as she saw his image, she saw a thug, short hair—a crew cut and a scarred face. He had 'love, hate' tattoos on his knuckles and an apparent lousy attitude. The man standing before her now looked like an upstanding citizen. His hair was neat, he wore a suit, he had no scars or tattoos, and his face was friendly. She knew better than to stereotype though, just because a guy looked pleasant and amiable, it didn't mean he was. Doctor Harold Shipman was considered a good guy in society, and he turned out to be a serial killer. Archie's dad introduced himself as Michael, but apparently, she could call him Mike.

Mike pulled out a seat for Cat opposite his own. Archie sat down next to her, which was opposite his mother. Three of them were seated. Sarah, still dressed in her trouser suit, was now wearing a pink apron. She brought in two plates, placing them in front of Mike and Archie.

"Boys first," Sarah stated. She disappeared and then came back with another two plates. She placed Cat's in front of her; it looked genuinely lovely. It was a lamb chop placed on top of some creamy mash. Sarah made further trips to provide dishes of steaming vegetables and a gravy boat. She eventually sat down and joined them, and they didn't start eating until then. As soon as she sat, she said, "enjoy." and everyone tucked in. Cat only had a few forkfuls of mashed potato, which were heavenly when Mike spoke up.

"So Archie, tomorrow you have an English test. After what Mr Burden told me Friday, I expect you'll be making an extra special effort?"

"Dad, do we have to talk about this now?" complained Archie. Mike looked over at Cat. Cat immediately took the pot of mint sauce and spooned a little on her plate; she gave him a quick smile.

"I'm sure Cat doesn't mind us discussing school briefly. How are you doing at school, Cat?" Cat swallowed the most tender piece of lamb and answered.

"I do okay, I guess. I'm not failing in anything if that's what you mean." She caught another piece of lamb and dipped it in the sauce, putting it in her mouth.

"Archie is failing in English…" Mike stated, Cat looked at Archie, and he looked at her and winked. He slammed down his cutlery, making a loud clatter.

"Are you trying to embarrass me, dad?" Archie shouted.

"No, son, with that kind of behaviour, you're just embarrassing yourself. I'm just trying to have a conversation." Mike spoke calmly.

"Do you really think this conversation is appropriate in front of my girlfriend?" Archie demanded. Mike pondered. He placed his cutlery down gently and silently and linked his fingers under his chin as he looked at Cat.

"I'm sorry, Cat, Archie's right. This probably isn't the best time for this conversation. Let's just enjoy this delicious dinner, shall we?" He sounded genuine enough, but this wasn't what Archie wanted. He stood up from his seat.

"Actually, dad, no, let's have this conversation now so that mum and Cat know what you're really like. You probably would prefer to do this in private, wouldn't you, so you can really let rip." Archie was no longer shouting but spoke aggressively. Mike furrowed his brow.

"I don't know what you mean, son. I feel no need to do this in private—" Archie interrupted him before he could say anything further.

"Drop the act, dad, just admit it, you hate me, and you know what, I hate you too."

"Now just a minute," Mike stood up too now.

"Both of you, enough." Sarah remained seated and calm. "Sit down." Archie ignored her; Mike started to sit, but Archie wasn't going to let it go.

"Yeah, you heard me; I hate you. You're the most selfish man I know. Look at us eating at nearly eleven o'clock because your job is more important than us. I wish you'd just leave; I'm sure mum could do better than you. Or maybe you should just die and do us all a favour!" Mike's face turned a bright Crimson, and he went from being relatively calm to fuming.

"How dare you," Mike's voice was booming. "You ungrateful little boy, I've always told your mother that she spoils you."

"Someone had to, dad, because you just ignored me whilst kissing the asses of my brothers." Mike's forehead looked like it was going to explode. A vein was visibly pulsating—Cat could see it from where she sat. Mike thumped the dinner table with the flat of his fist, and Archie squeezed Cat's shoulder. This was the signal. Cat glanced over at the dining-room door. It slammed shut; the force caused the windows to shake in their frames. Everyone's eyes snapped to the door. Sarah, who was still holding her fork, dropped it.

"What the—" breathed Sarah. The chandelier which hung over them shook; the crystals clinked together. Archie screwed up his face in concentration. The plates then rose from the table then crashed down. The dishes shattered into tiny pieces. No one said anything; they just watched. Mike then looked at Cat; she was aware of his gaze. She ensured her face wore a significant amount of shock and horror, with her mouth hanging open. He then looked at Archie, whose demeanour didn't look surprised at all; his face was full of focus. Sarah backed her chair away from the table and was frozen in place. Everything stilled and became silent.

"So, dad, I'm going to give you a choice. I want you to leave me alone from now on and get off my fucking case. It's up to you how you go about that. You can either leave us, but I expect you to continue supporting us, or you can stay and just let me do what I want to do. Or you can just see what else I can do. This is just the tip of the iceberg, a party trick. I am capable of so much more."

"Archie, please." Sarah wailed. She was crying now. "Honey, I love your father; I don't want him to leave" Archie frowned at his mother.

"You support what he's been doing to me?" His eyes turned

dark.

"I don't know what you mean, honey. All your father has done is try to make sure that you live up to your full potential. I'm sorry if it made you feel like he didn't love you because he does. He's always telling me how worried he is about you. Everything he does, he does with my support." Archie squeezed Cat's shoulder again, and she looked up at him.

"Babe, I don't want you to be afraid. I won't hurt you, I promise, but I think I need to show my *parents,*" He spat the last word, "what I'm truly capable of. To show them my *full potential,* as mum put it." Cat gave him a searching look. His parents were already afraid; she could see it in their eyes. Sarah was trembling, and Mike's cheeks were streaked with tears. His whole body language was defeated. He no longer sat up straight, and he slumped in his seat. He didn't need to see anything else; they'd achieved their goal, and she was confident his dad would no longer give him any problems. Mission accomplished.

"I think you should calm down, babe," Cat whispered. Archie's eyes narrowed. He still kept his hand on her shoulder. He squeezed hard, and Cat winced. He hissed through his teeth.

"We're doing this, or we are over." Cat was taken aback, and her eyes started to fill with water. This was not the Archie she knew. His warmth turned to a bitter coldness, so much so that she shivered. She loved him, though; perhaps his dad brought the worst out in him. She refused to believe this was the true Archie. When this was over, he'd be back to his usual, loving self. She nodded. Archie closed his eyes—for theatrical purposes only. This was the big finale—Cat concentrated on the depths of the house. She imagined the foundations, the dirt and the bricks. There was a low rumble below them; then, the floor began to move.

The table shook, clattering the broken crockery. The chandelier tinkled like a wind chime, the windows shook, and dust started to fall from the ceiling. Cat looked up at Archie; he was smiling. She glanced at Mike and Sarah. Mike gestured to Sarah to crawl under the table, and they disappeared as they took cover. Paint started to come away from the walls, and the wallpaper wrinkled as the bricks moved behind it. More significant pieces of plaster started to drop and crumble as they hit the floor. Archie opened his eyes and was startled by the state of his dining room. He ducked away from another falling piece of debris.

"Okay, I think it's time to stop now," he whispered loudly. Cat gave him a grave look.

"I already have stopped. To make the whole place shake, I needed to upset the foundations, problem is, I have a feeling it's made the whole house unstable," Archie grabbed her shoulders and pushed his face up to hers.

"Are you telling me that my house may completely come down?" Bricks were tumbling down from the walls.

"I don't know, but I think we should get out." He shoved Cat hard, and she fell on her bottom. It hurt.

"You stupid whore, you ruined everything!" Archie ran from the dining room with his arms over his head, shielding himself from the rubble, leaving Cat and his parents behind. Cat ducked down and searched under the table. Mike's arms were over his wife's head. Cat called out to them.

"Come on! We need to get out now; I think it's all going to collapse." Mike pushed his wife ahead of him, and she scrambled on her hands and knees toward Cat. Mike followed, and they both emerged from under the table. They sprinted to the door, but the whole ceiling collapsed in front of them, blocking their escape. They were trapped. Cat searched the room—there were no other escape routes apart from the windows. Mike saw where she was looking.

"It's Hammerglass, practically unbreakable. We can't get out that way," said Mike, his face apologetic.

Cat's mind cast back to when she was seven. It was almost the same, but there was no fire. She remembered the dust from the rubble clogging her nose as the house came apart and the noise of wood creaking and splintering. The same thing was happening, but this time Toby wasn't here to shield her. The dread built up in her gut, and she felt sick. Her mind was everywhere. She needed to get Archie's parents out; this wasn't supposed to happen. There was only one way she could help them. She concentrated on the fallen rubble in front of the doorway. Bit by bit, the pieces floated upward. She glanced at Mike and Sarah, and the realisation hit them as they watched her clear the way. She shot a look in their direction.

"Go quickly, I can hold it, but we have to move. I don't know what state the rest of the house is in!" They nodded and bolted for the exit; Cat followed them through the gap she'd created. They were now in the hall; the hall had a high ceiling, balconies and another chandelier. Cat already spied the light fitting plummeting down toward them. Mike and Sarah saw it too, and they crouched to the floor, but before it could reach them, Cat stopped it mid-air and threw it aside. Sarah and Mike braced for impact, but they slowly came out of their crouch when nothing happened. They saw the chandelier in pieces on the stairs. They stared at Cat with fear and gratitude on their faces. She may have saved them from being crushed, but if it weren't for her, none of this would have happened in the first place. They made a run for the front door; the door was left open from when Archie escaped. Cat could see him through the dust. He was standing in the road holding up his phone. *Was he recording this?* Just as Sarah and Mike reached the door, the lintel gave out. Again, Cat stopped it, and they ran onto the pavement to safety. Cat was still inside as the building disintegrated, and Mike and Sarah called out to her.

"C'mon, get out." Cat dived through the opening and landed hard on the path, scraping her elbows and knees. She looked behind her—this was it, the whole thing was about to go. She crawled away from the damaged site as fast as she could. Mike and Sarah were there helping her get some distance, and there was an almighty crash as the roof caved into the house's cavity. Dust spewed into the street. They were all now on the other side of the street. All except Archie—he was still in the road filming. He was laughing now and covered in dust. Cat felt exhausted, not just physically but mentally. She coughed, then stood and stared at the ruins of what used to be an attractive house.

Cat could hear sirens in the distance; they got louder as they closed in on the street. It was fire, ambulance and police. There were also several news vans, cameramen and people with microphones rushing out. They were all standing in the road, just like Archie. She noticed a female reporter approach him; he was showing her his phone. As they chatted, an ambulance crew member stood in front of Cat, blocking her view of Archie and the reporter. The paramedic was talking to her.

"Miss, are you hurt?" Cat didn't answer—she tried to look

around him to see what Archie was doing, and she caught a glimpse of him passing the reporter something. *What is he doing? Why isn't he over here checking that I'm okay?* She thought. Archie turned, and they made eye contact. He grinned a cruel smile. His eyes were dark, and he blew her a kiss. Cat looked away. She'd been a fool—she should've listened to Jake and Toby; he was scum. She gave the paramedic her full attention and told him she wasn't seriously hurt, just a couple of scrapes. Cat sat in the back of the ambulance with a foil blanket draped over her shoulders as they dressed her wounds. Mike and Sarah approached her. Their faces were grey with dust, and they suffered the odd cut here and there on their hands and faces, no doubt something to do with the smashing glass and crystals from the lighting. Cat was wary—she didn't know what to expect from them, but their faces were soft and not at all aggressive. Her shoulders were tense as they drew closer.

"We just wanted to say thank you. Obviously, you were the one doing those things in the house, and we also know it was our son who put you up to it," Sarah said softly. She put a hand on Cat's knee. Cat sagged her shoulders and sobbed loudly.

"I'm sorry," she wailed. "this was never supposed to happen." Sarah pulled Cat close.

"Shh, it's okay, it's not your fault. We knew Archie had problems. We just didn't know how bad."

"He said that you hit him." Cat sniffed; she was looking at Mike. He shook his head. Cat already knew it was an outrageous lie. Mike was a good man—she could see it in the way he stroked his wife's hair and the compassionate way he was looking at Cat; this wasn't the type of man who could hurt another human being on purpose.

"I'm sorry, Cat, my son, has done a bad thing. I don't know what to do with him," said Mike. At this point, Archie strolled over with a skip in his step with a smug smile on his face.

"This just about says it all about my family's loyalty. You do realise that this freak has just destroyed our house?" Cat gasped. *Freak?* She was horrified by what she was hearing; only an hour ago, he told her she was special to him. Mike stood in front of Cat protectively.

"Only because you told her to. You manipulated this poor girl to get even with me. She didn't deserve that; she obviously did it because she cares about you,"

"More fool her." He looked around his father to set his eyes on Cat. "Did you really think I'd be interested in you? You were a bet." Cat frowned. A *bet?* "Everyone knew you were a virgin. My mates reckoned I couldn't get you, and I bet them twenty quid that I could. You weren't easy, I'll give you that, but do you know what the best part was?" Archie didn't wait for a response. "The plan was to bed you and leave you, but then you told me your secret. Let's just say I was intrigued; perhaps you had more to offer. But now, you are of no value to me. You've wrecked my house; my parents are dicks, and they now know I don't have amazing powers. So now it's time to cash in my bet. They won't be paying up without proof, though. Luckily I have it right here." He raised his phone to her face. Cat swallowed hard. it felt like her heart stopped. She knew what he was about to say.

"You didn't," she said. Archie's grin was huge, and his eyes were cruel. Cat then realised what he was probably passing to the reporter.

"Yep, got it all on video, don't worry. I'm sure Miss Hawkins of Channel four news will be discreet and only show your stone snake trick. I've permitted them to show my body as long as they blur out my ass cheeks." Archie laughed.

"Archie. No." Sarah slapped him around the face. His head snapped to the right. He rubbed his cheek, but he was still grinning. Temper rose from deep down inside of Cat. The phone in Archie's hand suddenly flung itself away and smashed on the floor at Cat's feet. Archie looked stunned initially, then shrugged his shoulders.

"No worries, I have copies. Now I can afford to buy a better phone. As for you two. Mum. Dad. The TV network is going to pay me quite royally for my video footage. I'm sure others will follow; newspapers and Magazines. They'll all want to hear my story of how I dated the super freak and how she knocked down my house. So, I won't be needing you anymore either. I'm moving out, and I'm going places." With that, Archie turned his back and waltzed off. Pausing for a moment, he turned and winked at them all. "See ya."

* * *

Toby and Sean were sitting on Sean's bed watching a David Attenborough documentary. A killer whale was chasing a seal; it was ducking and diving, but Toby knew it wasn't going to make it. The pod arrived, and the Orca had back-up. The poor little guy was cornered on a piece of ice. The whales were tipping it, and the seal was sliding off. Toby's phone beeped—it was a text message. He tried to watch the TV and look at his phone simultaneously, and the seal fell into the water. The text was from Max, his other buddy. A whale glided through the water and grabbed the seal in its mouth. Toby read the message; it was brief:

TOBY MATE, TURN ON THE NEWS NOW. IT'S YOUR
SISTER.

Toby grabbed the remote control and immediately changed
the channel to the local news. A video recording filled the
screen. First, it showed a crumbling house from the town. It
wasn't far from Sean's. They faintly heard sirens earlier, but
that wasn't unusual. Sean lived next to a busy carriageway;
sirens were quite familiar with all the road accidents down
that stretch of road. In the footage, people were running out
of the house. He squinted his eyes and looked closer—there
was a girl in the doorway. Bricks and debris were floating
over her head.

"Oh. My. God," he whispered. The screen changed back to
a reporter, Rhonda Hawkins.

"It's unbelievable. But in case we have sceptics out there
looking at the screen, wondering to themselves what sort of
trickery this is, we have additional footage given to us by a
reliable source. There is some nudity in this video, so faces
and intimate areas have been blurred out."

Now there was another recording on the screen; it was a
female voice, and she was talking about moving things with
her mind. She went on to talk about Toby and their mum.

"Shit, man, that sounds like your sister," said Sean. He was
staring at the screen, and he turned up the volume—the whole
nation, and soon the whole world, would know about Toby's
family. Sean stared at Toby in bewilderment. "Mate. Is this
true? Are you like a family of superheroes or something? Or
like the X-men?" Further footage showed the crowds outside
the ruined house. A cameraman zoomed in on the girl sitting
in the back of the ambulance—it was Cat. He could then see
more people around her, one of which was Archie. It looked

like she was crying, and he was smiling as he walked away. Toby stood up, grabbed his bag and went for the door. "Hey!" called Sean. "Where are you going? I've got so many questions, mate."

"They'll have to wait; I need to see my sister." He marched out of Sean's home. Sean's parents were watching the television too. They stared at Toby, mouths open as he walked from their house. Cat had a lot of explaining to do.

* * *

Mae was watching the exact same story as Toby. She flicked to other channels, and every one of them was showing the same thing. Mae shook her head frantically. She needed to leave immediately. Mae tore the lines out of her arm, blood trickled in tiny rivulets down to her wrist, and she unclipped the pulse oximeter from her finger. Her clothes were stacked on the chair next to her bed; she dressed quickly, not bothering with socks as she pushed on her trainers. When she was leaving the private room, she heard Rhonda Hawkins finish her story.

"The girl in this footage is known as Cat Phoenix. Her brother who she speaks of in the video is Toby Phoenix. It turns out they are, in fact, twins. Do we have a couple of superheroes in our town, or are they dangerous? You can see behind me that this girl has caused quite the catastrophe. Stay with us to get the latest updates on the siblings. The media has branded them 'The Phoenix Twins.'"

Chapter 16

Whilst Cat was sitting down to dinner with Archie and his parents, Jake decided to see how she was doing. She texted him when she found out her mum was in the hospital, and he'd replied, saying he would come round and see her later. She said 'okay' in response. He'd not heard from her yet; he thought she may still be at the hospital, but he planned to be there waiting for her when she got back. Jake knew where the family hid the spare key. He had access rights whenever he wanted—even Mae was okay with it. She saw him as part of the family; he was there often enough.

He made sure Jennifer was fast asleep before he left. His mum was passed out on the sofa with an empty wine bottle lying on the floor beside her. He didn't like leaving his sister when his mum was like this, but Jennifer knew what to do if she woke up and needed anything. She had his number, and he would be home in fifteen minutes. He lived a half-hour walk away from Cat's house, but he would run. If they didn't have this arrangement, then he'd never be able to go out.

It was just after ten-thirty, and it was pitch black, but it was mild weather with the lightest breeze. Jake thought back to his conversation with Cat about how he would let go of any ideas about them ever being together. He felt good for making this decision. It was like a weight had been lifted. He was always going to love her, and he imagined any girl he met in the future could never match up to her, but hopefully, he would be the best thing in that girl's life, whoever she may be. He needed to be happy, which was never going to happen whilst waiting for a person who didn't want him. There wasn't anyone else he had any interest in at the moment. The problem was, his circle of friends wasn't even a circle; two people can't make a circle. It was always him and Cat as far back as he could remember. He got on alright with Amber and Angela, but they were Cat's friend, not his. He needed to branch out and make new friends; he was a likeable guy, he had a lot to offer. He wondered if he should join a club.

As Jake pondered his social life, he walked past a rental car on the side of the dirt track; it was black. The rental company was advertised on the side of the vehicle. With the corner of his eye, he slyly glimpsed into the car—it was empty. It was the middle of nowhere. Where could the driver possibly be? He assumed it might be a dog walker, although it was pretty late to be out walking a dog. He continued down the dirt track; Cat's house was now in view.

* * *

The man watching the Phoenix household had been loitering around for a while. He was about to enter the house, but then he saw the two teenagers leave. This wasn't what he expected—he thought they would arrive home then stay there. First, he felt his luck was in when the boy left, but then the girl came out being met by another boy; it definitely ruined

200

things. He made a call.

"Things are fucked up; they went out. Yeah, I know. Well, I'll wait for as long as it takes; we're just going to be a little behind schedule. Hey, it's not my fucking fault. I have just as much at stake as you, the car accident was risky, and it was my ass on the line. If you think you can do better, come down here and do it yourself. Yeah, I didn't think so." He hung up the phone and shoved it back into his pocket. He hated that guy, such a control freak.

It was hot sitting in the hedge wearing a beanie hat; he was wearing a balaclava too, but it was rolled up off his face for now. He'd be suffocating otherwise. His legs and back were aching too. He alternated between crouching and standing, but all he wanted to do was lay down. The collision less than twelve hours ago screwed up his already damaged body, and he was thinking he was probably suffering from whiplash. Where there's blame, there's a claim; not for him, unfortunately. But when this was over, he'd be getting something a whole lot more satisfying.

He heard footsteps; perfect. Someone was returning. He readied his knife in one hand, and with the other, he poured a clear fluid onto a handkerchief. He pulled down the balaclava and crouched further into the bushes as the footsteps grew closer. Shit, it was the boy. They were after the girl, but there was nothing to say that she'd be coming back at all, so the boy would have to do. He allowed the boy to walk past him—he was scuffing his feet and kicking gravel across the driveway. Just as he was a few feet ahead, the man in black came out from the hedge. He grabbed the boy from behind and pressed the handkerchief over his nose and mouth; The boy was taken totally by surprise. He struggled slightly, but the chloroform took effect quickly. Jake sagged into the man's arms, the man almost falling under him. Jake was a dead weight, but the man didn't expect him to be quite so heavy. He regained his composure and started hauling the boy to the car. He was parked about half a mile down the road on a dirt track.

The half-mile felt like ten miles. When he finally reached the car, he dropped the boy to the floor and leaned on the car's roof. He was panting hard. When he caught his breath, he opened the rear door of the vehicle. He took some more breaths to ready himself, and he heaved the boy into the car. It was not a graceful procedure; initially, the legs were sticking out the door, but the boy's body fell across the seat when he got the legs in. The man was soaked through with sweat by the time he finished. Eventually, the boy was sitting up with a seatbelt, securing him in place. His hands were cable tied together and tethered to the seatbelt. The man collapsed into the driving seat of the car, and he lit a cigarette. Now the heavy lifting was over, all he needed to do now was drive—he couldn't wait to get home. Before leaving, he took his phone out of his pocket and made another call.

"Hey. Yeah. I've got the boy. I know, I know, but I get the feeling the girl isn't coming back tonight. It was either the boy or nothing. It was easier than I thought, actually. Okay, I'll see you in a few hours."

* * *

Jake awoke with a start. He tried to move but found he was very well secured to his seat. He was on the passenger side of the car. He looked diagonally across the car and could see the side of a man's head; not much of it though, he was wearing a hat quite low down; he didn't recognise the man. The car was quiet except for some road noise and the noise of posts swishing past. The window was open slightly—the man was smoking a cigarette. Jake looked at the clock on the dashboard—it was just after midnight. Jake looked out of his window and noticed they were on the motorway. The man began to indicate off the main road—they'd just passed a sign for Cheltenham at the next junction. They were in Gloucestershire; it was where Cat's family were from.

Jake tried to get his hand to his pocket to reach for his phone, but it wasn't there. This guy certainly was no fool; he must have taken it. He needed to let someone know where he was, but he had no idea how. The man threw out his cigarette butt and closed the window. Jake quickly closed his eyes. He decided that being awake would do him no favours right now. He was curious to know what was going on, but he was also scared to find out—he'd wait.

They travelled for a further half-hour; Jake peeked out the window to get an idea of where he was. It was just fields; it was like they were going to the middle of nowhere. They turned off the A-road, and it started to get bumpy. Jake was still faking sleep, so he allowed his head to flop here, there and everywhere. He was beginning to feel sick. It had little to do with motion sickness, although it didn't help. The car finally came to a stop. This was it; he was about to find out what was going on—or at least what would happen next. He knew for sure it wasn't going to be good. The driver got out, but he didn't come to get Jake immediately. Jake cracked his eyelids open slightly. They were outside a large barn structure. It looked run-down, probably no longer in use. He saw the large barn door close; the driver had gone inside. He tried to listen but couldn't hear anything. Then the door swung open, and two men walked out—Jake squeezed his eyes shut. His door opened.

"You fucking idiot," One man said. He assumed it was the one he hadn't met yet; his voice was deep.

"What?" This must've been the driver. He had a much higher voice, almost squeaky, but that might be because he was under pressure.

"This isn't Toby, you asshole".

"What do you mean? He was going into the house."

"What... You think people don't get visitors to their homes?"

"Listen here, it's not like anyone gave me pictures, and it was dark."

"Yeah, but you're the one who's been spying on them for the past week. Did you not take any notice as to who lived there and what they looked like?"

"It's not like I sat and drank tea with them; for fuck sake, I had to be hidden, which meant I never got a good look at them myself. What the fuck do we do now, then? I ain't going back. What are we going to do with 'im?" There was silence for a moment.

"Let's find out who he is first. If he's useless, we'll have to dispose of him." Jake didn't like the sound of that. He hoped he would be helpful for his own sake. He felt a shove on his right shoulder.

"Hey, wake up," The deep-voiced man barked. Jake stirred, the same as he would if he were waking from sleep. He opened his eyes, feigning surprise.

"Who the hell are you? Where am I?" He impressed himself with his acting skills.

"I'll ask the questions," This was the deep voice guy again. He looked rough and ready; his hair was short and cropped, his eyes were cruel and small with a scar under one of them and his lips were thin and set in a line. He was huge; tall and large, clearly not all muscle, but you still wouldn't want to get in a fight with him. "I'm gonna cut these cable ties. Give me any trouble, and I'll cut off a finger." Jake's buttocks clenched. The cable ties were clipped from his wrists; Jake rubbed them, they looked red and sore. He was grabbed by the arm and shoved across the dirt path leading to the barn entrance. He fell over; his legs had fallen asleep whilst in the car. He was heaved up and pushed into the barn. He looked at his surroundings. The barn was separated into pens—it must've been used for livestock. The big man led Jake to a pen with a metal chair, the type you get with a patio set. He was thrust into it. They stood before Jake. The driver concealed his face more now; he was wearing his balaclava. Both men stood with their hands on their hips. The big guy did all the talking.

"So, who are you?" He appeared to be chewing the inside of his cheek—it was very intimidating. Not that he wasn't scary as hell already.

"M-my n-n-ame is Jake, Jake Matthews." Jake wasn't acting now; the stammer was authentic. He was apprehensive.

"Okay, *Jake Matthews*, what were you doing at Mae's house?"

"I was going to see Cat; she's my friend. Mae was in the hospital, so I wanted to check that Cat was okay." The big guy rubbed his stubbly chin. Jake wasn't sure, but this could be the pivotal moment that this guy decided whether he was usable or disposable. He gestured to the driver to step out with him, and they stood several feet away and conferred. They would occasionally look at him; sometimes they shook their heads, and sometimes they nodded—Jake didn't know which was better. They came back.

"I've got some good news for you, well… it's good as long as you cooperate," Jake said nothing. He just tilted his head and waited to hear what the big guy wanted from him. "Give me his phone, The big man demanded. The driver slapped the phone into the big guy's hand. He moved closer to Jake then kneeled on the ground in front of him. He put the phone up to him, showing him the black screen.

"I need you to unlock your phone, and then I want you to make a video with me. Not that app which gives you long dog ears and the slurpy tongue, though—can you do that?" Jake nodded quickly. He looked over the big guy's shoulder and saw the driver staring at him whilst fiddling with a sizeable jagged-bladed knife. Jake's nausea returned with a vengeance. Jake signed into his phone with his four-digit PIN code; however, his trembling hands made it difficult to type in the number, the big man looked impatient. He navigated to his camera and switched it to video mode. Jake handed the phone back to the big guy. His hand was shaking so much that he almost dropped it. The man took the phone, smiling as he observed Jake; he wasn't happy about something.

"No, this won't work. You see, Jakey-boy, you're going to be the co-star in this movie, and you don't look quite right. Now, we don't have any make-up on us, so I'm going to have to fix it myself. Just consider yourself the co-star and stuntman." Jake didn't know what he meant by that. The stuntman? The big guy raised his hand. Jake knew what was coming, and he braced himself. The big guy backhanded him across the front of his face. He felt the blow to his nose, and his head snapped to the right as he fell off the chair. Jake grazed his cheek on the ground, and he groaned—his face felt like it was on fire. The big guy picked him up and put him back on the chair. Jake could feel the blood trickling down from his nose. It ran down his lips and dropped off the end of his chin into his lap.

"Sorry about that, Jakey, but that looks so much better." He looked at Jake like he was a portrait he'd just painted, and he reached out and smeared the blood around a bit. Satisfied, he put the phone up, facing himself and put it into selfie mode. The big guy was facing away from Jake, but the phone looked toward him; he was in the background. His face looked worse than it felt, and for that, he was grateful. The big guy pressed record.

"Hey, little girl! It's your daddy!"

Chapter 17

Toby walked home; he was so angry he could barely think straight. He tried calling Cat more than ten times, but she wasn't answering. He hoped she'd gone home. She didn't have anywhere else to go now that her boyfriend's house was rubble. As he approached the house, he could see some of the lights were on. He jogged to the door and let himself in. As soon as he entered the hall, he started to bellow Cat's name.

"Cat," He searched the ground floor; she wasn't there, so he went upstairs to her room. He smashed the door open and there she was, laying on the bed with her face buried into a pillow. She turned her head; her eyes were red and puffy, her cheeks were soaking wet, and her chin trembled as her startled eyes made contact with his. He looked around her room. It was a mess; her mirror was smashed, and ornaments were in pieces over the floor. He approached his sister, and upon closer inspection, he could see blood on her knuckles. His eyes softened. He was still seriously pissed off, but Cat was clearly not in a good state. He sat on the edge of her bed. She began to sob loudly into her pillow, now smeared with black mascara. Toby laid a clean pillow in his lap and transferred her head from one pillow to the other; he stroked her hair and rubbed her back, and let her cry it out. It took about five minutes; then, she quietened to a sniffle. At this point, he pulled her up into an upright position. She hung her head, and her hair covered her face. He pulled her hair aside like curtains as he lifted her chin to make her look at him—she did.

"I'm sorry, I'm so, so sorry," she cried. She hung her head again.

"Cat. Don't start crying again; we need to talk. Saying sorry really isn't going to cut it this time." Cat knew that. She'd made a massive mistake. "I need to know what the hell happened. I heard some of the stories on the news, but I need to know your version." Toby sat patiently as Cat told the story about Archie. He grimaced as she spoke about the virgin part, and he turned scarlet when she told him about the bet Archie and his friends had.

"You have to understand, Toby. I loved him, and I thought he loved me. I would never have told him about us otherwise. I believed I could trust him. But he tricked me." She started to cry again. He rubbed her back, but his head was somewhere else. He gazed into nothing, and it felt like there was a screw in his head. The more he thought of what Archie did to his sister, the tighter the screw got until it wouldn't go any further.

"I'm going to kill him," Toby growled. He rose from her bed quickly, and he stamped out of her room. Cat bolted after him, following him down the stairs running; he was already at the door before she even reached halfway.

"Toby, no." she yelled, "thanks to me, we're already in a bunch of trouble. Please don't make it worse." Toby ignored her. He reached for the front door handle, but the door wasn't opening. A force was holding it shut. He turned to Cat, and she lifted her chin and raised her eyebrows at him.

"Cat. Let me open this door," Toby demanded. She shook her head.

"Fine," Toby replied. He pulled back his fist and pushed a hole right through the door. He pulled back the pieces of wood, snapping them, cutting his arms as he did.

"Toby, please stop. You're hurting yourself," She could see he wasn't going to stop, so she released the door; it flung open. Toby looked back at her. Blood was running down his wrists and hands, and she could see the rage on his face. Without saying anything else, he disappeared into the darkness. Cat sunk her body onto the bottom step of the staircase and hugged her knees tightly.

* * *

Toby knew where to find Archie. With his house gone, he'd be with his scum mates, and they liked to hang out at the skate park drinking. None of them skated. He'd never actually seen anyone there with a skateboard before. It wasn't far; it was a fifteen-minute walk. He could have gotten there in a minute if he wanted to, but he wanted time to consider what he would do to Archie. Almost the whole way there, Cat was phoning him; he didn't answer any of them.

Just before Toby arrived at the skate park, the phone rang again. He roughly pulled it out of his pocket, ready to decline the call, but it was a different number; he didn't recognise it, so he stopped and answered out of curiosity.

"Hello. Who is this?" He furrowed his forehead.

"Hi Toby, it's Alison," Perfect, this was all he needed. "I saw the news."

"Look, Alison, this isn't a good time."

"I need to talk to you." Toby was getting impatient. He had something pressing to be getting on with, and it involved a fist in someone's face.

"Alison, if you saw the news, then you have the answers you need, don't you? I'm busy, and I have to go."

"But— " Alison tried before Toby hung up the phone, but he pounded the 'off' key, and his phone turned black. He didn't want to be interrupted again.

He heard laughing. It sounded like Archie, or the 'Doof Nugget'. That was too kind now. Now he was a dirty motherfucking prick. He could see them all in the distance, Archie and three of his friends. Toby considered them more like henchmen; they only hung around him for the status. They were all sitting atop one of the ramps swigging from a bottle, taking turns. Toby didn't want them to see him coming, so he took the long route around the park so he could come up behind them. Now he could hear Archie.

"Yeah, she's a psycho freak, man, but I have to say. It was worth it. She was fucking tight" They all roared with laughter, but Toby's face heated to that equal of the sun. He clenched his fists tight. He stopped a few feet from them. He was on the ground, so he had to look up.

"Hey, Archie." They all looked around over their shoulders. "Or should I say limp-dick? That's how my sister described you anyway." The friends sniggered; Archie punched the friend's arm closest to him, who let out a yelp. Toby continued. "Come here; I want to urgh... talk." Archie looked at his friends—there was concern in those eyes. Toby was, after all, the gifted twin brother of the girl Archie had lied to, exploited, then ultimately dumped. Archie muttered quietly to his minions. Toby tilted his head and crossed his arms, then started to tap his foot. Archie then turned around.

"We can talk, Tobester," Archie said. Toby frowned, "I'm coming down. Just wait there." Archie slid down the ramp and walked around to where Toby stood. "So—" before Archie could even begin his sentence, Toby swung his right fist directly into Archie's face, connecting hard with his nose and mouth, and he fell to the ground. Archie perched himself up on his elbows and wiped at his face. His nose was bleeding, and his top lip split. He narrowed his eyes at Toby as he spat some blood out onto the floor and leapt back to his feet.

"Well, that was hardly fair. I had you pegged as a Queensbury rules fighter," said Archie. Toby smirked.

"You hurt my sister and outed my family's secret. We're not even close to being even. But hey, I promise to behave from now on. You ready?" Toby raised both his fists; his right hand and right foot were in front. This stance in the boxing world was known as Southpaw. Toby didn't pursue fighting as a hobby, but he did it for a short period. He couldn't help but think he had an advantage over the other fighters, so he stopped. His mother also disapproved. Despite that, he still remembered the training. Archie got to his feet. His face was severe, focussed. He lunged at Archie with his right fist, and Toby dodged it with ease—and very quickly. Toby returned with two jabs to his jaw, followed by a right hook to his stomach. Archie hit the floor again. He tried to get up quickly, but he was coughing too much. Archie managed to get up to his hands and knees. He eventually stopped coughing and was breathing hard, trying to catch his breath. His friends were muttering in the background, and he looked over his shoulder at them and nodded. They all slid down the ramp and stood behind Archie with fists clenched. Their stances were confident, but their faces told another story.

"Oh, I see," Toby laughed. "You've realised you're out-matched, so instead of putting your hands up and saying, 'hey mate, you win,' You decide to bring in your boys for help. Such bravery. You lame ass son of a bitch." Toby spat the last words. Archie looked at his friends and growled in response.

"Don't just stand there; get him." They all lurched in together to overpower Toby, thinking the three of them could bring him down. Archie was still portraying doggy style as he watched his friends fail miserably. They were all tall guys, but the smallest one went down first after a low force kick to the groin. The other two lasted a little longer. One had red hair and the others black. The redhead took a punch to the right cheek, then an uppercut under his chin—that finished him off. One of the others tried to wrestle Toby to the ground in a headlock. Toby whipped himself out of the hold swiftly and smoothly. He pushed him to the tarmac head-first and kicked him in the ass. With that, the guy jumped up and ran away. Toby stood there for a moment to survey his work—Redhead was unconscious, and the small one was rocking in the foetal position with his hands between his legs groaning; he may have been crying.

Toby switched his gaze back to Archie, who was now back on his feet. Archie scoured the scene also— clearly not liking what he saw; he turned and ran. Toby shook his head. *You're going to make me chase you now?* Toby went after him, and it didn't take any effort on Toby's part. He caught up in seconds. He grabbed the collar on the back of Archie's denim jacket.

"There's no use running from me. I won't even break a sweat." Said Toby amused. Archie turned to look at him.

The stern face he'd seen earlier was gone. His eyes were tearing, and he was trembling. The supposedly tough, bad boy dropped to his knees.

"I'm sorry, please don't kill me."

Archie's words echoed in Toby's head. *He thinks t I was gonna kill him. Was I gonna kill him? I guess maybe that's what I wanted to do. Do I still want to kill him?* Before Toby could answer his own questions, he heard another voice coming from behind him.

"Toby. Please step away from the boy. Now." It was PC Carrick; Toby recognised his faint Caribbean accent from the phone. Toby raised his hands; he heard the police officer's steps move closer to him.

"I'm sorry, Toby, but I'm putting you under arrest for grievous bodily harm." PC Carrick took Toby's hands and pulled them down behind his back. He cuffed and cautioned him. PC Harding was there too; he was calling an ambulance and helping Archie off the floor. Toby was led to the police car. PC Carrick tucked Toby's head down as he got into the back of the vehicle. As they pulled away, Archie stood and looked at him. The fear was gone now; how Toby wanted to wipe the smug smile off his face.

Toby said nothing in the car on the way to the station. The officer at the desk booked and placed him in a holding cell. Every officer in the station stared at him. He felt like a new attraction at a circus. They'd obviously all seen the news. The cold, miserable cell with the stinky toilet in the corner and the rock-hard bed was a relief; at least he was on his own. PC Carrick informed him he would be questioned shortly.

Toby reflected on his evening. He'd never behaved like this before; he was always the one in control. He always thought before he acted; he considered the consequences and usually made the safest and most reasonable choice. Cat was the impulsive one of the family. But tonight, he'd lost it. He might've even killed someone. Toby was disappointed with himself; he was better than this, but he was furious every time he thought about what Archie did to his sister. The scum bedded her for a bet, he used her for his own gains, and when that went wrong, he discarded her like dog shit in a shit bag. He'd lost all his inhibitions and the rage; he couldn't explain it. He couldn't care less about their secret, really. In a way, he was relieved that it was out there. There would be no more hiding and no more lying. He just needed to face it. From now on, he and his family would be known as freaks.

Toby was questioned in the morning—he didn't request a solicitor, and he was completely truthful. It was PC Carrick who led the interrogation. Toby admitted he went looking for a fight but only with Archie. As for the other guys who got involved, he pleaded self-defence. They all set on him three-to-one, which were fair odds in Toby's opinion, but he didn't say that. He was charged with the assault then released pending a court date.

Toby left the station. It was bright outside compared to the dinginess of his cell. He squinted. As he walked to the bottom of the steps, he was met by a familiar face. If she fronted up to him any closer, they would've bopped noses. Alison stood with her hands on her hips. It was the last place Toby expected to see her.

"How did you know I was here?" asked Toby.

"The perks of being a police officer's daughter." Toby blinked a few times and gave her a questioning look. "PC Carrick," she said. Toby looked up, searching his mind; he

215

was sure her surname was something other than Carrick. "I have my mother's surname," Alison continued, "Davies. They never got married, you know, they lived in sin. Well, they did before she ran off with a younger white boy." Alison shrugged.

"Oh, okay. So, what are you doing here?" Toby spoke impatiently. He was longing to get home for a shower. His clothes were still coated in quite a lot of blood, None of it was his own. At this point, she narrowed her eyes. It reminded him of the look his mum gave when she was going to tell him off.

"Well, if you'd let me speak on the phone last night, you would probably have never ended up here because you would have realised that you had bigger fish to fry." Toby tilted his head; he wished she would get to the point.

"And what fish is that?" asked Toby. Alison's body language changed. She went from looking quite aggressive to a more passive stance. She looked down at her hands.

"After the situation in the gym, I was curious. I knew you were hiding something, and I wanted to find out what. You weren't going to tell me anything, so I kinda spied on your house." Toby's eyes widened, and his mouth dropped open. "Wait. Before you get mad, let me finish, there's more, and you must hear me out." Toby relaxed his face and closed his mouth, and nodded, allowing her to continue. "One night, I was hanging around the back of the house. I came through the woods. I was nosey looking through some of your windows. I was hoping to see you doing some crazy shit. Then, I think it was your mum's study? Someone dressed in black came in, searching through the drawers in her desk."

"Wait, what? Someone was in my house? When?" Toby's eyes were wild.

"It was a few days ago, and he took something from the drawer, then he ran out of the back door. I had to hide so he couldn't see me, but he ran into the woods. I chose that time to leave myself. When I came out of the woods onto the dirt track, a car was parked there; I think it was his. I took a photo of the registration." Toby paced back and forth. He pushed his hair back with his hand then started rubbing the back of his neck, murmuring something. He stopped in front of Alison.

"Why the hell didn't you say something before? Why didn't you call the police or just tell your dad? He is the bloody police" Toby's face turned crimson.

"Look, he didn't seem to be planning on hurting anyone. If I thought he was dangerous, I would have done something, I swear. I was trespassing myself; I could hardly say anything. I didn't want to get into trouble, okay. I'm sorry." Alison hung her head. Toby sighed.

"So why are you telling me now?"

"I always planned to tell you at some point, but then I heard about your mum's accident. Dad told me that she thought it wasn't an accident. After what I saw, I wondered if she was right. Then that thing with your sister happened, and it made me think that maybe it was all related somehow. I wanted to call and tell you straight away, but you wouldn't listen, so here I am. Telling you now."

"I've got to go; I need to speak to my family." Toby dashed away, leaving Alison standing there alone. By the time she realised he was gone, he was already ten feet away; he could move fast.

* * *

217

Toby marched into the house; he called out for Cat. She appeared quickly from the living room, but she wasn't the only person to appear; his mum was there too. She looked terrible. She was pale, her face was bruised, and she could barely stand straight.

"Toby, where have you been?" asked Mae, her voice sounded tired. Toby shook his head. There was no time to explain.

"Mum, I'm sorry, I'm so, so, sorry," Toby started, but Cat interjected.

"Mum and I have already spoken. I've already apologised for what happened last night. I said we both regretted what we said to her. I've promised her that I'll be more supportive and…." Toby chewed his lip and interrupted.

"Cat, I'm not apologising about that, well, I do apologise for that as well, but there's more to it. Mum, you were right all along. A few days ago someone was in our house looking through your desk in the study, and they took something. I don't know what, but the things you said were happening around here. I believe you now, and I'm sorry I didn't before. I should have." Mae hugged him. Considering how weak she must've been, she hugged him tight; he was careful to be gentle with her.

Cat just stood frozen in place, looking into space, trying to figure out what the hell was going on. Had someone actually been in the house? Was Mum right? Could it have been their father like her mum had feared? She jumped as her phone vibrated and pinged in her pocket; she took the phone out. It was a video message from Jake. She almost didn't watch it. They were in the midst of something awful, and she didn't think it appropriate to waste time watching a silly video. But something in her head told her she should, and she suddenly became anxious. She felt a sinking feeling inside, like something terrible was about to happen. She tapped the video message. An image filled the screen. The first thing she saw was a man's face taking up most of the frame, and over his shoulder, she could see Jake.

"Mum. Toby. Come here. It's Jake." The panic in her voice made them come straight away. They stood on either side of Cat and watched the video; as soon as Mae saw Anthony's face, she gasped. She watched in horror as Anthony began his monologue:

"Hey, little girl, it's your daddy. Gosh, it's been a long time, hasn't it? I've missed you and your brother, but you know who I've missed more? Your mother. God, I miss her so much.

My plan went a bit wrong. You see, I was meant to have one of you kids here in this chair behind me, and then I would send a video to your mum. But then Jakey-boy here rolled up at your house last night, and my idiot associate got him by mistake. Can you believe it? You just can't get good staff these days. So here it goes. I'm kinda making things up as I go along now. I want you kids and your mum to come back to me. I'm willing to let everything go; my burns and my time in jail. I'm going to pretend it never happened. Now, if you refuse to come back, I'm afraid little Jakey-boy here will have a horrible day.

Don't disappoint me, will you? I want you here by six o'clock tonight, that allows you enough time to pack and to drive over to Gloucestershire. You will park in the services near junction twelve, and I'll send you the address. I know Mae likes to be early for everything, but I need you to arrive when expected, so I won't be sending it until five-thirty. If the police come instead of you, Jakey-boy is dead. I won't have anything left

219

to lose, so trust me, I'll do it. Love you, Mae. I'll see you soon."

Chapter 18

Anthony sat opposite Jake in another chair ten feet away; when Anthony wasn't sitting there, it was the driver. They were keeping around the clock surveillance on him. He was a commodity they couldn't lose. Anthony looked at his watch, it was a quarter past three in the morning, and he was getting sleepy. Jake appeared to be sleeping—he didn't think he was faking it, unlike earlier. He wasn't as good of an actor as he thought he was. It was apparent he was already awake; for a start, he stirred way too quickly.

He remembered when Mae used to fake sleep; she was better at acting than Jake was. He wasn't always sure whether she was or wasn't. It was always in the evening. They'd be watching a film in bed, and he'd be getting horny; he'd lean over her—she was always facing away from him—he'd kiss her cheek, then she would wipe at her face like there was a bug crawling on her. He would then whisper in her ear, asking her if she was asleep. She wouldn't answer but would make a moaning noise. This was at a time where they were only having sex about once every three months. When she was awake, and he tried something, she'd say she had a stomachache or was bleeding. He knew very few women who had a period for three weeks of the month; he knew she was lying; he just didn't know why. The first thought he had was that she must be getting it elsewhere; why else? She would deny it. But it usually triggered a satisfying night after a few days of constant accusations. Eventually, sex stopped completely; it was after those twins were born. She said it would be too painful, but he knew that was rubbish. He said before they were born that she would lose interest and be more interested in them than with him. At the time, she told him not to be silly, but he was right. Everything was better before those children came along; not once did she question him or defy him. The children were home for a couple of weeks, and then she left him. Babies were parasites, and he warned her not to let them get into her head, but she didn't listen.

They caused all of this; it was their fault, and he had no interest in them whatsoever. But he needed to make Mae think that he wanted them too; otherwise, she would never come back to him. He'd deal with them when they got here. Once they were out of the picture, the balance would be restored, and he would be back to being the centre of her universe, where he belonged. He smiled. Anthony was about to give in to sleep when he felt a tap on his shoulder; it was the driver.

"Mate. I not long ago woke up to take over from you. I was a bit early, so I sat in the car to listen to the radio for five minutes. You need to listen to it, mate. It's about those kids. It's on every station, massive news. I'll take over from you now so you can go and listen." Anthony stood up and made his way to the car, feeling intrigued. It wasn't like him to be so cryptic. Why didn't he just come out and tell him what was going on? Anthony slid into the driving seat of the car; the keys were still in the ignition. The current station was playing music, so he switched to another and there it was.

"...They are known as The Phoenix Twins; the amazing footage shows Catherine Phoenix manipulating the falling house through telekinesis, saving herself and two occupants of the home. Further footage showed Catherine doing tricks in private with stones, and she explains that it isn't just her with abilities. She talks of her mother, who makes anything spontaneously combust; she called it Pyro-kinesis. Her brother, who is faster than the average human being, can also create a shield around himself, keeping himself and others safe from harm. Is this real? Do we have real superheroes? Or even super villains depending on how you look at it, living among us, or is it just a clever camera trick? Keep with us, and we'll update you on this exciting story as soon as we can."

Anthony turned the radio off. He rubbed his chin; he was in serious need of a shave. This changed things. He knew what Mae could do, he had the scars to prove it, but he didn't realise the kids had abilities too. It made sense, though; if their mother had a freaky capability of doing weird things, it was bound to pass down to the children. He needed to make a call.

"Hi... Yeah, I know it's early, but we got a problem, have you seen the news? Seriously? You went to bed at eight? No. I'm not taking the piss out of you. Instead of me having to explain, I'll hold the line whilst you find a twenty-four-hour news channel. Yes, it's massive news. It will be on, without a doubt. As far as the world is concerned, they think they've discovered Supergirl, Superman, and perhaps Wonder Woman. Just do it. Trust me; if I had a TV in this barn in the middle of nowhere, I would have it on. I would love to see it all in action. Unfortunately, I've only been able to listen from the radio." He heard the television come on in the background; the sound of porn echoed through the phone's earpiece; it was clear what he'd last been watching. He listened to the murmur of people talking; it sounded like a news reporter. He waited on the line patiently; he heard the odd word, mainly consisting of *No shit, Oh my god. Shit, look at that.* He eventually returned to the phone; he was breathless. Anthony asked what they were going to do about it.

"…No shit, Sherlock. Of course, this changes everything. Did you know they could do this? No, I'm not suggesting anything. What are we going to do? This messes up the plan a bit, don't you think? You're really coming? Well, I'm looking forward to it, when will you be here? Okay then, I'll see you at four this afternoon."

Anthony hung up the phone. The guy was a psycho; he almost sounded excited about what these kids could do. Anthony didn't know who this guy was, but he seemed keener than him to get this family back here. He remembered when they met under the street light. The guy made him so many promises, and all he wanted in return was to get Mae back to Gloucestershire as well as those kids. He said Anthony could do anything he wanted with Mae, just as long as she suffered.

Anthony went back to the barn. He wondered how much this would impact the plan. He'd been expecting two defence-less teenagers and a not so defenceless ex-wife to show up. It would now appear that he should be expecting an arsenal of superhuman soldiers; this didn't sit well with him.

The initial plan consisted of making the authorities believe that Mae had killed herself and her kids. The local police had already seen her losing her mind; he and his associate made sure of that, and just in case there was doubt, they'd planted something in her desk. Mae wouldn't be dead, though. He would keep her alive. It would punish her for what she did to him, and he'd have her back forever. He hated her for what she did, but she was the only woman he ever really loved. It was challenging to keep this part of the plan from his associates because they both wanted Mae killed; he let him think this would happen because he needed their help. He couldn't do this alone. He needed to make sure he had alibis. When the time came, he would deal with both of them, but Mae was not to be touched.

He didn't think his plan would work now; maybe he'd have to make it look more like an accident. They would need to get the note back which was a ball ache. There's also the fact that these kids were now high profile; they're practically celebrities overnight, although this could all go in his favour. They're known to have powerful abilities. One of them already made a house collapse in on itself, and people saw it live on camera. They weren't equipped to take on all three of them. He could have controlled Mae by using the children, but now he needed to control them all. He supposed that this was where having Jake was a happy accident. He just hoped his relationship with the Phoenix family was as close as they were with each other. Anthony tapped the driver on the shoulder.

"Off you go, I'll carry on with the watch. I want to speak to Jakey-boy." The driver's eyes sparked with curiosity.

"You heard it didn't you? What does that mean for us? Does it change things?"

"I'll come and speak to you about it later; just go." His face was hard, and he started to chew the inside of his cheek. The driver didn't want to agitate him further, so he went out to the car.

Anthony watched Jake sleep; he watched the slow rise and fall of his chest. His chin was resting on his chest, and his mouth was hanging open. Could this kid be leveraged? He wasn't much to look at. Anthony tilted his head; a different aspect wasn't helping, but then looks weren't everything. He got up and kicked Jake's foot; Jake stirred, and he kicked him again but harder.

"Hey, wake up. I wanna speak to you." Jake's eyes shot open. For a moment, he'd forgotten where he was. He felt the sting of his cheek, and he could barely breathe through his nose; then, it all rushed back to him. He was confronted by the big guy, who he now knew as Anthony. His face was centimetres from his own. He felt his breath on his face; he could also smell it, which wasn't pleasant. It was a mix of cigarette smoke and gingivitis. He assumed there were no bathrooms around here for teeth brushing. He turned his head slightly, but it didn't help much.

"There he is. I hope I wasn't disturbing a lovely dream." He didn't; Jake couldn't remember dreaming at all. "I've woken you up because I've recently found something out. It turns out your little friend and her brother are quite special." Jake squished his eyebrows together.

"What exactly do you mean?" replied Jake.

"How long have you and my daughter been friends?" Jake knew immediately, but he pretended to think about it.

"Around ten years," Jake replied. Anthony sat himself down on the dirt; he leaned back on his hands, and his legs were outstretched.

"So, you've been friends for ten years, and she never told you?" Anthony lowered his head and looked at Jake. The shadows this aspect created, made Anthony look doubly menacing.

"Told me what? If you mean what happened with you when she was small, then no, she didn't. Her uncle told me, so I know about that." Anthony nodded.

"Okay. I'm worried, Jake. I'm concerned they may not care enough about you to come to get you alone. You see, your buddy has been hiding something from the world; it appears she hid it from you too. So, you'll understand why I have my doubts. If you were that close, wouldn't she have told you everything?" Jake's shoulders drooped. He had to admit it; he wondered this himself. Perhaps their friendship was more one-sided than he thought. He wanted to know what this secret was, and maybe there was a good reason for not sharing. Perhaps she was protecting him.

"So out of curiosity, what is it that makes her so special?" Jake asked. Anthony smiled, clearly trying to decide whether he would reveal or not. Anthony leaned forward; his eyes were bright. It reminded Jake of a schoolgirl who had juicy gossip to share with her besties, except his beaming face was frightening. Jake lurched his head back.

"Okay, I'll tell you. It turns out that your little friend and her brother have special powers. Their mum does as well, but I already knew that." Anthony pulled up his sleeve, revealing scarring. "I still have the scars to prove it." Jake didn't know what to say; was he winding him up? Surely he must be; he laughed.

"No, really, what is it?" said Jake. Anthony's eyes darkened in response.

"Are you calling me a liar?" He did the thing with the inside of his cheek again, and Jake immediately stopped laughing.

The last thing he wanted to do was antagonise the man, but he honestly thought he was joking.

"No, no. I thought you were messing with me, you know, joking." Anthony moved from his seated position to standing. He bent down to be face to face again; the breath hadn't improved, and Jake grimaced.

"I don't joke. I'm telling the truth. I have first-hand knowledge about their mum's abilities; the scars that I just showed you. She did that. She set me on fire which in turn caused our whole house to burn down. She was prepared to leave me in there to die, but I got out." Jake was still confused.

"She set you on fire. With a lighter or something?"

"No, not with a lighter," Anthony snapped. "She did it with her mind." He aggressively pointed to his head. "She got angry; she thought I was going to hurt my sweet baby daughter. Maybe I was, maybe I wasn't, but I watched her as her face grew bright red. I thought she was just mad, but then her eyes started to glow. I'll tell you now, that was freaky; it scared the shit outta me. Then all of a sudden, I went up in flames. She grabbed the baby then ran out of the house, leaving me there to burn. Then she dared to say that I'd started the fire and the police believed her. Then I ended up going to prison for attempted murder. Fuckin' bitch." Jake didn't know what to say; this guy sounded like a madman. He wasn't about to question him again, but he was categorically more scared than before.

"So, Mae can make people go up in flames? Wow. What does this have to do with Cat and her brother?" The darkness was gone from Anthony's face; he turned into the schoolgirl again.

"Well, this is the amazing thing. They have special abilities, too; it was caught on camera. It's on the news everywhere, probably even international by now. Cat, she can move things with her mind; what's the word? Telekinesis. She brought down a whole house. Her brother, there is no evidence of this yet, but it's just what Cat said on a video. She said that he could move extra fast and he can create a protective shield around himself. Are you saying that you knew nothing about this at all?" Jake thought about this for a moment; was this guy playing around with his head, some weird mind game? It was so far-fetched that it almost had to be true. Jake said nothing; he stared past Anthony. He was trying to remember into the past. He experienced something once when he was with Cat that he found strange but thought nothing more of it at the time. In particular, he never connected it to Cat, just an odd thing or a miracle that happened whilst she was there.

Around four years ago, he and Cat took Jennifer to the park; she was only six years old at the time. They'd played for a while, he pushed her on the swings, and they all played tag. It was a lovely afternoon, and the sun was shining. It was hot, and his sister complained of being thirsty, so they decided to return home. On their walk, there was one major road to cross. The rest of the way was residential streets and a dirt road.

They approached the crossing for the busy road. They stood pretty far back; it wasn't bustling, but the cars moved quickly. It was a dual carriageway, and there was a small island in the middle of the road. They pushed the pedestrian crossing button; it was still a red man showing, but their side of the road was empty, so they decided to cross. When they reached the island, his sister saw a puppy on the other side of the road. To Jake's shock, his sister darted forward, her hand coming away from his. It was so unexpected; he grabbed for her, but he wasn't fast enough.

His sister ran into the road, and there were two lanes. The first was clear, but a BMW silver hatchback was closing the gap between it and his sister very quickly in the other lane. He ran into the road after her to try and grab her, but she was too far ahead. He looked into the eyes of the driver; he'd braked, but he was too close. It didn't look as though he'd be able to stop in time. Jake yelled, and he dived forward, clutching his sister's foot. Her head was in line with the right tyre of the car. Then suddenly, he heard a smash.

It was like the car hit an invisible barrier. The driver was thrown forward; it was fortunate that he was wearing a seatbelt. The back of the car lurched up into the air and then slammed to the ground. The force collapsed the rear axle of the vehicle, and the driver's airbag was deployed. Jake looked up and saw that the car stopped mere inches away from his sister. It was a miracle. The next thing he knew, Cat had run up to them both and scooped them up in a giant bear hug; she was crying. He didn't think for one second she had anything to do with what happened. He believed it was some divine force that saved his sister, but perhaps it was her. Did Cat save his sister? He gazed up at Anthony.

"Oh my god. Why didn't she tell me?" Jake's eyes were sad. Anthony smirked.

"Well, mate, that's what I'm worried about too."

Chapter 19

Cat put down her phone. Her chest felt like it was going to explode. Not only was this the first time she'd seen and heard her dad in real life, but she also saw her best friend hurt and held at this madman's mercy. She remembered the text that Jake sent her last night; he said he would come over. When she decided to go to Archie's house, she didn't even think about telling Jake she wouldn't be there. If she had, her maniacal father wouldn't have him now—it was her fault. She was a lousy friend, and she'd let him down. Her heart ached, her mouth was dry, and she felt light-headed. Mae was standing right next to her; Cat grabbed her mum's arm. Cat's legs gave out, and Mae caught her. Mae's ribs screamed, and she winced as the pain shot through her body. Toby relieved her quickly, and he swept his sister up in his arms and laid her on the sofa. Cat was still awake, but everything turned into a blur. She could hear people talking, but she couldn't tell who; it was like she was hearing them whilst underwater.

"What are we going to do, mum?" asked Toby. Mae knelt beside her daughter and stroked her forehead and cheek.

"I don't know, sweetheart. He's dangerous. I don't doubt he'll hurt or maybe even kill Jake." Toby paced the floor.

"But mum, we can't let that happen. It's our fault that he's in this mess." Cat could hear everything now; her head had cleared, and she sat up on the sofa.

"It's not OUR fault Toby, it's MY fault, just mine. Jake came here to see me; I knew he was coming. I didn't tell him that I wasn't going to be here. Dad has him because of me." Cat began to cry. "Mum, I know that you want to keep us safe and protect us, but this is my mess, and I need to go and help him. If anything happens to him, I will never forgive myself." Cat gave Mae a pleading look.

"My love. We're not going to let anything happen to him; I'm going to go and get him. You guys are going to stay here, and I want you to call Isaac. As soon as I get Jake out, I need him around to protect you guys." The twins stared at her. Both were shaking their heads.

"No way, mum, you need us with you. Besides, he said all of us needed to be there," replied Toby.

"We can help. Toby's speed and protection and my telekinesis could mean the difference between Jake living or dying. Hell, it could mean the difference between you living and dying. We have to come with you." Cat's eyes were desperate.

"Absolutely not, no. There is no way either of you are getting anywhere near that man. I barely got you away the first time. I'm not risking you, either of you. I'd die first." Mae, too, started to become emotional. The whole idea of her children being at risk, filled her with dread; it made her feel sick just thinking about it. Mae carefully lowered herself into a chair. She was extremely sore and tried not to show it. Toby approached his mum; he stroked her arms.

"Mum, I understand you're scared. I can't begin to know how you've managed to get us to where we are now. But I think we really can help you, we've had all this training, it's about time that we use it. You need to realise that you can't do everything alone. I know you have up 'till now. But this is bigger than you; either you'll wind up dead, Jake will wind up dead, or you both will, and where does that leave us? We'll be alone and forever thinking that perhaps if we'd helped, you'd still be alive. We'll devise a plan and look out for each other. Let us help you," Toby pleaded. Mae exhaled; her head told her that he was making sense, but her maternal instincts were screaming, *No way.*

"Okay," Mae whispered. Toby beamed at his mother. He held her tight; he knew how hard this would be for her, and he was proud. Cat joined them. They all held each other. Mae pulled herself away from the huddle; tears dripped from her chin, and she wiped them away with her hand.

"But... You must do exactly as I say. You do not go off on your own, and you stay together. Cat, you have great offensive skills; use them. Toby, you have an important defensive skill; whilst you're together, you both should be safe." Mae got up from the chair. "I'd better go check out my study and see what they took. I can't even think what it could be." Mae went away.

Cat and Toby sat in the living room talking tactics. It was challenging to come up with something when they had no idea where they'd be going. Their discussion was interrupted by a knock at the door; Toby got up and answered it. It was PC Carrick and Alison. He stood away from the door. Would PC Carrick usually bring his daughter on police business? He doubted it. Then why were they here? There was only one way to find out. He asked them in, and they stepped inside the door quickly. The media was outside snapping pictures and calling out. It seemed that the papers finally figured out where they lived; it was only a matter of time. He slammed the door on them. This was something else they would need to talk about when this was all over; how to move forward in the public eye. Life would never be the same again.

They all stood in the hallway; Mae walked into the hall. She had a piece of paper in her hand. She started to call out to Toby; then, she saw the congregation before her. She stopped with her mouth gaping open.

"Isaac. Hi. What are you doing here, and who's this?" Mae gestured to Alison.

"Mum. This is Alison; PC Carrick is her father," said Toby. Mae held her hand out to Alison.

"Nice to meet you, Alison. What are you guys doing here? Is it a social call? If it is, we're swamped at the moment; I'm sure you'll understand. Maybe you could come back tomorrow."

"Actually, it is a semi-formal visit. We have some information for you. My daughter is in some way involved, and I thought she should be here," said Isaac.

"Shall we go into the living room?" said Toby. He knew exactly what this was about.

Before Isaac could explain the reason for their being there, Toby felt it necessary to fill his mum in on Alison's involvement. He started at the beginning with the incident in the gym. Isaac didn't seem surprised about what Toby said, so he assumed Alison told him the extra details. He then explained how it was Alison who saw the intruder in the house. Mae listened calmly; with everything going on, she couldn't be bothered to be angry at Toby for being indiscreet or be upset with the girl who snooped around their property.

"So now that you know the background, Alison took a photo

of the registration number of the car parked down the track. I put it through the national database. It is registered to a hire car company in Gloucester. From what you told me about your ex-husband, I was curious. I knew it couldn't just be a coincidence. So, I made some calls. I found out the car was rented by Anthony Newton." He paused, waiting for a shock, horror response. Their stares were blank. "I guess I was expecting a reaction," said Isaac whilst scratching his head. Mae leaned forward in her seat.

"The thing is, Isaac, we already know that Anthony's involved." Mae touched Cat's arm. "Show him the video, Cat." Cat looked up, eyes wide.

"But mum, we can't. He said no police."

"Sweetheart, please, I'm sure that Isaac will understand the situation; I trust him." Mae looked over at Isaac and smiled. Isaac smiled back. Cat sighed and showed him the video. Isaac's attention was fixed on the screen. When the video ended, he leaned back in his chair.

"Mae, you have to report this. This is kidnapping, and this kid is at massive risk."

"Isaac, please. If the police show up there, he's dead. I think you know from the news reports that my kids and I are better equipped to deal with this than the police. No offence. We can do things that the police can't. If anyone can get him out of there safely, it's us." Mae searched Isaac's face; he knew she was right.

"So, how are you going to do this?" Isaac asked.

"Well, we're not overly sure right now. It's hard to create a plan when we don't know where they are until half an hour before." Isaac leapt from his seat, startling everyone.

"But we do know where they are. After I traced the person

renting the car, I got information on where the car was delivered. I looked it up; there isn't anything there apart from an abandoned barn. I can guarantee this must be where Jake is being held. I'm guessing they didn't bother covering their tracks because they hadn't counted on anyone seeing the car."

"Oh my god. This is perfect. Now we know where it is, we can make a proper plan. So what was the address?" asked Cat excitedly. Her hopes before this news weren't exceptionally high, but now this gave them a real chance. Isaac thought for a moment; Cat wondered why he was stalling.

"Before I give it to you, I want you to agree for me to come as well. I promise not to report it to the station, but I'll feel a whole lot better if I was around. At least if things go wrong, I can get back up. I will stay out of sight, and I'll only come into the fold if you guys get into trouble." Mae didn't want Isaac involved; it was just another person to look out for. But they needed the address. There would be nothing stopping him from following or even going without them anyway.

"Okay," said Mae. Mae was still holding the piece of paper that she had when Isaac and Alison first arrived, and Cat pulled on one of its corners.

"What's that, mum?"

"Oh yeah. Alison, you said the intruder took something from my desk. They hadn't. They were putting something in. Anthony had a plan to explain our disappearances; that was if things had gone to plan. According to this, I was so depressed and stressed out that I killed Toby and Cat and then I killed myself. It's a murder, suicide note."

"What?" Cat whipped the letter from her mum's hand and scanned it.

"Oh my god, mum, does he actually mean to kill us?" cried

Cat.

"Maybe it should just be me and Isaac that go," said Mae. Toby practically stamped his foot in frustration.

"No, no way. This changes nothing. The situation is no different. He meant to kill us before you read that letter. His plans for us have not changed within the last five minutes," Toby wasn't going to budge on this. Mae could tell, much like Isaac, what was to stop the twins from hatching their own plan in her absence; it was better they made a plan together, then she could keep the risks to her children down to a minimum. There was no choice but to see this through.

They planned to arrive at the barn several hours early and take him by surprise. Isaac would remain in his car and be there if they needed him. They brought the address up on google maps, aerial view. It was a barn in the middle of nowhere. They would not go through the primary access track to get into the vicinity. On the map, they spotted a place where they could walk through the woods and come out on the treeline opposite the barn. There were two access points to the barn itself; the main door at the front and a side door. There was a window at the back, but they dismissed this as a place to enter as they would probably have to break a window.

They decided the best way to get in was to create a diversion to bring him out. They could then slip in, get Jake, get him to safety, then bring the whole nightmare to an end. The plan wasn't ideal, but it was all they had for now; they didn't know what to expect.

Chapter 20

Mae, Cat and Toby collected up some things that they would need. They didn't have much use for weapons, but they felt it necessary to take some nonetheless, just in case. They didn't exactly have an arsenal in their home, but some everyday household items would suffice. They raided the kitchen drawers and grabbed a few sharp carving knives. Mae ventured to the garage and found a crowbar; there wasn't much else in there; she wasn't one for DIY. They put everything into a bag and dropped it near the back door. The insurance company delivered a courtesy car for Mae to use whilst hers was being repaired. It would be tricky getting to it with all the media outside, and they were bound to be followed. Isaac had an idea.

"To be able to do this, we need to get the media away from the house. Al…" He looked directly at his daughter; he very rarely called her Alison unless she was in trouble for something. "You need to stay here. I'm going to take Mae, Cat and Toby to my police car. That lot out there are going to assume that I'll be taking them to the police station. When I drive away, hopefully, they'll follow. As soon as they're gone, you need to load the car up then drive to our place. I'll make sure that I lose the paparazzi, and we'll meet you there. Mae…

" He turned his gaze to Mae. "You and the kids will then get in your rental, and then I can follow you. Al, you'll be safe and sound at home."

"But dad, I want to come too." Alison pouted and folded her arms.

"Al, please, this is not an outing. You're supposed to be at school. Just think yourself lucky that I'm not making you go there instead." Isaac took his daughter's elbow and distanced her from the others. "It's going to be dangerous, honey. The only reason Mae is allowing her kids to get involved is because they can handle themselves. They're not like normal teenagers, as you well know. I can't put you at risk like that, okay?" Alison hung her head, still pouting, but she reluctantly agreed to stay home.

They were ready; Alison stood by the door with the bag as Isaac walked out with the Phoenix family. The press was on them immediately, and they crowded around as they walked to the car. Isaac put his palms up, pushing away the cameras. He opened the rear door for them all to climb in. Cat went first, then Toby and Mae last. He slammed the door closed and climbed into the driver's seat.

Alison was watching from the small window in the door. She could hardly see the car; it was covered with people, like ants on a doughnut. The car inched forward; Isaac was careful not to run over anyone's feet. He slowly accelerated away. The press went after them on foot then climbed into their vans; they pursued his car just as he expected.

Alison waited for the last van to go out of sight. She walked out of the house and closed the door behind her. She made further checks to make sure there were no stragglers, but they were all gone. Alison threw the bag of weapons, or more like kitchen utensils, into the boot. It was a nice car, a Hyundai i20. She hoped she'd be able to drive it okay. She recently passed her test and got her license, but she learned to drive in the old Peugeot 206 back at home. It was considerably basic; even for a car of twenty years old, it didn't even have electric windows. This car, though, was brand new. She turned the key, and nothing happened. *Great, it doesn't work,* she thought. There was a piece of card on the passenger seat; there were operating instructions on it. The instructions stated that she needed to push the clutch and then turn the ignition key. She tried it and it worked; the engine fired up. She slowly drove the car down the drive. The car jolted several times as she tried to get used to the pedal's sensitivity. By the time she arrived at her house, she had the hang of it, and she turned off the engine and proudly sat whilst she waited for the others.

* * *

Isaac struggled to lose his tails; he thought they'd just go ahead to the police station, but they stuck with him on every detour and rat run they came across.

"Isaac, what are we going to do? We're not losing them," said Mae. Cat gingerly raised her hand the same way she would if she needed to use the bathroom in class.

"I have a suggestion," she said. Isaac glanced over his shoulder.

"I'm certainly open to them. What is it?" Isaac looked back at the road; he sharply turned right, then left and right again, hoping that this time he would lose them. But no. They were still there; he slapped the wheel and growled. "I'm all ears," he exclaimed.

"If you could find a narrow residential street with driveways, perhaps I could 'encourage,'" Cat made quotation marks with her fingers, "a car to roll into the road creating a blockage." Mae snapped her head around.

"No way, you are not using your abilities. Save them for later when we need them." Cat rolled her eyes.

"Mum, it's not like they're gonna just run out. I don't need recharging, you know. Besides, everyone knows now, it's no secret anymore, and unless we can get rid of these guys, we can't get on with the task in hand." Isaac looked around at Mae.

"She has a point, Mae. It's a pretty good idea." Mae frowned. She didn't want her kids getting used to using their abilities. This was a one-time-only thing.

"Fine," she sighed.

"Okay then. Cat, keep your eyes peeled. I know a reasonably small street about half a mile away," said Isaac.

Cat watched out the window; they were in the narrow street in just a matter of minutes. Many of the drives were empty, it was Monday after all, and most people had probably gone to work. Up ahead, she saw a van; it was around ten houses away. It was a long-wheelbase one; it looked like it belonged to a gas company. It was perfect. It would cover the road and the pavements, and there would be no squeezing around that.

"There. That van," Cat shouted. Isaac nodded; he saw it. He put his foot down to increase the gap between them and the news vans behind them. They were only ten feet behind. The street had a twenty mile per hour speed limit, and Isaac was exceeding it quite dramatically. The gap between the police car and the news van had now doubled.

"Get ready," Isaac yelled. Cat concentrated on the van; they

241

could already see it moving backwards as they approached it on their left. By the time they passed the van, it already started to move onto the road. Cat turned to look through the back window; the vehicle continued to cover the road, and she couldn't see the news vans. The blockade she'd created was now obstructing her view of them. She made the vehicle come to a stop; there was no room to pass it. The street was empty behind them as they proceeded down the road.

"Way to go, Cat," Isaac looked over his shoulder at her beaming. She smiled back at him. It felt good to do something well; there was no disaster, and no one got hurt. Mae continued to frown. Cat looked at her mother and saw the disdain on her face; she chose not to comment. She'd done good, and at least someone recognised it.

The police car pulled up behind the rental at Isaac's house. It was a small cul-de-sac, and no one else seemed to be around. Alison got out and rushed over to them.

"My god. You guys took ages. I was worried something happened to you." Isaac hugged his daughter.

"There was no trouble as such. We just struggled to lose the paparazzi, but Cat took care of it." Cat wasn't getting bored of the praise in the slightest.

"C'mon then, we got to get a move on," said Mae. Her mouth was set in a hard line.

"Good luck, guys. Hopefully, I'll see you soon," said Alison. Her eyes rested on Toby; he was the one she was most interested in seeing again. Toby saw her gaze; his movements were awkward as he flashed a quick smile and then jumped into the car's front passenger side. Alison said goodbye to her dad then ran up to the house.

Mae and Isaac stood outside the cars. Mae held a map in

her hand, and she laid it out over the bonnet of her rental. She pointed to where they would meet before going on to the barn. It was a small dirt road about a mile away from the barn. It was now ten-thirty in the morning; their ETA would be around two-forty-five. Mae didn't like that they had to do this in broad daylight, but they had no choice. Anthony was expecting them at six, but they would have a couple of hours to watch the barn and look at their options. Isaac and Mae parted and got into their cars. Mae pulled off first, and Isaac followed.

* * *

The first half an hour in the car was silent; Mae's eyes were fixed on the road. Toby watched the hedges whizz past his window, and Cat sat behind him, re-watching her dad's video repeatedly. She wasn't watching her father; she was watching Jake in the background. He looked frightened and vulnerable; blood was smeared around his face, and his eyes were watery. She always saw Jake as a strong guy, so to see him like this was heart-breaking; tears pooled in her eyes. She hoped they could save him, but she was afraid they couldn't. She longed for his warmth; he gave the best cuddles, and she always felt safe in his arms. Then she realised; she did love him. She never allowed her feelings for Jake to properly manifest because she feared losing him. She knew she was hard to be with. She was damaged goods. She assumed that if they had a full-on relationship, she would only mess it up and lose him forever. This was probably why she never told him about her past and abilities; she didn't want to frighten him away. He was too special to her. She needed him in her life.

Eventually, Mae broke the silence. "Guys," Cat and Toby looked at their mum. "I don't know how all of this is going to go down and in case something goes bad, I need to tell you something." Cat and Toby looked at each other then back at their mum. Cat leaned forward, and Toby angled his body to face Mae. Mae swallowed hard.

"Back when I was little, I was able to do more than just make things catch fire. In fact, everything both of you can do, I could do too. It's just the pyro-kinesis, as I call it, that seems to be my prime protective ability, a bit like your shielding Toby. But I can only really use it to protect others. I can't seem to defend myself with it. Maybe I could with some training, but to be honest, it's not something that I ever tried to hone. I didn't even know about it until I was thirteen when my brother was attacked.

The other abilities, though, I knew about for a long time. I think I was about seven when I first moved something with my mind. I was washing the dishes to earn my pocket money. One of the plates slipped out of my hand; it was one of mum's favourites. As it fell, I stared at it, thinking, *No, stop*. And to my surprise, it stopped. It just floated inches from the ground; I was so shocked by it, and I wondered if I dreamt it.

"I started to practice with things in my room, and I discovered that I had quite the talent for it. As I explored my gift, I found that I could do even more; I could move quickly, I was strong, and I could create a bubble. Nobody knew what I could do, until my grandmother came to stay for Christmas; this was my mum's mum. I was about nine years old. My grandma walked in on me one evening when I was practising my skills. I was lying on my bed. Cat, the thing you did in that video on the news, with the rocks going around in circles, I was doing the same but with my snow globes. I didn't expect grandma to come in to check on me. My parents usually only checked on me when they came up to bed, but my grandmother burst the door open, and she took me by surprise. I lost my mental hold on those snow globes, and they crashed to the floor. I tried to lie, and I told grandma that I threw them, but she knew better. That was because once upon a time, she could do it too." Both Cat and Toby's eyes widened. Mae was still staring out the windscreen as she continued.

"She sat on my bed with me and explained to me about our family. It was the maternal bloodline who was affected, but it skipped a generation with my mum. She knew the history of it all the way back to the seventeenth century. There were even members of our family burned at the stake for witchcraft. Every generation passed down the knowledge of our ancestors to the next, but this stopped when mum was born. Grandma said that my mum showed no signs of having our abilities, so she assumed that the inheritance of these abilities had stopped. But when she saw me, she realised it either skipped my mum or was lying dormant. She thought that I should be the one to inherit the knowledge. I wasn't going to share it with you two either, but on what we're about to be faced with, I thought you should know. I do have an old diary at home that explains everything." Cat popped her head between the front seats.

"So, does this mean that we're witches?" Cat's eyes were alight with wonder, and Mae laughed.

"I suppose it's a term that could fit. Our gifts are considered elemental, related to earth, fire, air and water. But even grandma was looking for a more plausible scientific explanation within this century. There has been much research into telekinesis; some scientists think that some people might have more access to different parts of the brain than others. There's the possibility that every human being could do what we can do; they just can't harness that part of the brain as we can. I, like grandma, believed that it could be explained with science; that was until you guys were born.

"You know those birthmarks that you have?" The twins nodded, "I thought them very strange when you were babies but dismissed them as one of those weird things that twins get. However, I don't know if you remember, but those birthmarks changed when we were in that house fire. Cat, yours was a triangle, then a horizontal line seared its way through it. I did some research, and this is actually the elemental symbol for air; it means the power of the mind. It makes perfect sense, don't you think? And yours, Toby, it's the same but inverted. This is the symbol for earth, and it means protection. I looked into it deeper and before the lines appeared; Cat, you had the symbol of fire, meaning creation and Toby, yours would have been water, meaning regeneration," Cat and Toby looked at each other. It was all fascinating, but what did it mean?

"Do you see? I had it all. I exhibited every power of each element. I could CREATE fire, I could PROTECT with the bubble, I could REGENERATE muscle to be strong and move fast, and I had the power of the MIND to move things around me. But with you two, the components of the elements have been divided between you. It was probably split inside the womb; so together, you have it all," Cat frowned,

"But mum, I've never been able to create fire," Mae nodded.

"This is something I have wondered about. I wasn't aware of my pyro-kinesis until I was older. It took a moment of extreme emotion and upset before I even discovered it," Mae took her eyes off the road for a moment to look into Cat's eyes, "This is why I've always worried about you. Toby's abilities have always been very protective in nature, but yours… ours can be destructive. I don't think that you have to be able to create fire; it can be anything. It may be something that we haven't seen yet, and perhaps we'll never know until such an event triggers it." Cat reclined back into her seat, contemplating this.

Mae's hand was on the gear stick, and Toby put his hand over it. Mae looked into his eyes. He looked thoughtful.

"You said earlier that you didn't hone your skills. Why?" asked Toby. Mae looked distant again.

"Your great-grandma told me a story. It was about something which happened to her during the second world war. She was a nurse in Queen Alexandra's Imperial Military Nursing Service. She didn't flaunt her gifts, but a select few knew what she was capable of. She played a big part during the war that few knew about.

Unfortunately, she and some others ended up in a prisoner of war camp; she could have saved herself from capture, but she refused to leave without her friends, and she didn't want to expose herself to the Nazis. Later, she tried to use her abilities to escape, but it failed, and the guards caught her best friend, Emma. If she didn't give herself up, they were going to kill Emma and any others who were remotely close to her. You see, they'd seen her use telekinesis. So, you can imagine the Nazis had quite an interest in her. For months they threatened her fellow POW's to compel her to do terrible things for them. It led to a lot of deaths, friendly and non-friendly.

She couldn't keep doing what they wanted; England was

losing the war. She flatly refused to help them further, and they executed Emma as a result. She had to make a tough decision between her country and her loved ones. The day finally came when we won the war. She was freed, and she never used her gifts again. It was too dangerous. She never talked of what happened to anyone until me. She told me this world had unbelievably bad people living within it. Therefore, we should keep ourselves hidden. These people can manipulate us. Archie is a prime example of that." Mae looked at Cat. Cat hung her head in shame. "They will use those whom we love, family and friends to make us conform. Jake is an example of that one. My grandma said that if I ever decided to tell the world, I should ensure that I spent the rest of my life alone. It was the only way to keep innocent people safe."

It was then that I stopped using my abilities. I was afraid of losing my parents, my brother and my friends. I practically forgot how to use them, it's like a muscle that needs to be exercised, otherwise you lose it. It's just the pyro-kinesis that I've not been able to subdue. I don't seem to have any control over it, but I wish I could stop it. The damage I did to that bully all those years ago when I was just a teenager made me not want to see it ever again. It's dangerous, and I could inadvertently kill someone. I vowed that you guys would learn self-control so you could never accidentally hurt someone or expose yourselves. But I failed, and I'm so sorry." Cat put her hand on her mum's shoulder.

"Mum, it's not your fault; you did well to protect us. It was my fault that we're in this mess. I understand why you wanted us to go underground and hide our abilities from everyone, but there's no going back once this is all over. People know about us now, and we HAVE to adapt. I refuse to believe that we have no choice but to be alone for the rest of our existence. Don't you think there's a reason we can do these things? Have you ever thought there's a bigger purpose to our lives? The world's going to shit, and maybe we are the answer. Perhaps we can change things."

Mae admired Cat's positivity, but she couldn't see how they could ever return to having a normal life. But she would worry about that later. They had something or someone more pressing to deal with. To lighten the mood, Mae put on some music. She liked her nineties hits, and the kids had no choice but to listen to them. The electronic beat of, Snap! With "The Power" pounded through the speakers. The song was appropriate; there was a power in this car that Anthony should never have messed with.

Chapter 21

Jake's face was hurting; it was also stifling hot in the barn. As his face sweated, the salt dribbled into the scrape on his cheek, causing it to sting and itch. He tried to bring his face down to his hand, which was tied to the arm of the chair. He was able to get his head low enough for his thumb to brush across his skin, giving him a small amount of relief. Anthony was staring at him, clearly taking a lot of pleasure in Jake's discomfort.

Jake didn't know what time it was; it was daylight now, and the sun had come up and streamed through the ventilation slits in the dilapidated barn. He thought it might be about six o'clock. He didn't manage to get back to sleep last night; he couldn't stop thinking about Cat and her family and the revelation of their extraordinary past life and abilities. He hated to find out like this—he just wished Cat trusted him enough to tell him herself.

Jake thought about Anthony's reasons for bringing the Phoenix family here. In the video, he'd said that he wanted Mae back. Jake couldn't help but get the feeling that having Cat and Toby back as well was merely an after-thought. He found it hard to imagine how a dad couldn't give a damn about his kids. Jake knew his father loved him; his father did things every day that let Jake know he was the most important thing in his life. Anthony was a monster. Jake was worried for Cat and Toby. Did he intend to start a new life with all of them? He doubted it, and from what Cat's uncle told him, it was unlikely that they'd go with him without a fight.

"What're you thinking about Jakey-boy? I can see the cogs turning from over here." Anthony leaned forward in his seat, resting his elbows on his knees.

"I was just thinking about Cat. I'm worried about her." Anthony sat back again and chuckled.

"And so you should be buddy, that is if she comes for you. I'm hoping that she does." Jake narrowed his eyes.

"What exactly do you mean by that?" asked Jake. Anthony laughed again; it reminded Jake of a villain from a Bond movie.

"Do you think I'd want a couple of gifted teenage brats running around? Before I knew that they could do these special things, I didn't want them. For a start, I seriously doubt that they're mine; their mother was a whore, but hey, I can forgive her for that. She was the love of my life, you know. But those two? No thanks, I'd always planned to dispose of them. Even more important that they disappear now. I can see them causing me some trouble otherwise. It would be like kidnapping Superman's mother. He certainly wouldn't sit around and let it happen, so they are now my priority." Jake just stared; his mouth was slightly open, and he blinked rapidly.

"Y-you're gonna kill them?" he stammered. Anthony's face mocked apologies.

"Afraid so Jakey-boy and not just them, you'll have to go too." Jake swallowed hard.

"Don't worry, I've got nothing against you personally, so I'll make sure it's quick." If only Jake had known he was signing his death warrant when he gave Anthony access to his phone to record that message. Not that he could've done anything about it. However, he wondered if he could've given a hidden message to let them know they shouldn't come. He didn't have a speaking role in the video, and Anthony would have seen any hand gestures before sending the video. If Anthony had seen him try it, he would've got another beating and would have recorded another video. No, there was nothing he could've done to stop them from coming. He just hoped for once in his life that Cat thought so little of him that she wouldn't come to the rescue; he honestly wished it to be true.

The driver strolled into the barn.

"Do you want to get some breakfast? I can keep an eye on him now if you like. I just came back from Mackey D's." announced the driver. Anthony gave Jake a look. Jake wondered if he was thinking about whether it was safe to leave him, now that he knew he was a dead man walking. He looked Jake up and down. Hunger won over the risks that Jake may conveniently escape then warn his saviours of their upcoming slaughter.

"Alright, I won't be any longer than an hour, but don't talk to him," Anthony ordered. There was a presence about him that would make a person do as they were told. Anthony and the driver switched places. The driver held a knife and twirled the point around on the tip of his finger as he watched Jake, which was somewhat dis-concerting. The guy barely blinked, and with the balaclava hiding the rest of his face, his bright blue eyes looked demonic. Jake looked away. He heard the engine start-up outside as Anthony went off.

Three-quarters of an hour passed, and Jake was beginning

to feel sleepy. He moved around in his chair in an attempt to get a little more comfortable. The cable ties on his wrists had gotten tight. He must be swelling up from the heat and the friction. He knew it was pointless, but he thought he'd try to get some assistance. The driver wasn't looking at him; he was fiddling on his phone, and he was sure he heard the Candy Crush tune.

"Erm, excuse me," Jake said quietly. The driver looked up lazily.

"These cable ties have gotten really tight, is there any chance you could loosen them slightly? Please?" His mother gave him little advice during his life after his dad died, but what he always remembered was when she said, "Manners Maketh Man." Not that it did him any good in this situation.

"Why don't I just cut your hands off?" The driver smiled a mean smile, and Jake glared at him.

"No need for that. I suppose who cares about comfort if I'm going to die anyway. Never mind, forget I asked." The driver's eyes changed when he said that. He pondered whether the driver knew about Anthony's plans to kill three teenage kids.

"Who says you're gonna die?" The driver kept his voice even and nasty—his tone was almost humorous. It was clear to Jake that he knew nothing about this, but he didn't want him to know that.

"The other guy said so. Myself, Cat and Toby are all going to die, and he's only interested in keeping Mae alive. We will be surplus to requirements when he's got her." The driver nodded but said nothing further.

Anthony arrived back shortly after. He strutted into the barn, and the driver shot up from his seat, asking Anthony for a word outside. Anthony agreed. Jake strained to hear, but he couldn't hear a thing.

The driver grabbed Anthony by the arm. "The kid said that you were gonna kill him and the other kids. No one said anything about killing kids when I came into this arrangement. That woman, she deserves everything she gets; in fact, I'd love to kill her myself. But I ain't killing no kids." Anthony yanked his arm free from the driver's grip.

"I told you not to talk to him," he growled.

"Now I see why," yelled the driver. Anthony was wary about the volume of their voices; he pulled the driver further away from the barn. Anthony spoke in a hushed tone.

"Look, I'm not asking you to kill anyone—your job is to help me round everyone up. Leave the dirty work to me. There is no way I can keep the kids alive. Surely you get that. These kids are like superheroes. If we let them go, they'll probably kill us instead. We have no choice. The kid in there, he's a witness. I'm sorry to say this, mate, but he'll be on your conscience; it was only supposed to be the family involved. You're the one who kidnapped the wrong kid." The driver went to say something but didn't bother; he knew that it was his fault that this Jake boy had gotten involved. He did understand where Anthony was coming from about the other ones, but he didn't know how he could sit aside and watch kids get killed. What he said about Mae was true. He hated her—he would gladly slit her throat in cold blood, and he wouldn't lose sleep over it. But she was not an innocent party, and he had good reason to see her dead; he had nothing against the kids, though.

"Okay, as long as you know that I won't be the one doing it. What about Mae? The kid reckons that you plan to keep her alive, is that true?"

"No mate, he's lying. That bitch put me in jail for something I didn't do. Why would I want to keep her around?" The driver nodded; he had a good point. "That's why I told you not to talk to him. He's trying to divide us." The driver was satisfied, and they made their way back into the barn.

Chapter 22

Whilst her dad and Mae were pouring over the map, Alison saw her chance. They had the main door at the front of the house, but they also had a side door. Alison grabbed her camera as she passed through. She opened the side door and quietly eased it shut behind her. There was a hedge going down the side of their front garden. She ran down the side of it, allowing it to conceal her as she crouched low. She peeped over the hedge and could see they were still distracted. She darted from the cover of the hedge and went to the passenger side of the car furthest away from the pavement. The car itself was obstructing the view of her as she clicked the rear door open. She crawled into the back of the car into the near side footwell—she was small enough and flexible enough to fit quite nicely. It helped that her dad drove with the seat quite far forward, allowing more room. He also always kept loads of junk in the back of the car, so she'd typically travel in the front. But in this scenario, the junk was helpful. There was a jacket on the seat, and she draped it over herself—he would never know that she was there unless he wanted to wear the coat. But this was unlikely; it was boiling outside, probably about twenty-seven degrees. She was confident he wouldn't find her.

He came back to the car and slammed the door shut. He put the radio on; he didn't tend to listen to music. He listened to talk shows—people talked about different topics, and it bored Alison to tears. Today they were talking about the impact of leaving the European Union, and she wished she'd brought her earphones.

Her father had been driving for well over an hour now. Being so low down in the car, Alison was closer to the road noise, making her tired. With that and the radio, she couldn't help but close her eyes for a minute or two. She woke herself when she released a snore, and the car wobbled slightly.

"What the—" *Shit*, she'd been rumbled. Alison uncovered her head slowly; as the material came away from her eyes, she could see her father straining over his shoulder. He gave her a sour look and turned again to look at the road. "You might as well get up in the seat and put on your seatbelt now." Alison grimaced as she got up and strapped herself in.

"Are you annoyed at me?" she asked. She already knew the answer.

"No, I'm not annoyed. I'm fucking furious!" Alison's eyes widened; he'd never sworn in front of her like that before. The worst thing she'd ever heard him say was 'shit', but the 'F' bomb was unheard of. "Well, I can't turn around and take you back home because I'll never be back in time to help Mae and the twins. So, I have no choice but to take you with me. This is so dangerous, Alison; I doubt you really realise that. If you did, you would've stayed home." He smacked the wheel with his palm and shook his head; she could see the redness of his cheeks. Alison did realise it was dangerous. But this was her chance to get a real story, and not a silly story about how the lunch ladies at school spit in the food of kids who they

257

don't like. This was her ticket to being taken seriously and getting some recognition. Journalism was what she wanted to do, and opportunities like this didn't come around every day.

This kind of opportunity was unheard of. She'd stumbled upon a superhero by accident; she then discovers that he is part of an entire family of superheroes, and they've gone to rescue a fellow student from the deranged father who has threatened them throughout their whole lives. Alison already knew what her headline would be:

THE PHOENIX TWINS; RISEN FROM THE ASHES, STRONGER THAN EVER

Of course, she hoped for a good outcome. If it were a bad outcome, she probably wouldn't come out of it well, either. She looked down at her hands and prayed for it all to work out for the best; she wanted to write this story.

"I'm sorry, dad, I just really wanted to be a part of it. Toby did save my life; I feel like I owe him." Isaac was still shaking his head.

"I'm telling you now, when we get there, you are not leaving this car. Do you understand? You are getting nowhere near this; I don't know what you were hoping for. Maybe you want to be Lois Lane, getting into the thick of everything and risking your life, but that is not happening today." His voice was harsh.

"Okay, dad."

Three hours went by in total silence; it seemed that she had to suffer the silent treatment for the foreseeable future. She knew better than making small talk; it would only be met with a grunt. She'd been in the doghouse before. She was suspended from school for starting a protest about the school uniform. He seemed to think a local police officer's child should never be suspended from school. He thought people wouldn't respect him if his own child didn't. But it was like she said at the time. She respected her dad, just not school policies. It didn't go down well. He wanted her to be an upstanding student who was squeaky clean, but that was never going to happen; she was too much like her mum. Her parents were chalk and cheese.

Isaac drove off the main road, and they travelled down some quieter A-roads before turning off into a country lane. She could see the other car up ahead. The vehicles pulled into a lay-by; it was the entrance to a forestry commission footpath. He turned off the engine. Alison took a deep breath. *Here it goes,* she thought.

Chapter 23

Mae, Toby and Cat got out of their car, followed closely by Isaac and Alison. Alison got eye-balled three times; Isaac put his arms out in front of him, palms up.

"I know. She stowed away, and I didn't realise until I'd been driving for over an hour, it was too late to turn around. She has strict instructions to remain in the car." Alison hung her head; she started to get the feeling that no one wanted her here. Mae's face was thunderous. Cat was merely eye-rolling, and Toby was rubbing the back of his neck, shaking his head.

"For God's sake, guys. I'm no helpless damsel needing protection okay, I will stay out of the way, and I'll stand guard with the cars. Talking of cars, dad, I think you should put the police car elsewhere. No one will question the other car; it could be someone taking a dog for a walk. But if our guy drives past this," Alison gestured toward the police car. "Well, it might make him nervous." They all looked at each other, and Mae nodded at Isaac.

"You guys wait here; I'm going to hide the car, don't go anywhere without me, and Al. Just go nowhere."

Mae was in no hurry. It was only two-thirty, so they had plenty of time. They moved away from the car and went into the woods for cover, just in case. Mae considered what was about to happen; she was scared. More than that, she was terrified—not for herself but for Cat and Toby. She now had Alison to worry about as well, but as long as she stayed in the car, she shouldn't have to worry too much about her.

After the long drive from Cumbria, she needed to stretch, but her ribs were agony; this was not a good day for a battle. She hoped that it wouldn't come to a physical fight, but she was likely to lose if it did. She had to admit. If she'd gone this alone, she probably wouldn't stand much of a chance. She needed Cat and Toby to be there, but they wouldn't have to get too close with any luck.

Before they went in all guns blazing, they needed to consider the plan further. They needed to look at the barn and the surrounding area; a re-con mission was required.

Isaac returned; he'd only been gone twenty minutes.

"There was a field with a high hedge just down the road. I've parked it behind the hedge. It's not visible from the road."

"Great. We need to walk down to the barn; our plan based on Google maps is okay, but things might be different since the last maps update. We need to make sure that the plan will still work. We don't all need to go. Kids, I think you should all stay here. Isaac and I will go." Toby and Cat weren't sure. They were the ones going into battle, surely they should know how the land lies, but Mae's face had changed. For years, even though she was always neurotic about their safety, she was a typical warm, placid, and loving mother—they'd never seen her like this before. She seemed cold, and her eyes were brutal, the kind of look you'd see on a soldier. They didn't argue with her.

Isaac and Mae set off through the woods. When they looked

at the map previously, this lay-by was parallel to the dirt road that led to the barn. They should come out a couple of hundred yards away from the barn where Anthony was holding Jake. Neither of them said anything for the first half an hour of walking. Isaac was leading the way, and Mae was falling behind. The exertion was putting a massive strain on her body; every breath she took made her ribs protest. Her wrist was sore, but she could cope with that. Mae began to get light-headed. She stopped and grabbed hold of a tree. She rested her head against the trunk with her eyes closed. Isaac noticed that he could no longer hear Mae's footfalls. He turned. Several yards away, he could see Mae, and he ran back to her.

"Mae. Are you okay?" Isaac asked. He took her arm and encouraged her to sit down. She bent her knees and lowered herself to the ground. She reclined against the knobbly wood and exhaled a long breath.

"Not really," she laughed.

"Maybe you should go back. I can go ahead and see what the crack is. You need to rest." He placed a hand on her shoulder. Mae smiled.

"I don't think so, officer. I need to see it for myself. If I'm going to keep my kids safe, I need to know every inch of that place." Isaac sat down next to her.

"You've got a couple of good kids there, Mae. I think they'll be fine," said Isaac.

"They are good kids. But they're young. They think that they have something to prove. Especially Cat, she has a habit of not thinking things through. She can't keep doing that. She's powerful, more powerful than I am, and she could get someone killed. She may not mean to, but she would have to live with that. And now that everyone knows about us, she could see herself in prison or god knows what. I don't want people to think of us as dangerous. It could cause us an awful lot of trouble in the future." Mae rubbed her eyes. She was exhausted. Isaac gazed at her; it was like he was trying to search her soul. She had such a weight to carry on her shoulders alone.

"I don't think that you give Cat enough credit," said Isaac. Mae looked at him with daggers. "Don't get mad. This isn't a criticism. I wouldn't know the first thing about raising gifted kids. I have so much admiration for what you've achieved. But Cat seems to me like a smart girl. The idea that she had earlier with that van was great. There were other options that she could have used. The girl brought down a house, so I'm sure she would have been quite capable of destroying those paparazzi vehicles; maybe even turn them on their roofs or crash them into a couple of houses, but she didn't. She chose the option with the least collateral damage. No one was hurt, and it was a good result for us. Don't you think? In my eyes, that shows me that she did consider the consequences. She's no different than any other teenager; they make mistakes, she'll probably make more, but didn't you?" Isaac took Mae's hand. "She's a good girl, Mae. You've done well." her eyes met his.

"Thanks," said Mae. She squeezed his hand. Mae was thoughtful for a minute. "Isaac?"

"Yes?" he replied. Their eyes locked.

"Whatever happens today. I need you to know that I will be protecting my kids with my life. So, if something happens to me, I would like you to look out for them. They've never had a father figure to look up to, and I know that you are a good, honourable guy. If anyone can keep them on the straight and narrow, it's you. Will you do that?" Mae's eyes were wide, and there was pain in them.

"Hey, let's not have any of that talk. It won't come to that. We're going to get Jake out safely; you and the kids are going to be fine," replied Isaac. Mae tried to get up; she knew that Isaac was just trying to be supportive, but she needed to know that her children would be safe if she didn't make it.

"Isaac, please. Just tell me that you'll look out for them. Let's pretend that we are not in a perfect world, and things do go wrong sometimes," she snapped. Isaac was trying to help her to her feet, but she slapped his hands away. He stood back and watched her struggle.

"Of course, I'll look out for them, Mae. But could we please keep positive about this? No one is going to die today." Satisfied, Mae nodded. She had no issues about being positive, but they needed to be realistic. She would ensure that Cat and Toby would be okay; no one was getting to them without going through her first. But Mae knew that she wasn't in the best shape right now—she was probably the most significant liability of all. Mae took a swig of water and powered forward; Isaac followed.

* * *

Alison, Toby and Cat made themselves comfortable in a clearing of the woods; the siblings sat next to each other, but Alison kept her distance. They all sat in silence. To Alison, it was an uncomfortable silence, so she felt the need to lighten the mood.

"So, you guys are superheroes, huh?" Two sets of glaring

eyes met her comment, and both of their heads tilted to the right simultaneously, like a couple of robots who just received a direction to tilt their heads and glare; it was creepy to witness.

"Okay, perhaps not the best thing to say at a time like this. Do you guys mind if I ask you a few questions?"

"Depends'. Will it end up in the school rag?" Toby replied. Alison frowned; she knew how she should respond to that. She could lie and say no—she wanted the story. If she was truthful and told them yes, she would like to put it in the paper, she ran the risk of them not cooperating.

"Well, I would like to write about you guys. It's not every day that a school can say that they have two very gifted students. If you don't want me to, then that's fine, but the thing is, if everything goes well tonight—and I'm sure it will—you're going to face a lot of people wanting to know your story. You can choose to say nothing, and people can make their own assumptions, or you can talk to me. I promise that I will keep everything factual; I'm not the type of person that would misquote you. I want to show you in the best possible light. People are frightened of the unknown, and I don't think people should be scared. I don't think you want people to fear you either." Cat and Toby looked at each other; they shrugged their shoulders. What the hell.

"Okay, what would you like to know?" said Cat. Alison beamed. She leapt up to her knees and moved closer to them. She really was Lois Lane; she was interviewing the two most exciting people in the world. She had her hair in pigtails today, and the pink curls dropped forward in front of her chest. She threw them behind her as she sat up straight and removed a small notepad and pen from her bag.

265

"I never leave home without it," she giggled. "Okay. So, this question is for both of you. When did you first know about your special abilities?" Toby and Cat took turns as they described their history, starting from when they were seven. They didn't go into the same detail as their mother did in the car. Alison asked if it was hereditary, and they touched on their grandmother and how it went back centuries but didn't talk about the war; they both felt that some things should remain a secret. Alison continued.

"Now that the secret is out, what are you going to do?" Toby answered first.

"Honestly? I don't know. I never wanted this—I didn't want people to know about me; now that they do, there'll be expectations of me that weren't there before. Just because I can move fast and create shields of protection, does that mean I have to choose a career to use these abilities? Am I expected to be a police officer, a fireman or a soldier? Maybe I want to be a musician, a writer, or a painter, but would people judge me for that? Will they say it's a waste of my gifts and that I should be helping the community? I think this is why these comic book heroes have alter-egos. So that they can have the life they want, and if they had chosen to help others, they can do it in secret. Perhaps that would've been me, but I don't know now." Toby's revelation punched what felt like a shard of glass into Cat's heart. When the secret came out, and the video was all over the news, in a way, she was relieved. She no longer had to hide, and once she got over what Archie had done to her, she was ready to be herself. Cat never once thought of Toby. All the things she did in the past that risked their anonymity, and she didn't care—she was angry at her mum for holding her back. But here Toby was, talking about how he feels his life must be decided by society.

"I'm sorry, Toby; I had no idea that you felt like this." Cat reached out her fingers and took Toby's hand; he squeezed her fingers and gave her a tight smile.

"It wasn't completely your fault, Cat; I think Archie was more to blame, and it's not like I was able to keep our secret too well myself." He looked up at Alison and smirked; Alison didn't mean to, but she giggled like a little girl. She cringed at herself and cleared her throat to try a more adult laugh.

"Cat, what are you going to do?" Alison turned to Cat. Cat sighed.

"Unlike Toby, I hated to hide my gifts. I wanted the world to know. As far as I was concerned, these gifts were what made me worth something. I'm not particularly clever. I'm not going to do anything amazing with my life academically, so what does that leave me with? Working in a restaurant as a waitress? Doing admin in an office on a nine-to-five? I want more than that. I quite like the idea of being in the police force but not as your everyday PC. I have this dream of creating my own special department. I hoped Toby would be part of it, too; otherwise, it would only consist of me until other people came forward. I am under no illusion that we're the only ones out there that can do unusual, special things. I wanted to call it The HEAD task force. The Hyper Enhanced Ability Defence task force. I've put a lot of thought into it. So, if something is going on, like a big armed robbery, we could be called in to help." Cat's eyes were lighting up as she talked, and she spoke faster as she became more excited with the idea. "We could even be called in for terrorist plots or maybe even do work for the military; we could go global—

"Wow, Cat, you really do have some amazing ideas!" Alison

interrupted. Toby was shocked to hear that his sister felt she had nothing going for her except for her abilities. Toby laughed to himself; all he wanted when he was growing up was to blend in and be his own person, and all Cat wanted was to stand out and be the people's person. Considering they were twins, they had very opposite outlooks for their lives, although her taskforce idea did sound cool.

"So now that we are more acquainted, I would love to see your abilities in person. I mean, Toby, to be fair, I didn't actually see what you did. All I knew at the time was that I was on the floor unhurt when I should've been underneath a demolished climbing frame. Please?" Cat was the first to stand up.

"In case you haven't heard, I'm the family show-off, so I'll go first." She gave Alison a side glance and winked at her. Alison sat back onto her bottom; she had pins and needles in her feet from sitting on them for so long. She leaned back on her elbows, eyes glowing. She watched as Cat was looking into the trees considering what to do. Cat nodded to herself. She switched her gaze from the trees to Alison and stared unblinking at her. Alison tensed, and she sat up straight. *Why's Cat staring at me like that?* She thought. Then out of nowhere, there was a strange feeling in her stomach. It reminded her of when her dad was driving quickly over a hump or small hill in the road. Alison's eyes widened as her backside rose from the ground; Alison grappled for the ground in a panic, but she was moving up higher and higher.

"Alison, relax! Don't be afraid. I've got you." Cat's voice was calm. Alison tried to relax her body; it felt like she was cradled in someone's arms, and the fear left her. She looked down. She saw the ground about six feet below her, and she laughed.

"Oh. My. God. I'm flying; I'm frickin' flying. This is awesome," Cat moved Alison around a little—she wanted her to feel like she was really soaring through the air like Peter Pan. She moved her between the trees, swooping high and low.

"Cat. I don't want this to end because it is the best thing ever, but I kinda feel sick. Could you let me down?" Cat laughed and nodded. Alison slowly sank to the floor. Cat placed her down gently, feet first, directly in front of her. Alison had a permanent wide smile stretched across her face; the corners almost reached her ears.

"My god Cat, thank you so much! I would be so, so happy to run the Public Relations for your HEAD task force. I'd even accept minimum wage if you did that at least once per week!" For Cat, this was the best thing ever. She loved showing people what she could do. The wonder on Alison's face and Archie's made her feel amazing before she knew he was an ass. This is what she wanted for her future. Alison then looked at Toby.

"Can you top that?" Alison teased. Toby shook his head.

"On the basis that I'm the introvert of the family. I am nowhere near that much of a showman. This is only going to last a few seconds, so make sure that you're watching. And don't blink." With that, Toby was gone. Alison looked left, right, front and back; there was no sign of him.

"Up here," Toby called. Alison looked up. Toby was in a tree.

"How the hell did you get up there?" Alison yelled.

"I jumped." He flashed a small smile. It made Alison wobbly at the knees—he looked so cute when he smiled. "I can jump about ten feet, and I can run quite fast. I'm not as fast as the Flash, but I'm faster than Usain Bolt."

"Flash, smash. He's fictional; who cares? Have you ever timed yourself?" Alison asked; she had to shout as he was still quite far up the tree. Toby had, but it was a long time ago. When he was thirteen, curiosity got the better of him, and he decided to set a watch. He found a straight road near where they lived; he measured the distance and started the clock when he set off.

"It was a few years ago, but yeah, I clocked about sixty miles per hour. But I can't do that speed from a standing start; it's a bit like a car. I have to gain momentum."

"Can you show— " before she even finished her sentence, he leapt down from the tree in front of her and sprinted off into the woods. It may not have been sixty when he set off, but it was still damn fast. He returned as quickly as he left.

"Can I stop being a performing monkey now?" Toby laughed.

"Sure. I think I've seen enough. I'm sorry to say, Toby, but Cat is my favourite." Cat held up her palm for a high-five, and Alison slapped it.

"I like her," laughed Cat. Cat's abilities were Alison's favourite for sure, but Toby had that extra something that made him her favourite person—she kept this to herself.

They were all still laughing when Mae and Isaac returned.

"Sorry to break this up, guys, but we gotta get a move on," announced Mae.

Chapter 24

Mae, Cat and Toby traipsed through the overgrown woods; they weren't following a trail. They stepped over tree roots, nettles and ducked under low branches. What had begun as a sunny day was now overcast. The heavy grey clouds threatened rain, and the oppressive atmosphere was making Cat increasingly nervous. The lack of light in the dense forest was making it difficult to see. Cat tripped a couple of times, but Toby was there to steady her; she hated the dark. Mae's eyes were fixed ahead; any fear that she had for the woods were now gone. She was no longer the hunted. She steamed forward, not concerned with the obstacles that the woods created. She ignored the pain in her ribs—pain was just a state of mind. The trek felt like it lasted for hours, but it was just thirty minutes.

They soon approached the edge of the woods. Mae had already explained the layout; it was similar to the Google map images. Mae and Isaac had scoped out the barn earlier. They didn't see Jake or Anthony, but they confirmed that there were just the two entrances—the main door and the side door on the right side of the barn. The barn was made of stone but had a wooden roof. There were ventilation slits in the walls, but they weren't wide enough to fit their bodies through. A car was parked a few feet from the front entrance, but it wasn't the rental. There were several trees on the left side of the barn creating dark shadows. Mae decided that this would be an excellent place to look through the slits without being seen; they needed to know where Jake was before making their move in the building.

The plan was simple. Cat was to release Jake discreetly; she didn't even need to enter the building. Mae would cause a distraction to make Anthony leave the barn, and then Toby was to enter the barn, grab Jake and get him out quickly. They would then meet up outside, and Toby would shield them all back to the edge of the woods. Then the idea was to call in the cavalry, and Anthony would be arrested; Isaac assured her of this. But Mae had another plan that she hadn't told any of them about. Once they had Jake safe, she was going to send them all off to the forest. She would follow but then double back. There was no way that she and her family were going to continue to live in fear. He may go to jail, but once he got out, it would start all over again. She was going to end this for good.

* * *

Fifteen minutes had passed since Mae and the kids left. Isaac was sitting next to his daughter. He tapped the wheel, fidgeted in his seat and looked at his watch.

"Oh my god, dad. Will you please just relax," Isaac stopped

what he was doing.

"I can't let them do this alone; it's wrong. I need to be there." Alison rolled her eyes.

"Dad, she asked that you stay here. You're just supposed to be a back-up, you promised her." He started to tap the wheel again.

"I know that I promised, but how do I know that they need back-up if I'm nowhere near them?"

"It's called a phone dad, one of them will call if they need you."

"No, if they all got in trouble, they won't be able to call," Isaac replied. Alison sighed.

"Fine. Then go after them; I'll stay here. I'll be fine." Isaac turned to his daughter. He looked into her brown eyes.

"Are you sure you'll be okay?" Isaac asked. He was still unsure that he should leave her, but Alison nodded assuredly.

"I'll be fine. Off you go." Isaac softly stroked her cheek.

"Everything's going to be okay. Make sure that you stay here and do NOT leave the car under any circumstances."

"Okay, dad. I understand; now go." He kissed her on the cheek, then jumped out of the vehicle and jogged into the woods. Alison watched him go until he disappeared. She checked the time; it was just after four-thirty.

She messed about on her phone for a while, but the front seat was getting uncomfortable. She climbed over to the rear seats and laid down on her front. She took her notepad from her bag and began transferring her notes to her phone. She did this all the time; she was worried that her pad could be destroyed or damaged, so she felt better when she had it in digital form and saved on the "Cloud."

Alison had almost finished when spots started to hit the

back window, slowly at first, and then more and more drips melded into one. The water ran down the window. The rain became very heavy, and it was hitting the top of the car hard. Alison sat up; it was so noisy. She sat back; the windows were starting to steam up, so she climbed over into the driver's seat, turned on the ignition and opened a window. It was only then that she could hear something. There was a car coming; she closed the window and slipped down into her seat, slowly peeping up through the window. It was clear at the bottom from when it was opened, but it would soon steam up again. The car passed; she only saw its rear, but she caught the number plate—it looked familiar. Seconds after, another car passed. This one wasn't familiar, but they were travelling close together, and she wondered if they were going to the same place. Alison quickly opened her gallery on her phone and scrolled through her photographs. There it was, the car's registration that she saw on the dirt track by Mae's house; it matched the first car that passed. Alison put the car in gear and quickly pulled out of the lay-by. She needed to follow them—the only people they were expecting there were Anthony and whoever his partner was. There was no way they would have left Jake unguarded. If her hunch was correct about the second car, they could have a third mad person to contend with; she needed to let them know if that were the case.

She caught up to the other cars quickly—her wipers were moving fast, and the rain was lashing on the windscreen. She was struggling to see through the mini waterfall that was cascading down in front of her. She backed off slightly; she was getting too close and didn't want to spook them. They turned off down a track; both of them, together. She knew it.

She drove past the entrance not to cause any suspicion. She pulled over when she could and tried to call her dad.

There was no reception, and the phone refused to call out; she hoped that the mobile Wi-Fi was better, so she sent a message through an online messaging app, but it wasn't showing as received despite the message being sent. It was no good. She had to go after them and warn them. She drove back to where the cars pulled in. It was a narrow track lined with hedges; it was only wide enough for one car at a time. Alison chose to go up the path on foot. She looked at her watch—she hoped that she'd make it in time. She left the car near the track entrance and sprang out. Alison silently moaned as the rain doused her hair flat against her face. Her hair was going to frizz up like mad when it dried. She cursed to herself and jogged down the track.

* * *

Mae and the twins broke away from the trees—they were all gripping a weapon. Cat and Toby had carving knives whilst Mae clutched the crowbar. The ground was slippery from the downpour of rain. They crouched low behind the hedge. The coast appeared to be clear, and they ran toward the shady side of the barn, keeping low. Mae flinched as her ribs crushed together; the pain was unbelievable. They reached the barn wall. Mae put her back against the wall and breathed heavily. Her eyes were tearing, and her sight blurred—rainwater washed away her sweat. Toby crouched in front of her.

"Mum, are you okay?" he whispered.

"Yeah, I'm fine. It's just my ribs; they hurt like hell."

276

"Mum, maybe you should go back, you're in no—"

"No," Mae hissed. "There is no way that you two are doing this without me, so forget it. We have a job to do." Toby stepped back. It was no use; she was staying.

Cat was stretched up on her tiptoes, trying to look through one of the ventilation slots, but it was too high. Cat was disappointed that she could make other people fly but not herself. Maybe one day with more training. Toby saw her struggling. He left his mum whilst she caught her breath and gave Cat a leg-up. She could now see inside. The lack of windows made it dark inside, but she could make out the pens; she assumed they were for livestock once upon a time. She couldn't see anything to the right of her, which was toward the main entrance. She looked to her left, she struggled to see any detail, but there was a shadow.

Cat jumped down and gestured to move nearer to the rear of the barn so that she could get a better look. Mae stayed where she was as Toby and Cat moved to another slit in the wall. Toby once again cupped his hands as Cat stepped into them and heaved herself up. She looked through the narrow gap. Immediately below her, she could see Jake. Cat sighed in relief; he was okay. He was strapped to a chair. Opposite him was another figure. He, too, was sitting down, but she couldn't see his face; he wore a balaclava. He was dressed all in black, and he looked pretty slender. She wondered if it was her father. If it was, why did he conceal his identity? He didn't attempt to hide it when he made that video. Cat remembered back to the video where Anthony said his assistant made a mistake and took the wrong person; this must be his accomplice. Her mother really was right all along; this was why he had an alibi for all of the strange goings-on back at home. Cat felt ashamed for doubting her. She climbed down.

"I think we have a problem," she whispered. "There's someone in there with Jake, but I don't think it's dear old dad. If we're going to do something, we need to do it fast before company comes along." Mae didn't need telling twice. Mae crept to the front corner of the barn and checked that it was clear. There was no one in sight. She moved past the parked car and the front entrance. A fence adjoined the far corner of the barn, and Mae climbed over it clumsily, trying to avoid hurting her side. It wasn't easy, especially when she was trying to carry a crowbar as well. She landed on the other side of the fence softly; it wasn't high. She ran to the back of the barn near the side door. She stopped for a moment to catch her breath. She clutched her ribs and grimaced in pain. She looked out into the field and saw the hay bales that they'd spotted during their re-con. They'd decided then that this would be a perfect distraction. Mae took some matches from her jeans pocket, ran to the hay, and lit a match. Shielding it from the rain, she laid it under the dried grass—it burned quickly. Mae lit more and placed them in the bales. It wasn't long 'till the flames soared; the rain made it smoke more, which was ideal. Mae ran back to the side door and scraped the crowbar down it. She darted around the back of the barn, waiting for the man to come out.

* * *

The driver couldn't help but keep checking his watch. Anthony was due back soon. Apparently, the big boss was coming. It was all very mysterious. This was the man that contacted him in the first place. He didn't meet Anthony till later. He still remembered their first conversation over the phone.

"What would you say if I told you that we had a common enemy?" The man said. The driver had no idea what he was talking about—he didn't get out much these days and didn't have enemies. He told the caller as such. "You don't remember Mae Reynolds then? She's called Mae Phoenix now. She's made quite a nice life for herself. She has a lovely house in the country, twin children in their teenage years, and she's very, very happy. Are you happy for her?" Just the mention of Mae Reynolds made his blood run cold. The caller asked if he was interested in joining a team. He said that like-minded people wanted to see Mae pay for the things she'd done. The driver agreed to the man's terms and was eager to get started. Before he ended the call, he asked the caller for his name. "Just call me Justice."

That was the last that the driver heard of him. The next call he received was from Anthony; He found out that he was Mae's ex-husband. They compared stories then arranged to meet up. Justice had left most of the plans to them, but he wanted to know where and when the final showdown would occur; he wanted to be there. Today was the day, and he was anxious to meet him.

He broke out of his revelry when he could smell something—it smelled like something was burning. He looked at Jake. He was sniffing and looking around too, which meant it wasn't just his imagination. There was a sudden scrape outside on the side door which was directly behind him. He picked up his knife off the floor. He went to the side door and listened; he couldn't hear anything. He eased the large disintegrating door open, and the hinges creaked loudly. As soon as the door was open, he could see a blaze out in the field; he stepped out four paces. Then there was a sensation that stung the back of his head, and everything went black.

* * *

Mae swung the crowbar hard. It connected with the back of the driver's head with a loud thump—he dropped to the ground and was still. Mae crouched down and scooped her arms under the driver's armpits. She tried to take all the weight with her shoulders but pulling this dead weight took her whole body. She dropped him several times as the pangs of pain made it almost impossible to move him. She eventually managed to drag him around the corner and to the back of the barn. Mae collapsed. She needed to rest. With Jake's watchman out of the way, Cat and Toby could get Jake out, and she would follow shortly. But she was fully intending on waiting for Anthony. She closed her eyes as she fought through the pain.

* * *

Cat stood in Toby's hands by the ventilation slit above where Jake was sitting. As soon as the driver stepped out of the doorway, Cat tried to get Jake's attention.

"Psst. Jake," Cat hissed. Jake started and looked up behind him. Cat's face was grinning at him through the small gap in the wall; his eyes were wide.

"I'm going to release you—once you're free, Toby will come around and meet you. He can protect you." Jake wondered how she would free him; then he felt his binds tighten on his wrists, and then there was a sudden release. The cable ties snapped, and his hands were free. He looked up at Cat again, and she winked. Cat leapt down, which allowed Toby to go to Jake.

Jake unsteadily got up from his chair; he was so wobbly. Anyone would think he was drunk. There was still dried blood on his face; he'd barely slept, he hadn't been fed or watered since he'd been there, his mouth was dry, and his stomach hurt. He got himself out of the pen and stumbled. The barn's main entrance opened, and Toby was there, the door slamming shut behind him. Toby was standing next to Jake in an instant, and Jake grabbed hold of him to steady himself.

"Hey mate, you're alright now; we're getting you out of here." Jake was happy to hear that; he could think of nothing better right now. Toby had just got a good handle on Jake when the main door burst open.

* * *

Alison was panting. She could see the end of the lane up ahead. The two cars were parked up against some trees on the left side. The engines were silent, so she assumed that whoever had been in them had gotten out. Alison could smell burning, and she could see smoke pouring into the sky far to the left of her. It was the distraction; she was too late; they'd already started to carry out the plan. She walked low just in case someone happened to be in one of the cars. As she neared them, she peered through the windows—they were empty. Alison stayed close to the trees.

Alison could see her dad in the distance; he was opposite

the barn in the treeline. He couldn't see her, though. He was looking at something in the other direction; he must've seen the new arrivals; he was probably watching them now. She went to turn the corner and noticed that there were a few yards of trees then the front of the barn. Ahead, there was movement in the trees. She backed back up to the corner and studied the movement; It was the man from the video. He was watching something or someone down the side of the barn. He was holding something in his hands, and she tried to squint through the mess of branches to see through the trees. Someone was walking toward him. She could only imagine that it was a member of the Phoenix family. She wanted to call out, but it would blow her cover, so she remained silent and watched.

* * *

Isaac had seen the two cars pull up. There was one person in each vehicle. One was the rental that Alison had photographed—Anthony was inside that one. The other man was dressed in black, and his face was covered. Whoever he was, he wanted to remain anonymous, even to Anthony. They didn't get out straight away. Isaac wanted to run across the dead man's land between the treeline and the barn, to warn the others that they had company, but it was too open; they would see him.

Isaac crouched down behind the hedge; it was then that he saw a small figure run from the barn side door to the hay bales. He knew that it was Mae. She was about to create the distraction. "No, no, no, no… fuck, this whole thing is going to shit," Isaac said quietly. He was no stranger to talking to

282

himself. He grabbed his phone to call in some help, but there was no reception. *Shit.* He knew that as soon as Mae lit that fire, they were going to realise that something was happening. But there was nothing he could do to stop her, and he wasn't going to try and get her attention. He was more likely to gain the attention of the men. He saw the bales go up in smoke. There were only a few minutes between the hay going alight and the two men leaving their cars.

The man in black ran across the front of the barn and to the end of the fence overlooking the field; he stood and watched the hay burn. Anthony followed, but he stormed out of sight behind the car parked near the barn's entrance. He must have stopped following for some reason because he didn't re-emerge to join the other man. Isaac returned his attention to the man in black. To Isaac's horror, he saw Mae emerge from the back of the barn. The man in black just had to move his gaze forty-five degrees to the left, and he would see her; it was agonising for him to stand by and watch, but he needed to remember that Mae was special. She could handle this.

* * *

Toby was gone moments after Cat got down. It was strange for her to experience his gifts; he so very rarely used them. She hoped now that the secret was out, he would see them as a positive part of him, and he might embrace it instead of trying to hide it. Cat made her way to the front of the barn. She wished the sun would come back out, being nestled between the woods and the side of the barn like this had her plunged into darkness. The hairs on the back of her neck stood up.

Something didn't feel right; she could sense something

wrong, the air shimmered and warned of danger. Her mum should be back by now, *where is she?* She reached the corner when she heard a twig snap. She turned quickly, but she didn't see who it was, the person reacted too quickly. Her head was shrouded by what felt like a hessian sack. She tried to struggle out from the person's grip, but they were strong. She stilled herself and tried to concentrate on the person who had her to make them release her, but she couldn't do anything. She'd always believed that she had to be able to see, to move things around her; what was happening now confirmed that theory. It was dark inside the bag, and she felt so vulnerable; for the first time in an age, she was scared and felt powerless. The dark was her Achilles heel.

Her captor dragged her away. She didn't know where he was taking her; he had just one arm wrapped around her waist and his fingers were digging into her sides as he pulled her reluctant body. There was a sudden noise—it sounded like a door opening—then she felt something cold across her throat.

* * *

As Mae came from the rear of the barn, she spied a dark figure in the corner of her eye—she froze. It was a man dressed in black, and he was looking at the fire in the field. Mae began to back up. She clenched her teeth, willing him not to turn in her direction. The man suddenly shifted his gaze, and their eyes met. *Fuck, fuck,* she thought. There was nowhere to run; it was a dead-end at the back of the barn, and she couldn't go back the way she came. He had her cornered. She tried to weigh up her options, but there wasn't enough time. The man leapt over the fence with ease and ran toward her. She broke left toward the burning hay, and he made a beeline for her. Her injuries were slowing her down, and she was slipping and sliding on the wet grass. She knew that she couldn't outrun him. She stopped in the centre of the field. She still had the crowbar in her hand, and she took it with both hands and faced him. She resembled a tennis player waiting for the opponent to serve. He stopped too; she could only see his eyes. The balaclava covered his whole face, including his mouth, but she could tell that he was smiling; she could see it in his blue eyes.

The man pulled a sword from his back, and Mae gaped at the huge, glinting razor-sharp blade. *Who the hell is this guy? A samurai?* Mae thought. She looked at her crowbar woefully. The man strolled up to Mae slowly, sword in hand, swinging it down by his side and closing the gap between them. He was six feet away when he stopped. They stared at each other. Mae glared at him; she was more scared than ever, but she didn't want him to see that. He raised the sword and lunged for her. She darted to the side to avoid it, but the tip of the blade scratched her right shoulder. It stung, but she'd felt worse. A small amount of blood seeped through her shirt. She countered with a swipe of the crowbar. He ducked, and she missed. Her shoulder pulled from the force of her swing. She huffed and almost fell. She staggered but remained on her feet.

He was coming at her again, sword high up in the air, slashing down. She dropped and rolled across the grass. She screamed as her side impacted the ground. In her mind, she converted the pain to anger, and adrenaline rushed through her body. She kicked at his knee, and he came tumbling down, and in a fluid motion, she swung the crowbar at the hand holding the sword—she managed to make contact, and he dropped it. She climbed on top of him and straddled him. He grabbed her face with a clawed hand, and his nails sank into her cheeks. He pulled her face to the side and rolled her over. He was now looming over her. He took a fist to her right temple; her head flung in the opposite direction with force. Her eyes watered, and she went dizzy. She tried to scramble away, but he had his elbow across her throat. He held her down and put both hands around her throat instead. Mae tried to pull his hands away at the wrists, but his grip was firm. His thumbs were pushing hard on her windpipe. He moved around to adjust his grip as he climbed over her; he was straddling her now.

Mae used her feet to push her body up; she then raised her knee. It went straight between his legs, and his grip loosened immediately. Mae rolled away quickly onto her front, and she reached for his sword lying in the grass. He recovered quickly, and he was on top of her again—this time, he sat on her back. She screamed as she felt her already broken ribs crack again. He could see what she was reaching for, and he tried to pull her head back. His fingers wrapped over her mouth and nose, and she couldn't breathe. She gasped for air, and his middle finger slipped into her mouth; Mae clamped her teeth down hard, and the man yowled and fell off her. Mae spat the finger out of her mouth. The metallic taste of blood made her feel sick, and she heaved.

Mae was still on the ground catching her breath, and the man stood a metre from her; he tucked his damaged hand under his other arm. He was standing looking down at her; he started toward her when he heard shouting from behind. A man in a police uniform ran toward him, but he was still quite a distance away. He could finish her, she was weak now, but he would indeed be caught. He was in no state to fight a fit police officer. He ran for the fence, climbed over it and disappeared around the front of the barn.

Isaac saw the man in black run-off. He considered going after him, but he had too much of a head-start; he doubted that he could catch him. Mae was lying on the ground, and she wasn't moving. Isaac took one last look as the man vanished around the corner, then went to Mae instead. When he reached her, he dropped to his knees, and she was moving again.

"Are you alright?" he asked breathlessly. She coughed, and blood sprayed from her mouth. She caught the droplets in her hand.

"I'm great; I'm sure that's a great sign of health," she said sarcastically. She wiped her bloody hand on her jeans. She tried to get up, but she felt crippled on her right side. She imagined what her ribs would look like on an x-ray. She was sure it would resemble minestrone soup. The pasta was the fragments of bone floating around in her insides.

"You've probably punctured a lung; how's your breathing?" Isaac asked. Mae tried to inhale deeply, but it set her off on a coughing fit with more blood. Her breaths were short and shallow. "I'm so sorry, Mae, I saw the other guy show up, but you'd already set the fire, and I had no way of letting you know what was happening; my phone has no reception here. I saw that you were in trouble and came over. I think I frightened the guy away."

"I gave as good as I got, even in my already damaged condition. I can't imagine he fancied taking you on, someone who clearly takes care of himself." Mae grabbed Isaac's bicep and squeezed. Isaac laughed.

"Well, Miss Phoenix, I'll take that as a compliment." Mae smiled back at him. Even though she was paler than a ghost, she could feel a blush coming on. She stopped smiling suddenly—she could hear something.

"Can you hear that?" They both paused. There were voices. The side door to the barn was still open from when the driver came through. "It's Anthony's voice, and I would know it anywhere. Help me up."

"Mae, you shouldn't move. You're bleeding internally; you need serious medical care. It would be best if you sat this out now, I can—"

"Help me, Isaac," Mae interrupted. "I'm doing this with or without your help, but my chances are better if you do help me." Isaac sighed and took her left arm; he pulled it around his neck. He lifted her to her feet slowly. Mae wanted to scream but kept it internal, not wanting to give them away. They moved toward the side door. There was a small post on the left side. Isaac lowered her down onto it, and she perched there whilst she listened. Isaac moved to the other side of the door.

* * *

Alison saw Anthony take Cat. She watched as he pulled her toward the barn entrance. She saw the knife in his hand and knew that this was bad news. Alison crept along with the trees and went up the side of the barn where Cat had come from. She slowly made her way down; she heard the voice inside the barn, and it was getting louder and louder; she moved closer to the sound; it was coming from the back of the barn now, and the words were becoming clearer. Alison paused and listened.

* * *

Toby gasped when he saw the shape of his sister, blindfolded by a sack over her head. Anthony stood in the doorway. Cat was drawn close to his body, he had a knife to her throat, and he wore a cruel smile. Toby poised himself to move.

"I heard that you're quick, Toby, but are you quick enough to get to me before I slice her jugular?" Anthony's voice was calm and smug. Toby tensed. He may be fast, but it just took a millisecond to slice a sharp knife through the skin. He couldn't risk it.

"Jakey-boy and Toby, my son," Anthony taunted. Toby scowled as Anthony continued to speak. "Move back. I want you to stand up against that wall." Jake and Toby did as they were told; they moved back to the rear of the barn. Anthony followed behind with Cat, the knife remaining at her throat. "Good, that's right, you're doing as you're told. It's not hard, is it? All you had to do was wait at the services for my text, and you would have shown up here at the requested time. Then I would have given you Jake, and he would've gone on his merry way, but you had to defy me." Anthony was enjoying himself. Toby could see it in his eyes. He was ashamed to know that man was his blood.

"That's a lie," Jake yelled. "He planned to kill you guys and me. All he wanted was Mae." Anthony feigned shock.

"Jakey, you telling tales on me? That's not nice." Anthony chewed the inside of his cheek. "He's right, though. For starters, I'm sorry to say kids, but I don't think you're mine. Secondly, even if you were mine, I didn't want you in the first place. If anything, you just totally messed up mine and your mother's relationship. She did not incline to leave me until you came along. You seemed to give her a fire that wasn't good for me." He laughed loudly. "You see what I did there? You gave her a *fire*. Jakey-boy's right, all I wanted was your mum. You're a by-product that I don't need, and you must be disposed of. So, where is your mother? I'm dying to see her."

* * *

Mae looked at Isaac; her eyes were fearful. He shook his head; he knew what she wanted to do. She wanted to go in and negotiate for her kids. But they'd heard it from the horse's mouth. Anthony had no intention of keeping them around. He was going to kill them. It was up to him and Mae to save them, and it wasn't going to happen by walking in there without a plan. Isaac was about to go to Mae, but a hand grabbed him from behind. There was a sting at the back of his neck as someone pushed in something sharp. Mae watched, her eyes wide.

"Hey Ant. We got company." The driver gestured for Mae to enter the barn. Mae observed him, it was the man that she'd clubbed around the head earlier. He was not the one that she'd fought; he still had all his fingers. It looked as though there were three men altogether—Anthony and two men in black. As she entered the barn, only two of them were present; she wondered where the other was.

"Mae, you've joined the party. You've brought a friend too; I didn't peg you as a black man's bitch." He showed all his teeth as he smiled at her. Mae glared at him. She'd forgotten how vile he was. She remembered his psycho ways, but his general ignorance and bigoted persona had been lost in her memory; it all just came flooding back. Mae walked toward him, and every step was agony.

"You're a fucking asshole! I would never come back to you; I'd rather die first." She spat at his feet. Anthony snarled.

"Be careful with that temper, missy. It's almost like deja vu, ain't it? But this time, if I go up in flames, so does she." He jerked the knife up under Cat's chin, and a small rivulet of blood ran down her neck. Cat squealed, and Mae backed off; she could feel the heat building up inside her. He was right. When they were in this situation last time, she surprised him—now he was expecting it. She knew he would have no qualms with going up in smoke if he could take one of her children with him. The man in black behind her coughed.

"Don't forget about me over here with your boyfriend; you try anything, he goes too." Mae shot a glance at him—Isaac's face was calm; he looked as if he were already resigned to dying. Mae couldn't see a way out. The only ability she had was useless, and from where Toby stood, he could only protect Jake. Cat was in darkness, so she couldn't use her abilities either. They were stuck. Mae looked into the eyes of the man in black.

"I don't know who you are, but can't you see that this guy is a maniac? If he's willing to kill three teenagers, don't you think you're expendable too? You're a witness, and you can't trust him. Whatever he's paying you, I'll pay you more to help us. Please." The driver laughed hard; Mae frowned. *What the hell is so funny?* She thought.

"Do you honestly think that I'm doing this for money? I'm doing this for free, Mae Reynolds. On the basis that shit's about to go down, I think I should introduce myself." He kept the knife to Isaac's neck, and he used his free hand to whip off the balaclava. He had his head turned to the right, and Mae didn't recognise him at first. He then began to rotate his head. As his profile changed from the left side to the right, the skin became wrinkled and worn. The one side of his mouth was turned down, his right ear was missing, and his hair was gone. It looked like scars caused by burns. He smiled at her, but his lips only turned up on one side. She still couldn't recognise him, but it dawned on her that without the scars, she still wouldn't have known him—they were children when they last saw each other.

"You don't fucking recognise me, do you? I'm not surprised. The last time you saw me, I didn't have all of this." He gestured at his face. "It used to be worse. I had several surgeries, and it's not just my face. My face got off lightly. The rest of my body looks like a fucking prune!" He was getting agitated, and it was making Mae nervous, especially whilst there was a knife jabbing into the back of Isaac's neck. Isaac flinched several times during the introductions.

"Calm down, please. I don't want anyone getting hurt here. I know who you are now; from what I remember, you and your friends were beating on my brother for no reason—throwing stones at him, calling him a freak. It was three to one until I came along. Do I remember it correctly, Bobby?" Bobby's face reddened.

"So, the stones that we threw... Did they scar your brother's face? Did he spend a decade in and out of the hospital? Do you think that this was a fair punishment for my indiscretions as a naïve, stupid kid?" His voice was trembling. Mae had always felt bad about what she did. Nothing could have excused what she did to him.

"Bobby, I am sorry for what I did, I truly am, but I didn't know how far you guys were going to go. Once you started with stones, you might have continued with kicks, punches or worse. I was protecting my brother. You were in the wrong for what you did to him, and you have to be able to see that," Bobby's eyes were dark. There was nothing there that she could plead to. He despised her and would like nothing more than to kill her right there and then. Mae stopped talking.

* * *

Alison had heard enough. She had to do something. No one knew she was there, and everyone was in the barn as far as she could tell. She was afraid for her dad; this Anthony guy was a racist dick, and her dad would probably be the first one that he'd like to get rid of. Alison trod carefully down the side of the barn; she saw the car parked at the front. She opened the driver's door and checked the ignition. *Shit, no keys!* She thought. She checked under the front wheel arches, but there was nothing. But then, under the rear passenger wheel arch, there they were. She grabbed the keys and got into the driver's seat, turned the ignition, and nothing happened. She cursed silently. Then she remembered that she had to press down the clutch in the courtesy car to start it, and this was an equally new vehicle. She pushed her foot down onto the clutch and turned the key, and the car roared into action. She closed the door; she didn't know what she would do until she did it.

Alison put the car into first gear and pressed the accelerator. The car wheel spun on the dirt, but eventually, the wheels took purchase and pulled forward. She went into second gear, then third, and at this point, the barn doors were just a metre ahead of her. Alison gritted her teeth and screamed with determination, and the car crashed through the rotten wooden door and then came to an abrupt stop. The airbag went off in Alison's face, and she felt a snap in her nose. Alison's ears were ringing, and she felt dizzy. She looked up through the windscreen. It was mayhem—people were running around and shouting. Alison couldn't keep her eyes open; her eyelids closed, and all went quiet.

Chapter 25

Anthony was about to interject with Bobby and Mae's discussion when a car crashed into the barn. Anthony recognised the vehicle but had no clue who the girl was that was driving it. He was only distracted for a moment when Jake swooped past and knocked Cat from his grasp. Cat fell to the floor, and Jake lunged toward Anthony with his head down; it connected with Anthony's stomach, the air whooshed out of Anthony's mouth, then Jake managed to wrestle him to the ground. Unfortunately for Jake, Anthony was three times the size of him, and Anthony overpowered him quickly. The knife that he'd threatened Cat with plunged into Jake's abdomen. Cat tore the sack off her head and saw Jake sag into the dirt; he held his stomach, blood spilling around his hands.

"No," Cat screamed. She crawled over to him and pressed down on the wound, trying to stop the bleeding. Jake could see Anthony behind her. Jake shouted, "Cat, look out," Anthony grabbed her by the hair.

* * *

When the car crashed into the barn, Toby whipped Cat away

from Anthony, then immediately turned his attention to Bobby. He dashed over in a split second, and he snatched Bobby's knife away. Bobby was slow to react as he, too, was distracted by Alison's diversion. Bobby looked down at his empty hand and then at Toby, who was now holding his blade.

"I do believe this was yours." Toby smiled, and Bobby scowled back. Isaac realised that his hostage-taker was now disarmed, and Isaac swiftly turned and punched Bobby in the face; he went down quickly.

After Mae was happy that Toby and Isaac had Bobby in hand, she turned to Anthony. Mae was horrified when she saw Anthony behind Cat—he had her by the hair. The knife in his hand was dripping with Jake's blood. She could combust him from where she stood, but Cat would still be at risk. All he had to do was pull her to him then she'd be aflame as well. Mae needed to stop this. For good. She had a crazy idea. She concentrated deep within herself. Her gut burned, and her eyes burned even more. She could feel the heat flow through her veins—then something happened that had never happened before. Mae's own skin ignited, and it hurt; she could feel her skin beginning to burn. She didn't have much time.

Mae ran at Anthony. She jumped onto his back, and his hand tore away from Cat's hair. Mae wrapped her legs around his waist and her arms around his neck; he leaned back, away from Cat. He tried to throw Mae off him, but she held on tight. The fire transferred from her to him. He threw himself to the ground; he tried to roll to put out the flames, but Mae wouldn't allow it. The pain was indescribable, but she tried to hold on as long as she possibly could. He was screaming, and Mae was too. Her hair had burnt down to the scalp, and soon she wouldn't be able to hold him; she hoped that he would give in. He tried to pry her hand from his neck, but their skin had melded together; as her hand came away, so did his skin. He stopped fighting, and he knew that it was over. Still, a vile man, Anthony's last thought was, *"Till Death Us Do Part."* And he grinned.

Mae closed her eyes. She sealed off the pain in her mind, and she thought of Cat and Toby. She remembered their faces when they were born; she saw each of their birthdays in her head. She remembered the good times, the hugs and the kisses. The bedtime stories and her last birthday party. She saw her mum, dad, brother, and even Jake—he was part of the family after all—and her best friend Annie and her kids. Then she saw Isaac, the only man that she learned to trust. It was a shame that she hadn't met him years ago. Then there was nothing. Mae was gone—it was what she wanted. Her children were free from Anthony forever.

* * *

Toby and Cat saw the ball of flames rolling around the barn floor. Toby tried to make a bubble around his mother, but all it did was contain the fire inside. They wanted to pull her off, but they couldn't get close. Cat attempted to pull her mother away with her mind, but Mae wouldn't let go. They screamed at her to let go, but she couldn't hear them. Both their mother and Anthony shrieked as the fire consumed them both. Eventually, the fire stopped moving, and it fell silent.

Both Mae and Anthony were still, the flames still licked the air like a bonfire. As the flames died, Cat fell to her knees before the remains. The ball of fire had reduced to a smoulder of ashes. Toby knelt next to his sister, and he pulled her close as she sobbed. Toby needed to cry, too, but he would wait.

* * *

Stood by the side door of the barn was the man in black. His hand was wrapped in tissue sodden with blood. The moment that he heard the crash, he came running to see what was going on. The fight was in full swing, and he could see that his side was losing. He wouldn't stand a chance by himself. He watched Mae die, and that was all he wanted anyway, the ungrateful bitch. He just wished that he could have been the one that ended her existence. The children were still around, but he could work with that. He moved away from the door and jogged back to his car; luckily, it was an automatic, so he could still drive. He silently slipped away.

* * *

Isaac hung his head as he watched the children mourn for their mother. After this was all over, he had planned on asking Mae out for dinner. He thought they had a real connection. From the first day that he met her, he felt something. There was nothing that he wouldn't do for her. He was sad that he'd never find out what could've been. A tear rolled down his cheek and dropped—it hissed as it fell into the hot ashes.

* * *

Alison opened her eyes; her senses were assaulted with a God-awful smell. It reminded her of a barbecue, but the meat smells mixed with hair and other things she couldn't pinpoint. Her nose was hurting—she remembered the snap and hoped that she didn't look like a flat-nosed boxer right now. Dust and steam covered the windscreen. She couldn't see anything, but it was quiet. She opened the car door and pulled herself out; her head was spinning, and she was positive that she had a concussion. She stumbled forward. She was trying to focus her eyes, and up ahead, she could see fire. Two people were kneeling on the ground like they were huddled around a campfire; she could see her dad too, but he was standing and watching the same blaze unmoving. She made her way toward them, but before she reached their position, she spotted Jake. He was lying on the floor, his eyes were open and staring, and a pool of blood was soaking into the soil floor around him. Alison leaned over him and placed her fingers on his neck—there was no pulse.

"Oh my god. Jake." Alison tore open Jake's shirt, and there was a gaping hole in his abdomen. She lifted his chin then pumped his chest. She blew air in through his mouth, into his lungs. His chest rose and fell, and she pumped again. Cat heard her and ran over. She was so wrapped up in the death of her mother that she left Jake alone; she didn't think she'd left him that long. She watched Alison work on him; she seemed to know what she was doing. Isaac and Toby joined them. After ten breaths and several more pumps, Alison stopped. She looked up at Cat, her eyes full of sorrow. Jake was gone.

Cat couldn't take it; she'd lost her mum and now her best friend. Her head spun as she tried to process the events; her surroundings became out of focus. Cat put her hands to her temples as the agony of her loss took hold. She grabbed tufts of her hair and pulled hard. Cat let out a massive scream up at the ceiling, and the barn shook; dust was falling from the rafters. As the others watched her, they could see a blindingly bright yellow hue burst from her eyes. They all took several paces back and shielded their eyes, all except for Toby; he bowed his head and waited.

Cat screamed long and hard, and when she ran out of breath, she crumpled to the floor; she felt spent and empty. Her eyes returned to normal, and the barn was still once more. She laid next to Jake; placing her head on his chest, she put her hand over his stomach. Toby sat crossed legged above their heads. He stroked his sister's hair and put a hand on Jake's shoulder. All was dead quiet; the rain had stopped, and nothing moved. Nobody wanted to break the silence.

Then, Toby suddenly felt a strange sensation, and he gasped. The hand that rested on Jake began to tingle. Cat stopped sobbing and lifted her head; she too felt a tingle in the hand that covered Jake's stomach. Where Toby was stroking her hair, she could feel electricity. Neither of them had any idea what was happening, and they looked at each other with wide eyes. They kept their other hands on Jake, and the electricity heightened. They watched Jake intensely; they were scared to look away or let go in case it stopped whatever was happening. Isaac put his arm around Alison, mesmerised by what they were seeing. A bright blue current was flowing through Cat and Toby and going into Jake through their hands. Isaac noticed that both Toby's and Cat's eyes were glowing now; not like before, it was a soft illumination. Interestingly though, Toby's colour was different to Cat's; his was green.

The wound in Jake's stomach was decreasing in size, the flesh visually knitting back together. Jake's chest started to move; he was breathing. Then Jake opened his eyes.

It only felt like he was in the dark for mere seconds. Jake genuinely believed that he was dead. When he opened his eyes, he thought he was in heaven because he could see two glowing orbs. As his vision cleared, the orbs began to take shape, and it was then that he saw the faces of Cat and Toby. They were both smiling down at him, and then Cat landed a massive kiss on his lips. He felt amazing. He felt revitalised and rejuvenated. He was born again.

Alison watched on, amazed. Cat and Toby had brought Jake back to life, and she could barely believe her eyes. She was still confused about what went on. She looked around and couldn't see Mae. She asked her dad what happened. Isaac took Alison aside and told her everything, then showed her the pile of ash that used to be Mae and Anthony. Alison turned and hugged her dad. She knew that he liked her. Even though she only knew her for a minimal amount of time, she was sad too.

Isaac and Alison abruptly pulled apart as they heard a man screaming. It was Bobby. He was hurtling toward them with a knife raised above his head. He got within a metre of Isaac when he suddenly froze in place. His feet left the ground as he floated into the air. Alison and Isaac turned to see Cat standing there, and her yellow eyes fixed on Bobby. There was a rage in those eyes that burned deep. Isaac inched towards Cat; he was nervous.

"Cat. I know that you probably want to kill this guy right now. In this situation we're in, I probably wouldn't normally stop you. But we need to talk to him."

"What's there to talk about?" Cat growled. "He had a hand in getting my mother killed, and he needs to pay," said Cat through gritted teeth. Bobby screamed in pain, and he held his neck as he began to choke. Alison ran to Toby.

"Is she doing that? Is she strangling him?" She remembered back to when Cat made her fly. It did feel like hands were holding her, but for her, it felt gentle. Toby looked at her, and his eyes were hard.

"I guess she is. And I hope it's excruciating for him." He felt no pity for this man. Isaac moved closer to Cat.

"Cat, this guy and Anthony weren't the only people involved. There was a third." Cat's concentration faltered, and Bobby fell. His legs crumpled under him, there was a cracking noise, and he squealed in pain.

"A third?" said Cat. Isaac winced; he was pretty sure that either one or both of Bobby's legs just broke.

"Yes. Mae fought him outside before we were brought inside the barn. He ran off when he saw me. I think he's gone," said Isaac. Cat met Toby's gaze.

"I'll quickly go check," said Toby, and he vanished. Cat walked up to Bobby, and she stood over him. He was crying on the floor.

"Tell me who the other guy was," she demanded. His sobs quietened, and he looked up at Cat and snarled.

"Go fuck yourself! I ain't telling you nothing." Cat's eyes turned wild; she crouched down and grabbed him by the throat. Isaac lunged and tried to get Cat to release her grip. She looked at him.

"Don't worry, Isaac, I'm not killing him; I'm just getting the information that I need." Her voice remained level, and she sounded calm and in control. Isaac backed away. "Bobby. Tell me who the other man was." Bobby's face turned from angry to being completely blank. He looked as though he was in a trance.

"His name is Justice." Bobby's voice was monotone. Cat smiled at Isaac. Isaac stared, wondering what the hell was happening.

"Who is Justice, Bobby? Where do we find him?" Bobby shook his head.

"I don't know. We only spoke once on the phone. Anthony was his main contact." Cat released him. Bobby blinked. He looked around him.

"What the fuck did you just do to me? You were in my head! How dare you go in my head, you fucking freak!" Cat had lost her patience. She made a fist and punched him hard in the head. His head hit the ground, and he lost consciousness.

"Don't call me a freak, you asshole," said Cat. As she stood up, she was met with stares from Alison, Jake and Isaac. She wasn't sure that what she just pulled off would work. During Jake's healing process, Cat's mind was filled with knowledge, it flooded in, and she welcomed it. In that short moment, she was taught what she truly was capable of. Her mind was powerful, and there were no limits to what she could do with it. She wondered if Toby had a similar experience.

"Chill out; he's fine. Feel free to arrest him, PC Carrick." Cat walked away from him. She did want to kill Bobby. It took everything she had not to. But this was not the person that she wanted to be. She wasn't a killer, and her mother wouldn't have wanted that. It would be wrong to kill him in her name. Toby returned.

"There are car tracks; whoever it was is long gone," he said. It was frustrating. Cat had hoped that it was all over. Perhaps it was. If 'Justice' saw what they were capable of, maybe he'd be leaving them alone from now on. Cat wasn't convinced.

She vowed from that moment that one day she'd find him.
And she would be bringing *him* to justice.

Chapter 26

Cat and Toby had stayed with their nan for the last couple of weeks. There was a police investigation going on that they had to stick around for. The recent media attention about the Phoenix Twins had the local law enforcement concerned, and they didn't know how to deal with it. It was lucky that Isaac had been around; he was a good witness. He explained how Anthony and Bobby had tormented the family and that they went on to kidnap a young boy. He advised that everything that had happened to Anthony and Bobby was in self-defence.

Bobby was arrested. He had to spend time in the hospital—he had a broken leg. He was still there, and he had a twenty-four-hour guard. There was going to be a court case; now he was pleading insanity.

Gloucestershire police finally allowed Cat and Toby to go home. They were still considered minors, so they weren't allowed to go alone. Their grandfather agreed to stay with them for a while until they could figure out something more permanent. They talked about leaving Cumbria and going back to Gloucester, but Toby and Cat didn't want to. The small Cumbrian village had been their home for a decade, and they were happy there. Gloucester only held terrible memories for them; they were in no hurry to go back, ever.

Planning the funeral was awkward. Mae had always said that she wanted to be cremated. The problem was, she was already ashes; you couldn't really take ashes to a crematorium. So, they decided just to bury her ashes in the cemetery. Cat told Toby that she would like to visit a grave—it was somewhere to lay flowers and talk to her if she wanted. Toby agreed. The fact that Anthony's ashes were mixed in; wasn't spoken of by either of them. The funeral took place at the village church.

The funeral was meant to be a small affair, but the turnout at the graveside was phenomenal. The whole village was present to pay their respects, as well as the family. The press was also there; a representative from every newspaper must have shown up. What happened in Gloucester was big news both nationally and internationally. They were famous now. In some eyes, they were infamous, but as Alison said, people fear the unknown, and they were the first of their kind—that people knew about anyway.

The wake was being held at the house, in the garden. The media attempted to be respectful of their loss. Instead of camping directly outside the house, they rallied at the end of the road. The gathering reminded Cat of her mum's last birthday party, which was only a month ago. There were lots more people this time. Annie was there; she left the children at home but brought her husband for support—she and Mae were lifelong friends. Cat was sorry that Mae had spent such little time with her this decade. Cat gave her a long hug and made sure that she was aware that her mum loved her. Their nan and grandad, even though they were divorced, grieved for their daughter together. Their significant others sat aside and left them to reminisce. Sometimes they laughed, but mostly they cried.

Cat went into the house; her feet were aching from serving people drinks and nibbles. Toby was sitting at the dining table, his eyes red. Cat had cried enough for the both of them over the last couple of weeks, but she barely saw a tear from him. She knew that the dam would break eventually. She sat next to him and took his hand.

"You are allowed to cry, you know. It's okay being strong for me, but I can be strong for you too." He kissed his sister's hand.

"I know that Kitty-Cat. I've cried a bit, and I'm sure I will again later." He sighed.

"What is it?" Cat asked.

"What are we going to do now? Where are we going to live? We're still just seventeen. We won't be allowed to live here alone; Grandad won't stay here with us forever." There was a knock on the kitchen door—the door was open, and there stood Uncle Darren.

"Sorry to interrupt, guys; I overheard what you just said. I was hoping that I could help." Both Cat and Toby smiled at their uncle.

"No problem, come on in and take a seat." Darren sat opposite them.

"First of all. I didn't get a chance to pass on my condolences at the funeral. My sister and I have been distant for a while, much like the whole family, thanks to that ex-husband of hers. So, I feel her loss deeply, but I know it's worse for you two." Cat and Toby nodded with understanding. "I'm so sorry."

"Thanks, uncle Darren. It's only been two weeks, but I miss her so much," said Cat. They talked about Mae for a while, and he told the twins stories about her, and they laughed. Eventually, they fell silent.

"When you came in, you said that you could help us with something?" said Toby.

"Oh, yes. I heard you say earlier that you wouldn't be allowed to live here alone; well, I have a suggestion that could help us all." The twins looked at him expectantly. "I could move in. At the moment I live with dad. It's not a very big house, and it gets crowded, especially when Freya's kids visit. My job is in web design, so I can work from anywhere. As far as the social services are concerned, you will have an adult living with you, and I can get out from under dad's feet. What do you think?"

"It solves a problem..." said Toby. "What do you think, Cat?" Cat thought about it. They didn't know Uncle Darren very well, but what was the alternative? That they must leave their house and friends and live back in Gloucester with one of their grandparents. The thought of going back there made Cat shiver.

"I think we should do it. We'll make some calls tomorrow," said Cat. Darren pulled out his hand for them to shake on it—the hand was bandaged. Cat shook it gently. She'd seen him with the bandage on at the funeral, and she wondered what had happened.

"I meant to ask you earlier, what did you do to your hand?" asked Cat. Darren laughed dismissively.

"It was silly. I was trying to make a bird box in dad's back garden, and I got distracted and accidentally sawed off my middle finger!" Cat and Toby grimaced as they pictured it.

"Ouch," said Cat. Darren rose from his seat.

"I'm going to go back out there and get some food; I'll leave you to it. Remember, you two. If you need me, I'm always here; you're my niece and nephew, and I want to be here for you. You can trust me with anything. I'll see you soon."

"Thanks, Uncle Darren, we appreciate it." Darren got up and walked outside, grinning.

Epilogue

3rd August 1994

Darren stood in front of the bathroom mirror. His face was covered in dressings from the hospital. He hadn't needed any stitches; most injuries were superficial and would heal quickly without scarring. It was a shame. He already knew that he was unattractive, but at least scars would have added interest to his unappealing face.

The events of the day were beyond surprising. He could still see the boy in his head. Flames were exploding from his face and hair; he could still smell it. It brought a smile to his face. You couldn't look like Darren and not be a victim to bullying—this time was far from the first time. But on this occasion, the bullies got what was coming to them. He laughed to himself when he remembered Alfie's ears coming away from his head. He was slightly miffed that his sister was the one who got to have the special gift. It was hardly fair; she had good looks, was clever, and had a promising future ahead. It's not like she needed anything else going for her. But then, did it matter? As long as he had her around, he'd be untouchable from now on.

Darren and Mae hadn't spoken about what happened yet.

310

They didn't tell their dad; they didn't tell anyone. He thought it was about time that they had a chat. He left the bathroom and went to Mae's bedroom. The door was closed; he knocked on the door.

"Mae, can I come in?" he called. Mae opened the door slightly. He could only see one eye, and it was red and puffy.

"What do you want, Darren?" Mae said.

"We need to talk about what happened, Mae. What you did, was—"

"Horrible," Mae said, finishing his sentence.

"I was going to say amazing. Can I come in, please?" Darren insisted. Mae fully opened her door and allowed him inside. He sat on her bed; her room was still pink. Since she was six, it had been pink, but the walls were now covered with boy band members. "They got what they deserved, Mae. Look at me. Look what they did to me; who knows what would have happened if you didn't do what you did." Mae remained standing, and she shook her head.

"I can still see him, Darren. I can't close my eyes without seeing him engulfed in flames and hearing his screams. I didn't do a good thing. I might have killed him," Mae cried.

"But you didn't. The policeman at the hospital said that he was stable. Well done, by the way, about the story with the lighter. They didn't suspect a thing." Darren smiled.

"Of course, they didn't suspect anything. If someone tells a story that a girl put them on fire with her mind and then the girl says, 'don't be silly, they did it by accident with a lighter.' Which is the most feasible story? Making a person spontaneously combust with your mind is not normal," She was shouting now. When she realised that her dad might hear her, she toned down her voice. "Darren, we're never going to talk about this again. What happened today was a horrific thing that I just want to forget." Darren's face fell.

"But Mae. I need you. Do you think those are the only bullies that have attacked me? There are so many more, even at my school where most people are like me. Even they taunt and punch me. I want them to leave me alone, and you're the only one that can make them." Darren's lip began to wobble. Mae sat next to him.

"Look, Darren. I am not the answer. You need to stand up for yourself. I can't set fire to every bully that comes along. It's wrong. Besides, it's not going to last forever. You'll soon be leaving school. You're sixteen; you won't have any problems after that." Mae took his hand. Darren pulled it away from her.

"It's so unfair. You have a gift, and you're wasting it. I should be the one that has it; why do you get to have everything, and I have nothing?" Darren was yelling, and Mae tried to calm him down.

"Darren, please stop yelling. Mum and dad will hear you." He stood up and faced his sister.

"I don't care. I hate you, Mae. I wish you were dead," Darren stormed out of the room. He went to his bedroom and slammed the door. He was so angry. He never thought that he could hate his own sister, but he did.

* * *

Darren's feelings towards his sister only worsened as the years went on because she was wrong. The bullying didn't stop after school; in fact, it worsened. Taunts were rare, but punches became more common, and she just turned a blind eye to all of it. It wasn't her problem, was it? Her life was perfect; she always came out of it smelling of roses; even after he'd burned her house down.

He recollected the moment where he saw the first tendrils of smoke rise from the house. He knew they were all asleep, because he checked. It was unfortunate that Mae had fallen asleep in the lounge but he hoped the plan would still work anyway. He disabled all the smoke alarms by replacing the working batteries with dead ones. He replaced the components of the fuse board with some of his own, which just happened to be faulty. He'd spoken with an arsonist to get advice on how to accelerate a fire without leaving proof behind; he was given some very useful tips and laced the hallway and bedrooms with a clever concoction. He put so much work into it, just to make sure there were no survivors. When no one left the house, he thought he'd been victorious; he was so pleased with himself, she'd got what she deserved.

Then, some firemen walked out; and with them were three other people, one adult and two children. Darren punched the roof of his car; He didn't know how they got out of it. Looking back, he guessed it must have been because of the children's abilities. If only he'd known then. But this just proved his thoughts of his whole existence:

There really was no justice in the world.

The End

About the Author

The Phoenix Twins is my first novel. I wrote it throughout the 2020 lockdown. I had been furloughed for four months and this gave me a chance to get writing without having to worry about finding the time.

I am an office manager for my day job, so I have a Monday to Friday, nine-to-five. I have a wonderful husband who has supported me throughout this whole project and a beautiful son.

It was always my dream to write and publish a book. I have several unfinished projects on my hard-drive that I may just revisit because I have caught the bug. The feeling of actually finishing a piece of work that I've tried so hard to complete is overwhelmingly satisfying. The Serotonin seemed to rush through my brain and I want to feel it again.

Watch this space for more books. Be sure to checkout my short stories as well; they happen to be a prequel to this novel.

You can connect with me on:

🌐 https://www.maria-furlonger.com

📘 https://www.facebook.com/Maria.furlonger.author

Also by Maria Furlonger

This is the first of "The First Phoenix" short story series. It is set centuries before The Phoenix Twins. It tells the story of Sancha, she is the first hybrid within her tribe. Her father, the chief of the Cocharan tribe comes from the fire faction of the tribe, whereas her mother is from the Air faction.

See below for further details:

The First Phoenix - Playing With Fire
Sancha, is the daughter of Chief Nuallan of the Cocharan tribe.

It is Sancha's wedding day. Just as she is joined with her new husband, the sacred ceremony is interrupted by a sudden battle, led by the Romans.

The tribe have elemental powers that can usually end any war in moments, but the sheer numbers of the Roman army have them fearful that they may not win this battle.

Sancha and her people must do all they can to protect the tribe. But is it enough?